A SIGHT TO BEHOLD

Sparks flew as a flint was struck and a small pool of yellow light flickered to lfe. Golde's gaze immediately latched onto the baron where he stood encircled by horses and the remaining liegemen.

Her heart leapt upward to clog her throat. Sword drawn and legs braced, it appeared he looked directly at her. A lusty barbarian. A savage who would enjoy a contest between himself and the devil. A powerful chieftain of yore who would embrace her unholy eyes as a sign of good fortune, not evil.

His gaze shifted away. . . .

She sighed. Would that the baron could see, and that his fearless heated look was meant for her. . . .

LOVE AT FIRST SIGHT

SANDRA LEE

BANTAM BOOKS
New York Toronto London
Sydney Auckland

LOVE AT FIRST SIGHT

A Bantam Fanfare Book / January 1999

FANFARE *and the portrayal of a boxed "ff" are trademarks of Bantam Books,
a division of Bantam Doubleday Dell Publishing Group, Inc.*

All rights reserved.
Copyright © 1999 by Sandra Carmouche.
Cover art copyright © 1999 by Franco Accornero.
No part of this book may be reproduced or transmitted in any form
or by any means, electronic or mechanical, including
photocopying, recording, or by any information storage and
retrieval system, without permission in writing from the publisher.
For information address: Bantam Books.

If you purchased this book without a cover you should be aware that this
book is stolen property. It was reported as "unsold and destroyed" to the
publisher and neither the author nor the publisher has received any
payment for this "stripped book."

ISBN 0-553-58008-6

Published simultaneously in the United States and Canada

*Bantam Books are published by Bantam Books, a division of Random House,
Inc. Its trademark, consisting of the words "Bantam Books" and the portrayal of
a rooster, is Registered in U.S. Patent and Trademark Office and in other
countries. Marca Registrada. Bantam Books, 1540 Broadway, New York, New
York 10036.*

PRINTED IN THE UNITED STATES OF AMERICA

OPM   10 9 8 7 6 5 4 3 2 1

For Prudnuts,
who cut the diamond,
and for Juice,
who continues to polish.

PROLOGUE

❧❧❧

~ *England 1074*

Anxious to hide the smirk that besieged her lips, Golde lowered her head and pretended to study nonexistent images in the flickering reflection of a small silver plate.

Patience, she admonished herself. Had she not awaited this opportunity almost the entire twenty years of her life? To visit vengeance on the hateful Dorswyth?

Though it was full noon outside, few threads of light penetrated the wattle and daub of the windowless cottage. It could scarce be more perfect were it midnight, Golde thought with relish. Before the glow of a lone candle, she should appear fey as the fairies she claimed to consort with.

Summoning an ominous look, she returned her gaze to the wide-eyed woman who sat across the table from her.

"'Tis not good wot ye see?" Dorswyth's reed-thin voice cracked. "I know'd it!"

Golde scowled against the prick her inwit gave her. She would not feel pity for the woman, she vowed.

Dragon-hag. Grendelskin. That was what she should be remembering—the names Dorswyth had tormented her with in childhood. It mattered not that Dorswyth was hardly the adversary she'd once been; that at three and twenty her face was already lined from years of toil in the fields, her limp hair showing the first strands of gray.

Golde blinked. 'Od rot! What was she thinking? Had she not just vowed to feel no pity? Counseling her features to reveal nothing of her consternation, she picked up an egg that lay beside the silver plate.

Dorswyth clenched her rosary in a begrimed fist. "Mercy, Lord God. I always been yer loyal servant."

The egg trembled in Golde's palm. Dorswyth would never see the tiny needle-hole in the brown shell. Once the egg was cracked, she would be too horrified to notice aught but the bloodstained cow's hair—a terrible omen.

Truth tell, 'twas only berry juice, but Dorswyth would never know.

Yet Golde paused, fidgeting, unable to crack the egg. Considering their longtime enmity, Dorswyth had shown great courage in asking Golde to read her fortune. Only her husband's recent disappearance had prompted the request, for Dorswyth hoped to hear there was another man in her future. Otherwise, she and her children would be reduced to begging.

Nay, and nay! Golde longed to bang her head on the table. She would feel no sympathy. Instead, she forced herself to recall Dorswyth's rhyme about her unholy eyes.

> One eye black
> T'other eye green
> She dances wi' the devil
> On Allhallows e'en.

"Well? Go on." Dorswyth's fretful voice broke into her dark musings. "Crack the egg and have done."

Golde tried to reclaim the anticipation of retribution, but it eluded her. Rather, she could see naught but Dorswyth's anxious, work-worn features. "I think I should use the runes along with the egg," she hedged.

Dorswyth gaped. "Ever'one knows the runes is not safe."

"They will give me a more accurate reading," Golde lied. Laying the egg aside, she picked up a small leather pouch. "Here. Shake it gently."

"But—"

"Do as I say and no harm will befall you."

Golde crossed herself and closed her eyes against Dorswyth's anguished countenance. *Dragon-hag. Grendel-skin.* As Dorswyth shook the pouch containing the runes, Golde focused on the hurtful names, letting them sluice through her head until mortification settled like worms in her stomach.

Her lip curled at how the village folk, including Dorswyth, believed her disparate eye-coloring marked her as the devil's seed. Indeed, her existence was tolerated only because everyone feared her truculent great-grandmother, Mimskin: the village witchwife.

"Enough," Golde intoned without opening her eyes, determined anew to have her revenge. "Lord God, I appeal to you for aid. Say it thrice, then place the pouch in my hands."

Dorswyth's voice shook, cracked, and finally broke on

the third appeal. "I ar'nt always the best of persons, Lord God," she whimpered, then pleaded, "But it's fer me children. They done nothin' wrong."

Before Golde could prevent it, respect welled up to claim her. Unwilling respect for a woman able to admit her own shortcomings. Respect for an adversary who would humble herself before an enemy on her children's behalf. Respect, more powerful for the very fact that it was so hard to give.

Dorswyth's breath hitched as she placed the pouch in Golde's hands. And Golde knew in her heart she would not vanquish her old foe this day, or any other. To begrudge Dorswyth's hope would be too cruel. No woman deserved to watch her children go hungry.

Opening her eyes, Golde untied the drawstring and spilled the stones into the silver plate. A dozen black pebbles of varied shapes, their polished surfaces etched with gray symbols; what they meant, she knew not. Mimskin deplored her fraudulent practices and would not tell her. "Ye destroy yer swevyn with the sellin' of yer false prophesies," Mimskin would oft grouse.

Dorswyth sniffed, pulling her from her thoughts. "Ye can tell me wot ye sees. I ar'nt no babe."

"Sss," Golde hissed, turning her attention to the stones. Would that she could make sense of just one. Would that she had Mimskin's Celtic gift of sight, and that she could see some hope for Dorswyth's future.

Nothing.

Angry, Golde felt like pounding the runes until they released their power—like the toad she'd once beaten.

Part of a spell that would change the color of her cursed eyes, the toad had struggled. It had croaked, pleading for release, when she'd raised a rock over its head.

Golde caught herself before she winced. The toad

had died for naught. Her eyes had remained the same, just as she would remain a fearsome miscreation to her dying day.

Of a sudden, she felt like weeping. For the poor toad. For the lonely little girl she'd been. For the oncemighty Dorswyth, who now commanded only pity.

Golde stared at the useless runes. 'Twas well and good she was adept at deception, she thought, as a most logical idea struck. If Dorswyth would clean herself regularly, she would stand a much greater chance of attracting a man. Not that she could say such to Dorswyth without insulting her.

Abruptly, Golde pushed two stones off the plate. "The sun shines around you. There is a man who will bring you much happiness."

With each prediction of good fortune, she moved another rune from the plate as evidence. At last, only two remained. "And you are to purify yourself by bathing twice each week until you find a man."

Dorswyth's face shone with the light of redemption. "That is all? Wot about the egg?"

"'Tis not necessary."

Eyes shining, Dorswyth rose from her seat and held out a small silver coin. "'Tis all I can spare."

Golde shook her head and stood, flinging strands of black hair over her shoulder. "I cannot take your money."

"Wot?" Dorswyth puzzled.

Taller than most men, her body more solid than her slender appearance indicated, Golde propelled Dorswyth toward the door. "'Twas a bright new tunic I saw you wearing in my vision. Your money is meant to buy cloth."

"But—"

"Off with you."

She fair slammed the door in Dorswyth's face, then

scowled. A new tunic, indeed. Marching back to the table, she plopped down on the stool and glared at the candle.

Whatever ailed her? 'Twas the third time this week she'd refused coin for her services. At this rate, she'd soon be paying her culls. The money she'd saved against the day her father grew too old to work would dwindle away. Then where would she be?

A shriveled old beggar-woman, she answered herself, for no man would take a spawn of the devil to wife.

And what of her father? Though he'd e'er eased her hurtful childhood with words of love and affection, had he been embarrassed by her, too? Were there even now occasions when he secretly wished she'd never been born? She'd brought naught but misery upon him since her birth. Even as she'd drawn her first breath, her mother had died.

Sighing, she rested her elbows on the table and cupped her chin in her hands. If her father's future comfort were to be ensured, she must cease feeling sorry for her culls.

Extending a finger, she darted it back and forth through the candle-flame. If only she could garner a new group of culls, people she didn't know, perhaps some of the wealthy Norman elite . . .

Without warning, the door swung open. Thinking Dorswyth had returned, she swiveled about, only to find Mimskin.

She inclined her head as her great-grandmother ushered a narrow-set man into the cottage. Attired in an immaculate blue tunic with matching braises and sporting a knobby Adam's apple, he appeared just past the middle of life.

"This fellow has need of yer aid," Mimskin supplied

in her usual brusque tone. She tilted her white-tufted head back to squint at him. "Who'd ye say ye was, boy? Spurvul?"

" 'Tis Sper*ville.*" His nasal tone emphasized the *ville.* "*Sir* Sperville, chamberlain to Sir Gavarnie Delamaure, Baron of Skyenvic."

Mimskin snorted. "Ye looks more like a Spindleshanks."

Golde pursed her lips to hide her amusement. The oaf's dignity would suffer permanent injury were he not careful with her great-grandmother.

"The boy's liege lord, this Delamaure, has lost his sight." Mimskin's watery green eyes bore into Golde's. "He wishes to acquire yer services to heal the man. Ye'll have to travel, though to reach this Skyenvic."

Golde couldn't prevent the smile that curved her lips as she rose. She'd travel to the mythical Valhalla if she must. Sir Sperville was the answer to her prayers. "Come and sit, sir. Might I fetch you something cool to drink?"

The chamberlain shook his balding head. Though he tried to stare down his thin nose at her, he was little taller than she, and the ploy failed.

Mimskin beamed. "Let us discuss matters, then."

Golde's smile dipped at the corners. If Mimskin thought to appear angelic with such a look, she'd failed. She more resembled a goblin about to devour a small child. Indeed, it could mean naught but trouble that Mimskin would suddenly promote the fraud she claimed to abhor.

Before Golde could ponder further, Sir Sperville commanded her attention. "Your great-grandmother says you are a great mystical healer. Thus, I am prepared to offer you fifty pieces of gold to heal my liege lord's eyes."

Golde frowned as a sense of foreboding rippled

through her belly. Mimskin had even called her a great, mystical—

Abruptly her brows climbed her forehead. *Fifty pieces of gold!* No wonder Mimskin was willing to suspend her disapproval of Golde's duplicitous practices.

Golde's thoughts raced forward. Why did Mimskin not heal this Delamaure herself? She could easily do so without ever leaving her cottage. Her great-grandmother must think this Delamaure was unworthy of a cure, and deserved to be fleeced. Thus, the trick would be for Golde to secure the fifty gold pieces without restoring the man's sight.

"Money cannot cure blindness, sir," she intoned, instinctively slipping into her mystical role even as she wondered how she was going to accomplish such a feat. "However, you are come to the right woman."

ONE

SQUINTING AGAINST the midmorning sun, Golde crouched beside Sir Sperville where he slumped with his back against the boat's bow.

The answer to her prayers, she thought sourly to the whining screech of sea gulls.

Seven days ago, they had left her home in Cyning. Upon reaching Portchester last eve, they'd secured passage aboard a small sailing vessel that would leave at dawn. A short ride across the Solent, Sperville had said, and they would arrive at Castle Skyenvic on the Isle of Wynt long before dusk.

Only, it appeared the chamberlain might not survive the "short ride."

"If you would drink this"—Golde gestured with the cup she held—"you would feel better."

The chamberlain puckered his thin lips and turned his head away.

Unable to brace herself against the sway of the boat, Golde was forced to sit beside the stubborn fool. "Why did you not say something of your problem with sea travel? I could have saved you this misery."

Sweat dripped down the chamberlain's pasty face and he closed his eyes.

'Od rot, Golde cursed. The three seamen who manned the boat glanced at her surreptitiously, as if she might call monsters from the depths of the Solent to sink them. Did they think she could not see them crossing themselves and making the sign of the evil eye at her? She would not be surprised if they pitched her overboard while Sperville was in his weakened state. And though the boat had remained in sight of land since leaving port, she could not swim.

Fear-borne determination knotted her jaw. She had not traveled in an ox-drawn cart over bone-rattling roads for six days, only to drown on the final day of the journey. Sperville would drink her potion or she would—

Abruptly the chamberlain's Adam's apple jerked spasmodically and he lurched to his knees. Golde grabbed the back of his tunic as he wobbled about to clutch the bow, his face aimed over the side.

"Faith," she muttered, rising on her knees beside him while maintaining a steady hold on the cup. "'Twill be a miracle if your toenails do not fly forth."

Sperville groaned, then heaved, and Golde ordered a cease to her sharp tongue. Remarks about toenails would hardly improve Sperville's spirits. Not that her spirits were any better.

Indeed, a sense of unease had plagued her since she'd left Cyning. A sense of disquiet that had ripened with each dawn, despite the clear days and tranquil weather. A sense of impending trouble that had begun with Mimskin's beaming countenance and sudden approval of Golde's false practices.

Sperville's ragged coughing broke into her thoughts. Wiping his mouth, he slumped back down against the bow.

"You will drink this—" Golde stuck the cup under his nose, "or I will shove it—"

The chamberlain grabbed the cup and gulped its contents. "There!" he rasped and flung the cup in the briny Solent. "With luck, your potion will kill me and I will be free of this wretched suffering."

"Pff," Golde huffed, hiding her relief that Sperville was finally speaking to her. "'Tis I who am in danger of being killed. While you snivel and whine, yon seafolk are plotting to throw me overboard."

"An idea that is not without merit," the chamberlain grumbled. Wrapping his cloak into a ball, he eased himself down on his side and pillowed his head.

Golde gritted her teeth. "How long before we make landfall?"

Sperville pulled the neck of his tunic over his head, ignoring her.

"You said it would be a short ride."

When the chamberlain did not respond, Golde scowled. "Your cloak and tunic will be wrinkled beyond measure."

Still, he said nothing.

Golde crossed her arms over her chest and shot a sullen look at the three seamen, who immediately began crossing themselves. Plague take them, and the useless Sir Sperville. She had yet to reach Skyenvic, and already she longed for home.

She smoothed the skirts of her blue tunic. At least her dearest friend's husband, the Baron of Cyning, would be attending the king's tourney five weeks hence. By co-incidence, the tourney would be held at Atherbrook on the Isle of Wynt, a mere half-day's ride by horse from Skyenvic. Lady Roscelyn's husband would fetch Golde when the festivities concluded, and see her home.

Everything was perfect, Golde told herself firmly. Her uneasiness was no more than a result of her ridiculous sentimentality over leaving home. She would have her fifty pieces of gold and return to Cyning a rich woman, a woman who would never have to beg, a woman who would never be dependent on anyone, least of all a hus-band—

"Do your shoulders always slump thus?" Sir Sperville interrupted her internal diatribe as he rose to sit beside her. "You appear to be malformed."

"Malformed!" Golde squared her shoulders and sat straighter. "What would you call your spindly shanks?"

The chamberlain's nose twitched as if there was a bothersome gnat flying about his face. "Must you always scowl? His lordship will find it most unbecoming."

"His lordship is blind," Golde sneered. "Once I heal him, his joy will be such that he will not care if I am a toothless dragon."

"All the same," Sperville sniffed, "your bearing is a reflection upon me. I'll not have the good folk of Sky-envic questioning my choice of healers."

Golde cast him a disbelieving look. "Ungrateful cur. You are recovered from your ceaseless retching by my good hand, yet you dare to insult me. Doubtless, your master is just as thankless, and my time will be wasted restoring his sight. I may as well order the boat about and return home."

Her tone belied the true sentiments behind her words, for the closer they drew to Skyenvic, the greater grew her discomfort. She would return home in an instant if Sperville agreed.

But Spindleshanks, as Golde decided then and there to think of him, demurred. "Think of me as you will. My shortcomings are indeed great. Unlike me," he continued, "Sir Gavarnie e'er places the needs of others before his own. Since his wife's premature death, none at Skyenvic go hungry, nor cold in winter. He is praised by Church and serf alike for his generosity, while wisdom tempers his judgment and manner so that he is never cruel or cross. Wishes for his long life and good health follow him wherever he goes."

Golde envisioned an elderly, white-haired man, a widower. A saint, no less, if one believed Spindleshanks. "It strikes me that your Gavarnie Delamaure is trying to assure himself a place in heaven by atoning for his sins here on earth. Thus, he's brought blindness upon himself that he will appear more worthy in God's eyes."

She waited for an enraged response from Sperville. Instead, his owlish eyes appeared fixated upon her, while his mouth hung slightly open.

Then he blinked and turned his head that she could not see his countenance. "I am no healer and cannot say what stole my liege's sight. I can only say that Sir Gavarnie will never be whole until he is able to see."

Golde's breath caught. 'Twas respect she'd seen in the chamberlain's eyes; respect for her. She was right in her assumptions about Delamaure bringing blindness upon himself.

Well, not exactly *her* assumptions, she admitted. 'Twas Mimskin who'd determined the cause of Delamaure's ailment, before she'd brought Sperville to Golde's cottage that day.

"Can't abide them snufflers wot inflicts hurts on themselves to gain God's favor," Mimskin had said later, after Sperville had taken himself off to dine. "No reason why ye shouldn't profit from the man's stupidity. All ye need do is make the man believe in yer magic, and his eyes will heal themselves."

Golde's gaze slid now to the chest that contained her clothing and medicines. Not that the medicines would be useful in curing aught but the most common of illnesses. Rather, Mimskin had instructed her to mix several potions together until they stank "worse than a buzzard's supper." Then she was to convince this Gavarnie Delamaure that the concoction would heal his eyes.

Which should not be difficult. Had she not spent the past four years of her life convincing people of her prophesies? Did any amongst her culls doubt her word?

Yet, she was unable to completely reassure herself, and her spirits tumbled further when the rudderman called, "Port, ho!"

In short order, they had docked in the town of New Market, loaded their belongings on a cart, and set off for Castle Skyenvic where Golde would collect her fortune.

'Twas the only thought that held her still upon reaching the castle's great hall several hours later. Despite the activity in the bailey that surrounded her—the shouts of men practicing with weapons, the servants wrestling with squawking chickens and clanging milk pails, the flash of guards' swords from the wallwalk overhead—she felt isolated.

Fifty pieces of gold. A fortune. The answer to her prayers. Golde repeated it over and again in her head as she stared heavenward at the great hall's massive, weatherbeaten timbers. 'Twas absurd that she should feel so intimidated. And cold. Despite the afternoon warmth, a shiver threatened to climb her back.

A brush against her sleeve redirected her thoughts. "Touch me again, Sperville," she threatened, "and you will draw back a stump."

The chamberlain's hand halted its quest to remove yet another imaginary piece of lint from her best blue tunic. Sniffing, he opened the massive oak portal, and ushered her into the great hall.

Golde squinted through the cavernous gloom. At the far end of the enormous trabeated room, a shadowed figure rose to stand before a table atop a dais. Again, a shiver threatened. Was this the saintly lord of whom the chamberlain spoke with such reverence?

Nay. This man had seen them. The Baron of Skyenvic, Golde reminded herself, was blind.

Sperville made a grab for her arm and she jerked it out of his reach. "I need not your assistance," she hissed. Did the chamberlain think her incapable of correctly placing one foot before the other?

Her lip curled as she moved to keep pace with his stately gait. Doubtless, Spindleshanks would split hairs over the length of a proper stride. And at the moment, she desired nothing so much as to meet this quintessential Gavarnie Delamaure, empty his coffers, and be gone. 'Twas hardly imperative that she wait five weeks for Sir Varin and Arnulf to collect her.

"Who have you there?" The cordial man queried as she and Sperville reached the foot of the dais. Fair-featured, he appeared to be kind in spirit and, were she interested, not bad to look upon. So why did she feel such discomfort?

A dry, coughing fit suddenly seized Spindleshanks.

His eyes widened, while his Adam's apple bobbed nervously to the twitching rhythm of his nose.

Golde's uneasy feeling intensified.

"Christ's blood, Sperville. Speak or remove your scrawny hide from my presence."

Golde started, and her gaze jerked to the spot from whence the new voice had emanated. 'Twas little wonder she felt such disquiet. How had she not noticed the man sitting in the huge dragon-carved chair at the far end of the long table? He fair exuded rancor. Dressed in black, he looked much like a great scorch mark that had been seared into the wood.

Sir Sperville cleared his throat. "Mistress Golde." He bowed toward her, then extended his hand to the dark-visaged man. "His Lordship, Sir Gavarnie Delamaure, Baron of Skyenvic."

Upon learning that this man was the baron, she understood nothing else the chamberlain said, so captivated was she by the lord's face. Swarthy and pox-scarred, 'twas as arrogant as 'twas bitter, forbidding as the sheer cliffs that rose defiantly above the English Channel. And like the battered cliffs that fought the sea's merciless onslaught, it was a face that knew not how to compromise. It would break before yielding.

A chill raced over her shoulders and down her spine.

In the next instant, heated anger prickled her flesh.

He is praised by serf and Church alike. Wisdom tempers his judgment and manner so that he is never cruel or cross.

A pox on Spindleshanks. He should be boiled in oil for the falsehoods he'd spouted.

Delamaure was no elderly saint hoping to reach heaven. Nor was he some bumbling lord with whom to trifle. The spells and potions that so becharmed her usual culls would have no effect on this man. He would recognize her mummery for what it was.

His teeth flashed white against his dark skin, and she marveled at how the pockmarks did naught to detract from his compelling looks. Indeed, they lent an irresistible, sinister quality to his features.

Inexplicably, a yearning deep within her pulsed for release. Like a flame to the moth.

A sharp kick to her shin interrupted her disturbed musings, and she realized the lord was speaking.

". . . brought some stupid wench who knows not the language?"

Stupid wench? She glanced around. Of whom did he speak?

"Nay, mi'lord." Spindleshanks' tone was conciliatory. "She is well versed in Norman French."

They were speaking of her? By the rood!

Golde summoned a practiced tone to conceal her outrage. "I speak English, and Gaelic as well."

The lord's black eyes shifted until it appeared he was looking directly at her, though the blankness of his gaze betrayed his inability to do so. "My offspring will not be exposed to a language fit only for grunting pigs. One word of English from your mouth and you will be dismissed."

'Twas no easy task to maintain her placid facade as all thought of returning home flew from her head. 'Twould be a pleasure to cozen the hidebound, arrogant bastard. Meanwhile, she would be certain to teach his offspring English. And Gaelic incantations as well. Let his toadship explain that to his pious Norman priests.

For the moment she affected a humble, concerned tone. Let the dolt think her some Saxon whelp instead of the Celt she was. "Mayhap you should seek the aid of a good Norman witchwife. I would not wish to distress you, considering your obvious aversion to all things English."

Spindleshanks kicked her shin again and she cast him a glance that promised retribution.

The lord's hard voice recaptured her attention. "Few possess the brazen ignorance to come into Skyenvic and insult me."

She'd thought her disdain well veiled, and redoubled her effort to sound sincere. "I meant no offense, your lordship. 'Twas my thinking you would respond more quickly—"

She gasped as pain shot through her shin, then loosed her ire on the chamberlain. "Kick me again, base-born mucker, and I will send your puling soul straight to hell."

Spindleshanks winced, but his voice remained level when he addressed the baron. "Mi'lord, I—"

The fair-featured man who'd greeted them cleared his throat and spoke smoothly. "Mayhap, Sperville, we should look elsewhere for a more mature woman to care for the children."

"Children?" Golde demanded. Of what did the man speak?

"Enough!" the lord bellowed. Slamming his fist on the linen-covered tabletop, he rose, his visage thunderous.

Golde clutched her skirts, preparing to flee. Glancing over her shoulder, she judged the shadowed entrance to the hall to be several furlongs distant, though surely it could not be. Her gaze darted to the bare walls on either side of her, but she could see no doors. The windows were perhaps three times a man's height, and even if she climbed the table trestles stacked beneath them, she would be unable to reach the openings.

Sir Sperville lightly patted her elbow as if to reassure her all was well. Obviously, the fool knew not when to fly.

"You will tell me, wench," continued Lord Delamaure, "to what purpose you are come to Skyenvic."

"Your forgiveness, my liege." The chamberlain spoke before she could reply. "I see now I have made a poor choice—"

"By the throat of Christ. You will hold your tongue, Sperville, else I will cut it from your head."

Spindleshanks responded without a trace of fear. "Yes, my liege, but—"

Golde could stand no more. "Know you what dangers your chamberlain braved to enlist my aid that you might regain your sight? For a week he traveled alone over roads thick with thieves and outlaws to reach me. You should be grateful to have a man of such courage in your service."

Rage twisted the lord's countenance and she took an involuntary backward step. From her lowly position, he appeared huge, both in height and breadth of chest. Indeed, he looked capable of breathing fire with the unholiest of dragons. 'Twas rattling how his black eyes honed in on her as if she were a hare and he the wolf.

"My chamberlain was *instructed*," he spat, "to locate a nursemaid here on the isle for my children. He has been gone a fortnight, to where I know not. Indeed, there has been much speculation concerning his demise. And instead of a nursemaid, he has brought me a tart-tongued, arrogant wench to heal my eyes, a fruitless task already attempted by the king's own physicians."

He paused long enough to draw breath, and his sightless eyes shifted in Spindleshanks' direction. "Now I discover the man not only disobeyed my orders, he is a

dunderwit as well. Only an imbecile would traipse about
the countryside accompanied by no more than an idiot
woman."

Golde tilted her chin upward and forced an even
tone. "How fortunate Sir Sperville is to have one of such
great intellect for master. I assumed his reckless actions to
be a result of unyielding devotion, not witless foolery.
And since your concern is so great, be comforted that we
had a full escort from Cyning all the way to the Solent."

Delamaure raised a brow. "So, the Baron of Cyning is
behind this scheme." He snorted, though when next he
spoke, much of the anger had left his voice. "Sir Varin
risks losing his wits each time he empties his bowels, and
you may tell him I said so." His blanks gaze swept the dais
area. "Nigel?"

"Here, sir," the fair-complexioned man answered.

"Remove this troublesome female from my presence
and see she is returned to Cyning forthwith. And you,
Sperville, shall remain. There is much I would say to
you."

TWO

GAVARNIE DELAMAURE, Baron of Sky-envic, confidante of the king and master of the Solent, shifted his bare rump on a hard wooden stool in his bed-chamber. Though no little time had passed since Sperville's afternoon arrival, he wondered how it could already be morn. The ale-induced thunder that cracked about his skull would require much more sleep before it dissipated.

He fixed his sour attention on the area where he could hear the quick shuffle of Sperville's steps, followed by the spill of pouring water.

"Where is Roland?" he grumbled. "Why does the task of filling my tub fall to you?"

The chamberlain grunted. "Your squire is running errands."

"By whose command?"

"Mine," Sperville snapped, sounding uncommonly flustered.

Gavarnie frowned. Nothing short of death would rattle the chamberlain thus. The child, Nicolette, must have died in the night of the lung fever.

He bowed his head, anxious to betray no trace of the inexplicable sentiment that suddenly gripped him. How was it he could care so much?

Nay.

He raised his head.

He would feel naught but relief. The girl was well rid of him, was she not? As he was of her.

Yet, despite his disavowal, breath continued to leak from his chest, stealing away with part of his very soul. Worse, an image of Nicolette's little elfin face rose to torment him. Her tremulous smiles whenever she caught him staring at her; smiles he'd pointedly ignored for nigh on two years now. The lisping prayers he'd overheard when he chanced to pass her chamber at bedtime. "God bwess Papa . . ."

He jammed the heels of his palms against his eyes. He'd insisted she refer to him as "sir" instead of "Papa," though she could not have understood the reason. She'd never been told what her mother, his wife, had done.

At the sound of water splashing into the bath, he tensed. Was Sperville watching him? Was he making a fool of himself in front of the chamberlain? He rubbed his hands over his eyes and affected a yawn, hoping to look tired rather than expose his womanish grief. His blind eyes made him appear weakling enough.

Still, he could not bring himself to ask after Nicolette. Instead, he crossed his arms over his chest, concentrating hard on the many offenses the chamberlain had most recently committed.

"That tart-tongued magpie you attempted to foist upon me yestereve. She is gone?"

"The witchwife?"

"The witchwife?" Gavarnie whined, mocking the chamberlain's nasal tone. "Do not pretend ignorance, conniving worm. I may yet kill you. That you would have the gall to bring that mean-tempered hellhag into my presence." He scowled, continuing, "I now have no one to care for Ronces and Alory. The king's tourney is little more than a month off. I must prepare for hordes of hungry guests, and that dunghead, de Warrenne . . ."

His words trailed away when he heard the chamber door shut.

"Sperville?"

He narrowed his eyes. Even were the chamberlain in the wardrobe or garderobe, he would respond. Obviously, he'd left the room, and without so much as a by-your-leave.

Gavarnie clenched his fists and cocked his head, listening. No footfalls. No noise filtered through the slitted windows from the bailey below his second-floor bedchamber.

Strange. Where was the clangor of servants rushing to prepare breakfast? Why did no chirping birds or crowing cocks herald the morn?

His head snapped about as a strangled noise issued from the corridor beyond his door. It sounded much like a bleating goat whose throat had been slit.

The back of his neck prickled. Plague take his blind eyes. Had an assassin slipped into Skyenvic?

He rose slowly, his muscles twitching. Whatever the noise, it was drawing nearer.

An image of the chamberlain, throat gushing blood,

assailed him. His eyes rounded reflexively—a futile attempt to see.

He lurched toward the bed, sweeping his hands before him. If he could reach his sword, hidden beneath the pillows . . .

❧❦❧

GOLDE FOLLOWED SPERVILLE into the baron's chamber, then stumbled to a halt. Despite the little girl she carried, despite the urgency of the child's welfare, she could do naught but stare. Delamaure was completely nude where he stood midroom.

Indeed, he was a large man. The flesh strapped over his rib cage vied with sinewed shoulders and arms for her attention. Not to be outdone, the banded muscles of his belly hailed her gaze, as did his—

A deep-chested, raspy eruption instantly reminded her of her mission. Plague take her ogling eyes. She realized Sperville was halfway across the great chamber, heading toward a tub, the only indoor tub, she'd been told. Confining her gaze to the floor, Golde sped toward it. If the baron's small daughter did not gain immediate relief from her raging fever, she was like to die. The only alternative was the outdoor bathing barrels.

Golde caught up with the chamberlain just as he reached the bath. Heedless of her long sleeves, she dropped to her knees and immersed the little girl in the cold bath Sperville had prepared.

"Your forgiveness, my liege," the chamberlain began.

"Speak up, man!" Delamaure bellowed over his daughter's coughing.

Sperville cleared his throat. "I lied. 'Tis not morn, and I did not draw the bath for *you*."

"Get rid of that racket. I can hardly hear you."

Sweet Mother of God, Golde thought. Could the demanding baron think of none, save himself?

"'Tis your daughter," she shouted.

❧❧❧

STUNNED, GAVARNIE STOOD motionless. Anguish over Nicolette's impending death bit into his very soul, gnashing and grinding until he was naught but a bloody pulp. Why was it that men knew not what they possessed until it was taken from them?

Had he not prayed day and night for Nicolette's recovery this week past? Had he not pledged to make amends for his atrocious behavior toward her?

Why must Nicolette suffer, when it was Gavarnie who deserved God's punishment?

Still, it was his chance to tell her . . .

Tell her what, his inwit demanded?

So sorry, Nicolette, but your mother spread her legs for another man. You are his child, not mine. That is the reason for my cruelty toward you these two years past. I hope you will forgive me.

Whore's gleet, Gavarnie swore. What sort of man would burden a five-year-old with such on her deathbed? And that only to ease his own guilt. He might as well confess that he'd killed her mother while he was at it. Then mayhap Nicolette would be glad she was not his—

Abruptly his brow furrowed. His daughter? By his command, none referred to Nicolette as such.

Who would dare?

His lip curled. That voice.

The hellhag. Did she think to make him listen while Nicolette drew her last breath?

"Worthless get of a toothless serpent!" he roared at Sperville. "You will rid my chamber of that presumptuous she-goat this instant."

Nicolette's ragged coughing wheezed to a low gasp, and he heard water swish.

"I will need drying cloths, Sperville," the hellhag directed.

Did no one hear him, Gavarnie wondered? "I forbid it!"

Another croupy outburst rent the air, and he edged his way toward the sound. Where was the dimwitted chamberlain? Why did he not respond?

The barking noise trailed away, followed by a weak moan. What was the hellhag doing to Nicolette? Had the child not suffered enough?

His knees bumped something solid and his hands connected with a head. Ha! The hag. He grabbed a fistful of braided hair.

"You will get yourself gone, wench."

Water splashed and he tightened his grip on the braid as her head bobbed forward.

"Sperville," she croaked.

Faith, but the woman reeked of sweat. Wrinkling his nose, he snapped, "The chamberlain will not help you."

Abruptly he froze. She'd grabbed his—

"Sperville," he ground between clenched teeth. Was the imbecile going to stand about while the woman castrated him?

Then his jaw dropped as another thought struck him. Surely the fool chamberlain had not abandoned his lord to obey the hag's bidding and fetch a drying cloth.

Nicolette whimpered, the sound burning his ears and churning his belly. The rage that gripped him only added to his misery.

He clutched the thick, damp braid. Gladly would he sell his soul for a few moments of sight. He would hack his tormentor limb from limb. His thoughts conjured a pinched-faced, sour dowd. The warts on her chin would quiver with fear.

His grisly musings were interrupted when the dowd's fingers tightened about his *coillons*.

By the rood, he would break the bitch's wrist, he vowed, seizing her forearm.

"Only a fool would burn his fields to keep the crows away," the woman grated over Nicolette's mewling. She applied more pressure.

Gavarnie sucked air. Though he yet felt more discomfort than pain from her brazen hold, the muscle that bunched 'neath her skin bespoke strength and determination. Despite the large span of his hand, he was just able to close his fingers 'round her forearm. The wench must be the size of an ogress.

An image of a hairy, snag-toothed woman-beast captured his thoughts until he realized the flesh beneath his hand was sleekly smooth. A hairless, snag-toothed woman-beast, then. But the thick braid he clutched destroyed that vision as well.

Confused, and more than concerned with his position, he released her hair and arm, then loosed his pent-up breath when her hand left him. Moving backward, he stumbled over the uneven floorboards in his haste to remove himself from her range.

"Mi'lord!" Sperville called from the wardrobe across the room, his tone fretful. "Allow me to assist you."

With each word the chamberlain's voice drew nearer until Gavarnie felt a steadying hand on his elbow.

"I would sooner place my body 'tween the jaws of Fenris." He jerked his arm from Sperville's grasp. "Death from that monstrous wolf's bite is preferable to the misery you have visited on me this day."

Stretching his hands before him, Gavarnie groped toward the wardrobe, intent on dressing himself. Sperville had done naught to aid him thus far, and he'd be boiled in oil before he'd ask the churl for help again.

"Mi'lord, I beg you," the chamberlain persisted, and grabbed his arm.

Balling his hand to a fist, Gavarnie swung at the spot from whence the pleading issued. He would knock every tooth from the idiot's head. But the chamberlain managed to avoid the blow, and as Gavarnie staggered forward, arms wheeling for balance, Sperville caught him.

"Release me, fool."

"As you wish, my liege." The chamberlain loosed his hold.

Gavarnie straightened, then scowled. Though he'd regained his footing, he'd lost his direction. Which way to the wardrobe? Plague take his wife, Isabelle. Had she not taunted him with her infidelity, she would yet live. There would be no hag in his chamber, and he would not be forced to hear . . .

He titled his head and listened.

". . . sweeting. All is well now," the woman-beast soothed. "Be still that your fever may cool a bit more."

"Don't wanna be still. I don't wike baths."

The hellhag had stuck poor little Nicolette in the tub to rid her of fever? Of all the dullwitted—

He clamped his teeth together. 'Twas none of his affair. He would not allow himself to grow attached to the child at this point, not when she was about to die. 'Twould only bring him more misery.

"I am c-c-cold," Nicolette spluttered.

He refused to acknowledge the stirring in his heart at

the child's chattered complaint. At least she'd quit that horrid coughing.

"What is a little cold to a girl as brave and strong as you?" the ogress queried softly. "I would swear the fairy queen, Titania, guards your soul."

Her deep, velvet voice whispered in his ears like waves slipping ashore from the Solent on a warm, star-clad night, inviting him to take his ease.

He shook himself. Concentrating on the matter at hand, he turned. Judging from the dowd's voice, the tub was now behind him. The wardrobe should be ahead of him.

He shuffled forward, arms outstretched, until he stumbled into the bed. God be damned. He must appear the most incompetent of lackwits.

Inhaling deeply, he felt his way 'round the foot of the mattress, then paused. Frowning, he tried to recall the room's dimensions. Only three months had passed since he'd last seen his private chambers, but it seemed an eternity. The thickly curtained bed stood in the center of the room, its smooth, polished posts near reaching the ceiling.

Unbidden, his wife's glazed blue eyes surfaced in his thoughts, along with the memory of her dried, crimson-black blood where it had splashed over the sheets. 'Twas the last thing he'd seen before—

He lurched forward.

The wardrobe—its doorway should be a little to his right. He adjusted his approach accordingly, and within moments his hand struck the wall that separated the storage room from the bedchamber. He halted, and the dowd's voice again captured his attention as she wove a tale of fairy lore for Nicolette.

"The walls of their little palace are made of spiders' legs, and the roof of bats' wings dipped in moonlight."

'Twas devil's magic that the hag sounded so alluring. Her voice swirled through his senses like a lazy cat's purr. Lulled by her tone, he absently slid his hands along the coarse wooden partition, moving to his right.

"'Tis the other direction." Sperville's words pulled him from the woman-beast's spell.

Unaccountably annoyed by the interruption, he groused, "If 'tis your wish to assist me, then place your scrawny neck between my hands that I may have the pleasure of strangling you."

"Yes, my liege."

Plague take Sperville and his droll retort. Gavarnie's jaw clamped together and he reversed direction until he located the opening to the wardrobe. Edging forward, he breathed the tallowy scent of the beeswax used to polish his storage chests. Again he paused.

". . . her gossamer wings of silver—"

"I don't care about bat wegs and spidew wings," Nicolette interupted, saving Gavarnie from falling victim to the ogress's seductive voice a third time. "I hate baths."

Gavarnie focused on recalling which chests held his clothing. Whore's gleet. How was he to remember what was where? He never dressed himself. His squire, Roland, performed that task.

But nay, Sperville had ordered the boy on some errand. Bending, Gavarnie swept his hands before him and lumbered on. Something *would* be done about the chamberlain's disrespectful insouciance, he vowed. The gall, that the mutton-head had ordered *his* squire about. His hand struck a chest, and fumbling with the latch, he threw open the lid. Instantly the coppery scent of polished silver filled his nostrils.

A shiver crawled over his neck. 'Twas much the same odor as Isabelle's blood. For a moment he could not force himself to reach out and close the lid, afraid of what he might touch.

Cold, viscid flesh.

Fool's get, he chided himself. The chest contained no more than silver plate. The murder charges against him had been dismissed on the basis of Isabelle's adultery. He was guilty of naught, despite that whoreson de War-renne's insistence on a trial. Straightening, he swiped at the lid and heard it clap shut.

Still, his hands trembled as he sidled to his left, open-ing each chest he came upon. Moments later he found his clothes. Grabbing the first pair of braies and tunic he laid hands on, he fumbled about, dressing himself. At one point he was forced to sit, bare-assed, on the floor. But once finished with the task, he pulled on some boots and shuffled to the opening that led from the anteroom to the bedchamber.

"If you would be still." The ogress's tone held a forced sweetness.

"I am dwy awweady," Nicolette rasped stubbornly, then coughed.

Take that, ogress! Gavarnie silently cheered. From whence had Nicolette acquired such mettle? Were the child not facing the throes of death, he would—

Nay. He would not allow his thoughts to run in that direction. If Nicolette lived, there would be time enough to make up for his mean treatment of her. Meanwhile, he had no intention of standing about and listening to her die, and he did not care if it was God's punishment. He had suffered enough for Isabelle's death.

Checking his bearings, he ran his hands along the framed doorway, then drew himself to his full height.

Ha! He had done it. He had dressed himself with no assistance. A smirk curled his lips. Nothing stood between him and the far bedchamber door, and he headed toward it. For the first time since he'd lost his sight, he would leave the room under his own power.

Then he would find his way to the great hall, by God, where he would command Nigel to see to the removal of the interlopers in his chamber. At least the steward had never failed to carry out his orders.

He'd taken no more than a dozen steps when a bundle was suddenly thrust against his chest.

"Your daughter, mi'lord," the ogress snapped.

He stiffened and felt a corresponding tension in Nicolette's small body where he clutched her. By the Blessed Virgin. He would not have the child die in his arms.

"A pox on you, hag. You will take this bit of stuff this instant."

"My liege," the chamberlain interrupted.

"Hold your tongue, Sperville," he commanded, then continued to address the woman-beast in an icy tone. "Now that you've insisted upon involving yourself with the child's welfare, you will care for her until—"

"Mi'lord!" Sperville blurted. "She is gone."

Disbelief snatched Gavarnie's voice. None dared walk away when he was speaking. Several moments passed before he managed to sputter, "Whe—wha—what mean you she is gone?"

"She has taken leave."

Nicolette coughed fitfully. From near-forgotten habit, Gavarnie jounced her as he had when she was a babe, the same as he had jounced his sons, Ronces and Alory. "Fetch the hag back," he demanded.

"I do not think she will return, sir."

"'Tis not your duty to think. You will do as I bid or I will flay you hideless."

"Yes, my liege, but what if she refuses to come?" Sperville's misgivings were evident in his tone.

"Whore's gleet, man. Bind her hands and feet, truss her like the Saxon pig she is. I care not how you go about it. But you will get her here. Now."

Nicolette wheezed, and her tiny fingers clutched his shoulder. "Papa! She woo make you nose tuwn bwack and faw off."

Gavarnie stilled. Despite his cruelty, despite the fact she was near death, Nicolette was still concerned for his welfare. Guilt rushed to clog his throat until he could scarce speak, though he was determined to ease her fears this once.

"No one can make my nose turn black and fall off," he managed to choke.

But the child misread his tone, which sounded gruff even to his ears. Her fingers left his shoulder and her body again grew rigid.

He scowled. What had he expected? That Nicolette would magically comprehend his change in heart toward her? That the thought of her death made him realize how deeply he cared for her?

A pox on the cursed ogress. She'd accomplished in one day what he'd never dreamed possible. She'd made him more miserable than he already was.

The chamberlain's voice broke into his reverie. "Mayhap 'twould be best—"

"Why are you not fetching the hag?" he demanded. Closing his eyes, he took a deep breath, then affected his most reasonable tone. "Truth tell, Sperville. Do you simply wish for death, or is it your mission to render me witless with rage? I can assure you the latter will not come to pass. But if you will fetch my blade and direct my hand, I will cheerfully see to the former."

Nicolette coughed raggedly, and again he jounced her.

"I was going to suggest I take Nicolette back to her chamber," Sperville huffed, "and then fetch the hag."

Relief washed over Gavarnie. Escape was at hand. "Now, there is an intelligent thought." Holding his arms out, he waited to be relieved of his burden.

Several moments passed with no response. "Well? What are you about now?"

No reply.

"Shiew Spewville—" Nicolette choked.

When the child said no more, he prodded, "Sir Sperville?"

"Gone," Nicolette wheezed, then convulsed in a coughing spasm.

Rage boiled his blood anew. He jerked Nicolette to his chest and bounced her. He would murder the chamberlain. Yea, and he would do it by his own hand. He would have the spineless worm bound and staked to the whipping post in the bailey and carve his mean flesh to ribbons, then gut him while he yet drew breath.

"Sightless I may be," he bellowed, "but I will have the pleasure of hearing your agony when I cut your heart from your spindly chest."

"Pwease, Shiew Bawon," Nicolette whimpered. "You awe shaking up my bewwy."

Gavarnie froze. "You are going to be sick?"

He felt her nod against his chest and swallowed hard. What was he thinking with his bluster and blather? Nicolette could die any moment. The thought turned his limbs to mush until he feared he might collapse. Turning, he shuffled toward the bed where he could sit and hold her.

" 'Tis not Shiew Spewville's fawt," the child whispered as he maneuvered along. "That witch took his wits."

Was she frightened? Could she feel his terror at her impending death? "Witches are naught but the imaginings of simpletons," he whispered back, though whether he said so to soothe Nicolette or himself, he wasn't certain.

"She is a witch," the child insisted. "Her hair is bwack and so is one of her eyes. The other eye is gween."

Nicolette drew a shuddering breath. "She is skinny and taw as Shiew Spewville. And you could faw in a fit fwom her just looking at you."

"Shh," he coaxed gently. Faith, but it hurt to listen to Nicolette's strangled voice.

He inhaled her little-girl smell, the scent reminding him of the joy he'd experienced at her birth. *God bwess Papa.* The words of her overheard prayer tore at his heart with the sharpness of a well-honed blade.

If given a choice at this moment, he would kill Isabelle all over again. Only this time he would not do it for her infidelity.

Nay. She deserved to die for allowing him to love Nicolette those first three years of her life, a crime far greater than adultery, because it was doubly painful to then find out she wasn't his.

Why had the realization been so long in coming?

Despite the fact that Nicolette wasn't his daughter, he loved her as if she were. He'd been a fool to fight his feelings for her these two years past. He'd brought naught but misery upon himself, and the child.

God bwess Papa. He grimaced as his eyes stung. When was the last time he'd cried?

Isabelle was doubtless laughing at him from the bowels of hell.

THREE

NICOLETTE'S CRAMPED bedchamber sweltered from heated stones that had been dropped in pails of water. Golde swiped sweat from her brow and scraped sticky hair from her temples. Faith, she needed to bathe. Her best blue tunic looked as if it had been used to muck the sheep pen, and her gray chainse felt like a scratchy second layer of skin.

"'Tis important you continue steaming the room," she instructed the matronly servant, Hesper. "Once the child tolerates honey-water, then you may begin feeding her broth."

Golde snatched up her medicine jars and fair threw them into her chest. How could she, the mistress of deception, have been so duped by the blunderheaded chamberlain? Oh, but his eyes had appeared so properly heartsick when he'd wakened her in the undercroft. "I have need of your aid," he'd whispered urgently.

She slammed the lid on the chest. What had become of her vow to not involve herself in the affairs of her culls?

But nay. She'd had to await the morn to begin her journey home. And Spindleshanks had taken full advantage of the delay, pleading with her in the middle of the night to save Delamaure's daughter from death.

As if her thoughts had conjured the wheedling snake, Sperville hurried into the child's bedchamber. "Mistress, let us get you gone."

Before Golde could reply, Hesper cried, "She cannot leave." The older woman wrung the folds of her tunic while her second chin quivered pinkly above the red coals in the brazier. "Ye must convince her to stay, at least until Nicolette is healed."

Convince her to stay, indeed, Golde thought. There was not enough gold in all England to make her do so. She opened her mouth to say just that, but Spindleshanks spoke first. "Nay, Hesper. She has done enough. I would not repay her kindness by subjecting her to the baron's foul temper any longer."

Golde curled her lip. "'Tis a bit late—"

"I know not how to care for sick folk," Hesper interrupted. "What if Nicolette should worsen again?"

"I have told you—" Golde began.

Hesper allowed her no chance to finish. "What if the baron forbids me to care for her? I dare not gainsay him."

"There is naught we can do about the matter, should it come to pass," Sperville intoned gravely.

Golde frowned. The evil baron had seemed most willing to allow his daughter to die. And but moments ago, just before Spindleshanks had appeared, the lord's blustering threat to cut out someone's heart had fair rattled the castle timbers.

"'Tis no concern of this great lady's," Sperville was saying. "She has worked a miracle this night and we must pray for the best."

Golde raised a black brow. "Seek you to convince me to stay with sweet words of praise?"

Sir Sperville's features hardened, lending his visage a strength she would never have imagined. "I would not allow you to remain, even were it your greatest desire. Despite your skill and knowledge, you are . . ." A sheepish look overcame the chamberlain.

Golde inclined her head and stared pointedly.

"It matters not. You must away." He beckoned her with his hand.

Golde crossed her arms over her chest. "I am what?"

"Truly, you are everything I have said." Spindleshanks was clearly hedging. "Now let us get you gone."

Golde narrowed her eyes. "I will hear this great lack you have discovered in my nature. Why, of a sudden, must you spirit me off where before you did all in your power to keep me here?"

Spindleshanks glanced over his shoulder, then lowered his voice and stammered, "I had hoped . . . You appeared to be most—"

"By Saint Cuthbert! Cease your spluttering and speak."

The chamberlain's gaze darted away from her face and he bowed his head. "You lack naught. Few, if any, have the courage to betake themselves unto dealing with the baron's personal affairs. I had hoped to secure your great-grandmother's services, for I had heard of her wisdom and strength. When she refused, I grew desperate.

His lordship will never know peace until he recovers his sight."

He cast her a penitent look, then lowered his gaze again. "Though I am certain you could heal him, you are far too young and inexperienced to deal with the baron's temper. I can do naught but ask your forgiveness."

Golde sneered. "You tell me I have worked miracles, then speak of me as if I were a cowering, snot-nosed whelp too thickwitted to come in from the rain."

Sir Sperville's head snapped up. "I meant no insult." He fixed his attention on Hesper, defending himself to her, as if he feared looking at Golde. "Truly, you would not credit all mistress has accomplished. Not only did she compel Sir Gavarnie to dress himself, when I left him just now, he was holding Nicolette with a father's tenderness. And talking to her."

"Saints be praised," Hesper breathed.

The woman crossed herself, and curiosity near overwhelmed Golde. The baron had forbade her to bathe Nicolette earlier. And though the child's very life was dependent upon Golde's knowledge, Delamaure had attempted to force her from his chamber. At the time, she'd thought it was only *her* person that he objected to. But after listening to Sperville and Hesper, it sounded as if the baron also objected to his daughter.

Nay. Golde caught herself as silence descended over the chamber. 'Twas none of her affair. Indeed, if she'd learned aught in her youth, 'twas that children were cruel little beasts. Ever demanding and willful, they never spared a thought for the feelings of others. They were peculiar of habit, not the least of which was their penchant for mischief and destruction, and they required such . . . *devotion* was the only word she could think of.

Still, her feet refused to budge at her command.

Worse, an image of the baron's naked body wiggled its way into her thoughts.

She flapped the neck of her chainse. Imposing. Delamaure's body bespoke strength, hostility, and arrogance. They were present in tightly coiled muscles, in his powerful broad frame, in his regal stance. Legs braced, fists on hips . . . despite its dormancy, his sex when she'd grabbed him had felt—

Faith! What was she thinking? Worse, she was flapping the neck of her chainse with the speed of a bee's wing. She let loose of the material and glared at the chamberlain.

"'Twas you and none other who made me appear the fool. You knew full well the baron was expecting a nursemaid, not a witchwife."

Spindleshanks' head drooped lower. "Sir Gavarnie's pride e're prevents him from seeking aid of any type. I'd hoped to disguise your true purpose."

"Why did you not explain yourself from the beginning?"

Sperville glanced up at her. "Had you known of the deception, would you have agreed to come?"

'Twas as if a worm were squirming inside her. Obviously, he thought her too honorable to be involved in trickery. She felt as if Mimskin were standing there, shaking a finger at her.

Ye destroy your swevyn with your falseness and rob those who have true need of your help. 'Tis ashamed I am to claim you as kin.

Golde piled her braid atop her head and fanned herself, cooling the flesh that prickled not from the room's heat—or from thoughts of the baron—but from shame. Though why she should feel thus was a mystery. In this instance, Mimskin was as guilty as Golde of deceit.

Meanwhile, Sperville had deceived Delamaure into thinking Golde was a nursemaid. Had Mimskin foreseen the baron's foul reaction to Golde's arrival at Skyenvic, she would never have allowed her to come. But Mimskin hadn't consulted the runes on the question of Golde's reception, for Spindleshanks had implied that the baron would welcome her.

And what had Delamaure said earlier about Sir Varin?

. . . the Baron of Cyning is behind this scheme.

Aye. That was it. Delamaure assumed Varin had sent her.

. . . risks losing his wits each time he empties his bowels . . .

Which she would indeed tell Varin the moment she arrived home. For, according to what Roscelyn had said before Golde left Cyning, Varin believed Delamaure to be a friend.

Golde frowned at the ache that was beginning to throb in her head. 'Twas nigh impossible to determine who was deceiving whom.

Nor did her ruminations help solve her immediate dilemma concerning Nicolette's illness. Would the baron truly forbid Hesper to care for the child?

At last, she addressed Spindleshanks, her tone brusque. "I will stay until the child is well, provided you confess your maneuvering to your master."

A look of satisfaction appeared to cross the chamberlain's features, but before she could be certain, Hesper had clutched her hand and kissed it.

When she looked back to Sperville, he'd drawn himself up and was shaking his head. "Nay. I cannot allow it. You would be less than a mouthful for the baron's wolfish bite. As we speak, he demands your presence for no reason but to vent his spleen upon you."

The poor lighting and vapor haze had tricked her. Far from looking satisfied, Spindleshanks' eyes were round with fear.

Golde snorted. "If his lordship commands my presence, then so shall it be."

She marched past Sir Sperville into the hall. 'Twould be best to instruct the ill-mannered Delamaure at once on the proper treatment of her person, now that she'd decided to stay.

Four

IT SEEMED TO GAVARNIE he'd just drifted off again when something wakened him. Christ's blood. Would he never sleep this night? He started to roll from his back to his side when he left a tug on his boot. He forced himself to stillness as the evening's events surfaced in his thoughts.

The ogress.

By the rood, she was no more than a thief. 'Twas a common fallacy amongst the Saxon peasantry that Norman lords slept with valuables tucked inside their boots. A fallacy the hag would regret.

He concentrated on the movement at his feet until he knew exactly where he'd aim his blade. In one smooth motion, he hauled his sword from beneath the pillows and shot upward to his knees.

Blessed Virgin Mother! Could it be Nicolette?

His heart thudded and he jerked the blade sideways. The sharp-honed steel tore through the heavy bed curtain and bit into the massive post at the foot of the bed.

Sperville yelped, "'Tis I!"

Gavarnie gulped air and clutched the sword's hilt, hands shaking. "Whore's gleet! Have you no consideration for your safety, man? Had I not thought you Nicolette at the last moment—" He yanked the blade free of the post. "What were you thinking?"

"I was removing your boots so your rest would be more comfortable." The chamberlain's voice carried high and thin. "Nicolette has been returned to her chamber."

Still gripping the sword, Gavarnie sank back against the pillows. Swallowing hard, he waited for his heart to slide from his throat back down to his chest, where it belonged. Then he forced himself to speak calmly. "As ever, Sperville, your devotion to duty overrides your good sense. But I prefer you whole rather than in halves. And, if you would, please consider my sentiments before next you come creeping 'round my bed in the dead of night."

"My apologies," the chamberlain sniffed. "Might I remove your boots, that I may get some rest?"

Gavarnie rose again to sit. "You have yet to gain your bed? Why do you not rouse Roland to remove my boots? Or does he yet run errands at your command? And what has become of that miserable dowd I sent you to collect?"

"When we returned, you were sleeping. I assumed you would rather deal with matters on the morrow than be disturbed."

Gavarnie ran a hand over his face. "Faith, Sperville, you and Roland have much to do. De Warrenne will be arriving on the morrow. The silver plate needs counting and spices must be doled out to the kitchens."

He paused as his thoughts came full circle. "Nicolette. Is she . . ." He could not complete the question, so sharply did his inwit stab him.

"She is recovering."

Gavarnie's pulse quickened. The child was recovering? Before God, he vowed, Nicolette would never want for anything again.

"You would do well to avail *yourself* of the witchwife's miracles before you scare her off."

"Humph," Gavarnie snorted, feeling better than he had in years. "The hag is not afraid of the devil. Know you what she dared earlier? She threatened to castrate me with her bare hands. Had the audacity to clutch my—"

Wheezing gasps issued from the foot of the bed.

"That had best not be laughter I hear spilling from your mouth."

The windy mirth only increased, and Gavarnie drummed his fingers on the hilt of the sword. 'Twas not at all like the staid chamberlain to find humor in such base-born behavior.

"Your reasoning has deserted you," he remarked sourly. "Take yourself off and get some sleep."

Sperville cleared his throat. "The young lady is most resourceful, is she not?"

"Resourceful? Snakes doubtless flee at her approach. Spiders likely scramble to hide, lest she pluck them from their webs to eat."

More gasping merriment.

Gavarnie struggled to shove the sword back under his pillows, the length of the blade making the task difficult. It kept catching in the bed linens. At last he succeeded, then bent forward to wrestle with a boot.

"Young lady," he grumbled, and slammed one boot on the floor. "I'll wager she has not one tooth left in her ancient head."

"You have formed quite an image of the woman. Surely she does not frighten you." Sperville's voice quivered, clearly a result of his struggle to contain his mirth.

Gavarnie jerked the remaining boot from his foot and clutched the stiff leather in his fists. "Begone, imbecile, lest you find my boot between your teeth."

"As you wish, my liege. But my inwit would allow me no respite were I to leave you with such nightmarish visions. Golde is not as you think." The chamberlain's tone grew earnest. "Though I will admit she is no beauty at first glance, if you could see, you would find her quite striking."

"She is big as a horse, judging from the size of her forearm. And tall as you, according to Nicolette, with one black eye and one green. I'm not sure *striking* properly describes the wench. *Hideous*, perhaps. *Ugly*, of a certainty."

"Aye, she is tall, but in the likeness of a sapling that bends with grace before the wind. Far from big, she is lean in the way of woodland creatures that depend upon agility to survive."

Big as a tree and lean as a boar sow, he translated Sperville's description. "Get thee gone. You are moonstruck and I will hear no more."

He dropped the boot and plopped back on the mattress, pulling a pillow over his head. He'd never heard the chamberlain speak so warmly of a woman. Not that Sperville did not know beauty when he saw it. He'd oft remarked on serving wenches, and even a time or two on Isabelle's appearance. But 'twas always dispassionate, in the way a jeweler might examine a particular stone.

Removing the pillow from his head, Gavarnie rolled

to his side. On a whim, he squeezed the fingers of one hand around his forearm. His lips puckered.

Mayhap he'd been wrong. The hag's arm was nowhere near the size of his. Even so, she could not be skinny, as Nicolette claimed.

He hugged the pillow to his chest. One eye green, the other black. No pinch-faced sour dowd. No beauty, either. Striking. He tried to imagine her face. Oval, round, heart-shaped? Framed with black hair, by Nicolette's account. He remembered the thick, damp tresses he'd clutched earlier.

Bats' wings dipped in moonlight.

Her voice floated through his memory. Throaty, muted. A low murmur trailed through still water, rippling outward, caressing everything it touched. Like a woman skilled at seduction, he thought drowsily, allowing the layers of sound to drift ever lower. They lapped at his loins and laved his shaft in a resonant, husky chorus.

Abruptly lust tore for release, and he ground his hips against the pillow. It seemed an eternity had passed since he'd last—

Whore's gleet! He bolted upright. For all he knew, Sperville could yet be standing at the foot of the bed. He stilled, straining to hear the telltale whisper of breathing.

Nothing.

Fool! he railed at himself. Had he not covered his head with the pillow, he would have heard whether or not the door closed and known if the chamberlain had left to seek his bed in the undercroft.

"Sperville?" he whispered.

No reply.

Still, it felt as if every person in the castle were watching him. 'Twas not the first time he'd felt thus, but never had he sensed it so keenly.

He threw himself back on the mattress, willing away the despair that threatened to engulf him.

He would not remain blind.

He would not!

And by all that was holy, in future he would make certain of his privacy.

FIVE

❧❧❧

GOLDE SWATTED at the nettlesome hand
that persisted in shaking her shoulder. Despite the dripping heat, she was having no difficulty sleeping on a pallet beside Nicolette's bed. Indeed, now that the child's
cough had eased, providing a measure of quiet, Golde felt
certain she could sleep a full fortnight.

Her thoughts drifted to the stream that ran behind
the castle orchard back home at Cyning. An image of
clear water flashed crisp invitation. She hurried toward it,
stripping her clothes. Ah, to be clean and cool.

Her steps slowed to a halt. Delamaure stood on the
bank opposite her. The black-eyed stare he leveled at her
gleamed hard and sharp. His nostrils flared. His visage
darkened with heated blood. A wolf that had just scented
its mate. Though a black cloak concealed his body, he
exuded raw, randy strength.

Warmth pooled in her groin at his predatory gaze. Possession. 'Twas what he wanted. How she longed to surrender, to be held in his powerful embrace, to feel his hands on her. A blush crept over her face. None would dare ridicule her so long as she held the baron's favor. She would be safe.

The hand shook her more urgently.

Golde refused to open her eyes. "Get thee gone, wretched gnat."

"Lady, please," a young woman's voice quavered. "It's me duty to rouse ye. His lordship commands yer presence."

"The baron?" Golde rolled onto her belly and snuggled her face into the woolen blanket she'd used to pillow her head. 'Twas remarkable how comfortable the scratchy material felt against her cheek, despite its sweat-ripened smell. If only she could again draw forth the stream's cool image. And Delamaure.

"Lady," the girlish voice pleaded, "if ye don't obey the summons, Sir Gavarnie will have me hide."

Golde jerked to a sitting position, prepared to unleash a poisonous rebuke.

A freckle-faced serving girl gave her a horror-stricken look and backed toward the door. "Y-y-yer pardon, lady," she stuttered. "I will tell Sir Gavarnie ye are lamed up."

Golde forced a tired smile. She must truly resemble an old dragon-hag if the girl's distressed appearance were any indication. "My apologies for my ill-bred manner."

The maid halted her backward flight and nodded her redhaired head, though she yet appeared discomfited. Doubtless, the baron was no less cruel to his servants than he was to his daughter. The poor maid would likely suffer should she fail her task.

Golde rose, her body feeling leaden as a great iron cauldron. "I will attend the summons."

She checked Nicolette and found the child's skin cool to the touch. While the little girl's coloring was yet wan, 'twas no longer deathly gray. Golde smoothed a light brown ringlet from the child's brow. Who would guess that beneath the angelic features lay a stubborn little mule? And mule she was, if her reaction to last night's bath were any indication. Golde tucked the bed sheet more closely about the girl's chin, then stretched.

The motion did naught but drain what little energy she possessed. Dropping her arms to her sides, she addressed the young serving maid, who hovered uncertainly by the door. "Where may I find the baron?"

The girl bobbed a quick curtsy. "He is in the hall. If you will, follow me." Turning, she made to leave.

"A moment," Golde begged. "Are you not to stay and care for his lordship's daughter in my absence?"

The girl paused. "I gots me chores to finish in the hall, then me duties in the kitchen."

"Am I to wait for someone to relieve me?"

"Not so's I know. Sir Gavarnie only told me to serve ye the message that he wished t' see ye."

"Is his lordship aware there are none to watch over his daughter? Hesper was up all night and has gone to catch some rest."

The serving maid's glance darted back and forth between Golde and Nicolette. She chewed a fingernail, and her features grew apprehensive. "Do ye wish me to ask?"

"Nay. I would that you stay and attend the child. I will speak with the baron."

The maid flushed and her freckles appeared to take on a greenish cast. "I daren't do that, lady. Someone would tell the steward I wasn't at me chores."

The girl backed away as Golde strode forward. Fearing she might bolt any moment, Golde fair leapt to cover the distance between them. The servant flinched as she wrapped an arm about her shoulder.

"Calm yourself." She drew the maid back inside the room. "I will explain the situation to the baron. I am certain he will appreciate your attention to his daughter. The child should not be left alone."

The servant, a good head shorter than Golde, gave her an anxious look. "I ar'nt certain his lordship will care."

He would when she was finished with him, Golde thought. Patting the girl's arm, she fixed a kindly smile on her lips. "I assure you, the baron is most concerned with his daughter. Why, early this morn I carried Nicolette from his bed where she slept wrapped in the comfort of his arms."

The girl looked incredulous. "Truth tell?"

Golde crossed herself. "Before God."

The maid glanced at Nicolette and back to Golde. "Then I will stay. Please tell his lordship I shall work late if needs be to finish me duties."

Golde nodded at the girl's proffered sacrifice, then headed for the door, frowning. First Spindleshanks, and now the young maid. However did the mean-tempered baron manage to instill such loyalty?

The corridor felt icy after the bedchamber's heat and Golde crossed her arms as gooseflesh rose on her body. Once she reached the stairs, she quickly descended, scowling.

She'd intended to speak with Delamaure long before daybreak. But when she and Spindleshanks had returned to the baron's chamber, they'd found Sir Gavarnie and his daughter fast asleep. Sperville had convinced her to leave wolves to their slumber, thus she had returned the child to her bed without disturbing the lord.

A courtesy he'd not returned, she groused to herself. He'd had no qualms about disturbing her sleep. She reached the bottom of the steps and her stomach growled at the smell of cheese and bread wafting through the undercroft. The rude bastard could not even bother to see her fed before demanding her presence.

Golde marched through a screens passage, a free-standing wooden wall that partitioned the stairs and undercroft from the great hall. So determined were her steps, she near collided with a small boy spinning in circles. She halted and eyed the cooking pot perched atop his head. Grime encrusted the fine blue material of his tunic.

"Away with you, bug, lest I squash you 'neath my heel," she snapped.

The child, perhaps five or six, paused. Tilting his head back, he tried to stare at her, but his eyes refused to focus. He fell sideways, dizzy as a drunken sailor on a gale-blown ship.

Golde snorted. Were all children lunatics?

A sudden, high-pitched shriek erupted behind her, causing her to shudder. Before she could locate its source, something solid thwacked her rear.

"None attack my brother, but that they will be gutted!"

Golde spun to face yet another boy, this one seven or eight. Dressed in a filthy black tunic with gray braies, he brandished a wooden sword at her. Grabbing its tip, she tried to shake it from the brat's grasp, but he would not leave go.

Narrowing an eye, she taunted, "Only a fool would

gut a person's buttocks. Unless, of course, he lives in a privy and has learned to tolerate fetid odors."

The boy glared at her, dark eyes sparking with anger. With his black hair and dark complexion, she recognized immediately 'twas the baron's get. At the same moment, she realized the hall was silent as a tomb. Glancing about the enormous room, she noted that the servants had frozen midtask.

"Dare you imply my son is dullwitted?" a voice demanded from the dais behind her.

She would have known the sour voice, even had he not identified himself as the boy's father. Ignoring the baron, she continued to address the angry child. "In future, master swordsman, where will you gut a person?"

The little brat's features were hate-filled. "In the belly." He shoved the wooden blade toward her stomach with all his might.

Rather than resist the motion, Golde jerked the sword forward, pulling the boy with it. Taking advantage of his surprise, she swept a foot behind his and shoved him backward. He fell on his rear, loosing his grip on the weapon.

Golde placed one foot on his stomach. Flipping the blade in her hand, she pointed the tip at his throat. He flushed darkly, embarrassed.

"Now, master swordsman," she affected a threatening tone. "I will tell you something only dead men know."

The boy's eyes grew round and his throat worked as he tried to swallow.

"Never underestimate your opponent."

Tossing the wooden sword on the ground, she turned and approached the dais without looking back. If the child dared strike her again, she would beat him senseless, baron's get or no.

Climbing the steps to the raised platform, she nodded at the steward, Nigel, who stood grinning near the seated baron. His merriment only fueled her anger. 'Twas telling of a man's character that he would find pleasure in the humiliation of a child.

She frowned as a thought occurred. Had she not . . .

Nay. That she'd felt a sense of satisfaction at the boy's chagrin was different, she told herself. She'd done naught but teach the brat a well-deserved lesson.

The steward cleared his throat and addressed Sir Gavarnie in an overloud voice. "'Twould appear the servants will idle the morn away, my liege. Mayhap 'twould be an opportune time to dig a new privy."

Instantly the hall came alive with bustling activity. Breakfast remains were carted off and linen tablecloths snapped as servants shook crumbs from them.

Golde turned her attention to Sir Gavarnie. "What grave matter is so pressing that I am prevented from a moment's rest?"

Though his eyes remained blank when they shifted to fix on her position, the lord's features reflected displeasure. "I have e're impressed the importance of family on my children. They have been taught to defend one another. You have near destroyed the unity I worked to achieve with one swipe of your acid tongue. Do so again, and you risk losing the poisonous appendage."

Golde raised a brow. His threat would have more effect were he not dressed in such ill-conceived apparel. His pale-green, moth-eaten undertunic in no way matched his short-sleeved, faded-purple tunic. The leather thongs in the tunic's V-shaped neck were knotted to the point that only a wizard could hope to undo them. Edging nearer the table, she peeked at his lap. His braies were an odd mustard color.

Her mouth crooked in a half smile and she glanced at the steward. In contrast, Sir Nigel was immaculately dressed in brown braies and a yellow tunic.

"You shall care for my children until—"

"I will what?" Golde whipped her gaze back to the lord's face.

The baron clenched his fists on the tabletop. "You will not interrupt when I am speaking. Nor will you walk away until I give you leave."

Inexplicably his mouth drew her gaze, then snatched her attention. Darkly inviting, his chiseled lips moved with the suppleness of molten gold. Would they feel as warm and smooth as they looked, or would they—

'Od rot! Did she yet dream? Concentrating her efforts, she managed a glib retort. "My apologies, sir. I was distracted by your elegant choice of attire. Prithee, continue."

The baron frowned. "Of what do you speak?"

Golde shifted her gaze to focus on his black eyes, anxious to avoid the absurd feelings his mouth aroused. "'Tis naught. You were saying?"

His features grew stony. "You will tell me to what elegant attire you refer."

Faith, but it appeared the baron's gaze was fixed on her breasts. Unaccountably her nipples hardened, pulling taut some invisible string attached to her woman's core. As if she had waited too long to attend her bodily functions, she was struck by a maddening desire to cross her legs.

"'Tis a most . . ." She licked her lips, and marshaling her thoughts, began anew. " 'Tis quite an impressive arrangement of color you have chosen to wear."

There, she congratulated herself. She'd successfully affected a light tone. Confidence restored, she continued.

"Did you select the garments yourself, or was more than one person required to coordinate such an array of shades?"

She scarce had time to blink before the baron had seized her forearm and risen from his chair. Would that she had not edged so near to view the color of his braies. His grip was hard, his callused, dark fingers unyielding. 'Twas unsettling to have to look up to see his chilling features; doubly so, considering her height had ere given her the advantage of looking down on people, including a goodly number of men.

"We shall continue this discussion in my chambers," he snapped. Spinning her about, he grasped the back of her tunic and propelled her toward the dais steps, forcing her to lead the way.

Her first thought was to drive an elbow into his belly. But as he bunched the material at the small of her back and the tunic tightened across her chest, her wits deserted her.

Straining to acquire all possible contact with the binding material, her nipples again hardened, the treacherous louts.

"My liege," Sir Nigel spoke, his blue-green eyes sparkling with humor. "Do you wish me to accompany you?"

"Nay." The baron's deep voice vibrated as if his mouth were pressed against her ear. "Since it appears she is the only person bold enough to point out the shortcomings of my raiment, the hag can escort me."

Instantly rage consumed Golde. Hag, was she?

Shuffling forward at a pace slow enough to accommodate a snail, her thoughts ran to vengeance. A toad in his bed. No. Too childish. Fleas, then. There was an idea. She descended the first dais step. But fleas were hard to catch.

"Should we not finish discussing preparations for the king's tournament before you retire?" Sir Nigel inquired. "At last count, it appears we shall have to provide for several dozen barons and their retinues."

"I will be gone but a short time."

Golde took the second step and felt the baron descend behind her. To see the mean-tempered bastard scratch welts for a week would make fleas worth the effort. Her right foot landed on the third step.

"But de Warrenne will be arriving this afternoon," Sir Nigel persisted.

Her left foot was yet in midair when the baron jerked to a halt. "I have said . . ."

Golde teetered, struggling to maintain her balance, but her forward momentum was too great. She stumbled to the fourth step. The lord's grip tightened on her tunic for the barest moment. Then he slammed against her. Unable to bear his weight, her legs buckled.

Cursing, she tumbled headlong over the remaining step to sprawl belly-down on the rush-strewn floor. Gavarnie landed hard atop her, crushing the breath from her.

A chorus of gasps spiraled around her. The hiss of air echoed off the high-timbered walls with increasing volume until her ears rang. She labored for breath as a heated emptiness expanded in her stomach, then spread to engulf her arms and legs.

'Twill pass, she assured herself as anxiety stole over her. She'd had the wind knocked from her before. Any moment now, she'd draw a chestful of air, and all would be well.

She raised her head as several pairs of wooden-soled shoes appeared in her line of vision, only to become hazy and indistinct. She widened her eyes, straining to see, but a white fog rapidly enveloped the room until all was thick and motionless.

Had she fainted?

Nay. Her eyes were open.

She struggled to move, but 'twas if she no longer had a body to command. Dread, suchlike she'd never experienced, consumed her senses.

Had she died?

Abruptly she became aware of the baron's solid body atop hers. His chest expanded so gradually against her back, she could feel each slight displacement of his ribs as they moved to accommodate air. His indrawn breath rustled in her ears like a slow, gentle breeze, bearing her up, arousing her senses to levels of alertness she had never dreamed possible.

Comfort, fuzzy and warm. Her terror vanished and she reveled in a cool mist that drifted over her.

The baron's heart thumped once, reverberating, the pulse-beat rippling over the fine hairs that covered her flesh like so many divining rods. How safe she felt. As if Delamaure were protecting her. As if he would never allow harm to befall her.

Then his breath seeped outward, draining away her sense of ease, bleeding over the fog.

Stained crimson.

Rage?

Not hers.

Delamaure's?

Or was it directed at the lord?

The crimson color separated into browns, reds, golds— sifting through the mist—spinning faster, drawing her into the vortex—until the shades merged to form a solid image.

'Twas the baron's bedchamber.

Tapestries, wild and fantastic, hung on the walls.

How had she not seen them last night?

Strangely dressed horsemen, oddly shaped castles, their pastel hues, time-faded. She felt their texture, fine and worn soft. The riders' ululations called, echoing dimly in her ears. She tasted bland grittiness on her tongue. An elemental odor transcended the scent of arid heat.

Was it brine?

Nay, 'twas sharper, more bitter.

The great four-posted bed drew her attention. There was something there. She should not look. Away, her thoughts whispered urgently.

But 'twas as if some giant serpent had captured her will. The bed dragged her onward until she hovered directly over it.

Good lack!

A beautiful blond-haired woman stared heavenward, her blue eyes death-shrouded.

Now she recognized the cloying smell.

'Twas blood. Everywhere.

Splattering the woman's waxen face. Covering her bare torso. Raging over the white bed sheets like a flash flood.

Hatred. Fear.

The woman's?

'Twas as if her cold, dead fingers were reaching out, clutching at Golde's insides, drawing her into some visceral pit from whence she would never return.

Churning emotions buffeted her and sweat broke on her brow. Breathing, harsh and ragged, filled her ears.

'Twas hers.

She had to escape.

Suddenly a white-hot light flashed from the midst of the sanguine fog. It lanced through her eyes and shot to the tips of her fingers and toes.

Golde yelped.

Quickened by the stab of agony, her arms and legs at

last responded to her command to flee. She shot from
beneath the baron like a stone from a sling, then scrambled to her feet.

"Whore's gleet, wench," the lord snarled.

Panting, she looked to see him push himself to sit
from where he lay on his belly.

"She tripped you, Papa!" the sword-wielding brat
howled.

Ignoring the boy's accusation, Golde's gaze swept the
hall. Servants stared silently at their lord, many with
hands covering their hearts. Bright sunlight spilled
through the windows, illuminating the room where before she'd seen naught but fog. The bug-child struggled to
remove the pot from his head, but the bar-handle kept
catching beneath his chin and he began to wail.

Golde wrapped her fists in the folds of her skirt as her
body trembled. Saint Blaise! What had happened here?
All appeared normal, yet she could not deny what she'd
just seen.

". . . not to blame, Ronces." Delamaure was grous-
ing to his sword-wielding son. "'Twas God who created
those great bumbling feet of hers."

Golde attempted to muster some anger at his remark,
anything to restore her bearings, but 'twas no use. Instead, she lowered her head, anxious that none see her
discomposure. Was she going mad?

"Allow me to assist you, mi'lord," Sir Nigel offered.

She watched from beneath lowered lashes as the
steward hurried toward Delamaure.

"I need no aid." The lord's tone could grind granite.
Golde glanced surreptitiously at him when he made no
move to rise. In opposition to his forbidding countenance, she could yet feel the solid reassurance of his body
pressed against her back. The comforting beat of his

heart. The gentle hush of his indrawn breath, urging her body, her soul, to awareness. Whatever had made her feel thus?

She squared her shoulders and gathered the reins of her wild imaginings. 'Twas exhaustion, and lack of food, and, and . . . And the overgrown lackwit would have crushed her to death were she a smaller person.

Her anxious feelings subsided and her breathing slowed. Who would not be stricken with thick-comings?

She tripped you, Papa. Her lip curled as she thought on the brat's accusation. Now, she supposed, the baron would rebuke her for causing his fall. And she hoped he would, for she welcomed the opportunity to respond in kind. 'Twas his fault she'd been scared witless. Brushing bits of straw and dirt from her tunic, she anticipated his ire.

Instead, he addressed the brat, Ronces. "Collect your brother. I would have you and Alory escort me to my chambers."

Ronces scampered to remove the pot from the bug, Alory's, head—yet a younger, chubbier version of his lordship, Golde reflected. Then both boys raced to grab their father's hands. They pulled him to his feet, a task not unlike two ants drawing a bear onto its hind legs.

"Where is the wench?" Sir Gavarnie demanded.

A pox on the man, Golde swore. Had he not just ordered his sons to assist him to his chambers? What need had he of her?

Ronces turned him in her direction, but before the lord could speak, the brat tugged urgently on his sleeve. Cupping his grubby little hands around his mouth, the child whispered in a voice loud enough to be heard the length of the hall, "Never oppose your opponent."

The baron's lips twitched as if he might laugh, then he pursed them and his features grew stern.

"Come along," he commanded, motioning in her direction. "I now have protection from those oversized feet of yours."

Golde searched his severe, pock-ravaged features. His comment stung and . . .

Nay. She was no longer a child. Never again would such hurtful taunts affect her.

She glanced over her shoulder at the great entrance doors. The urge to run through them and return home was so acute, her muscles twitched in anticipation.

Instead, her legs carried her straight to the baron. 'Twas impossible to deny him. Despite the macabre scene her demented thoughts had just conjured, she could not forget the comforting feel of his body atop hers. Never had she experienced such soul-snatching awareness.

Nor have you known such terror, a voice whispered in her head.

SIX

"I AM NOT too slow," Alory huffed at Ronces, his cherubic features acquiring a mulish cast.

"Papa is no baby to crawl up the stairs like you," Ronces returned hotly.

If the baron heard aught of his sons' squabbling, he gave no indication. Golde glared at the boys' backs. She would not be surprised to see horns growing from their heads.

Upon gaining the head of the stairs, Delamaure paused. "Is Hesper caring for Nicolette?" he asked, his head swiveling in the direction of the girl's chamber.

Before Golde could respond, the redhaired serving maid appeared in the doorway. "'Tis Edna, yer lordship."

"Aye . . . Edna?" The baron appeared nonplussed.

"I be Hesper's niece," the girl supplied.

Delamaure's face cleared. "Well, then, Edna. Keep a

close watch, and should you need aught, the ha—er, the witch . . ."

Golde folded her arms over her chest as the baron stammered.

"That is, mistress here," he nodded over his shoulder, "will be in my chambers."

With that, he nudged the boys forward, and Golde followed the threesome down the corridor.

She halted just inside the baron's chamber door, distracted by the tapestries that hung on the walls. In one, men in flowing white robes galloped dun-colored horses across a background of swirling, cream-colored—was it sand? Faded red, blue, and gold streamers trailed from ornate headgear, which resembled nothing that English men wore. Another scene depicted whimsical buildings with round roofs perched atop columns.

She moved closer, inspecting the images. Though fresh, salty air drifted through the unshuttered chamber windows, she caught a whiff of some night-sweet, smoky scent she could not define. 'Twas obvious the wall coverings had absorbed the odor, but from what?

Suddenly the hair crawled along her nape. The tapestries appeared exactly as they had in her . . .

She'd had a vision! She closed her eyes and breathed deeply. Praise the Goddess Danu. And God, too. She crossed herself. She was not mad. Mimskin would be thrilled.

Abruptly her good cheer fled and her eyes snapped open. If her swevyn was accurate, a beautiful woman had been brutally slaughtered in this very room. Who was she?

A tingle of apprehension climbed her spine. Her gaze swept past the dark lord and his children to fix on the great four-posted bed. A gold-embroidered scarlet coverlet covered the bed. The material looked to have been spun from rubies—or blood.

Her gaze leapt to the lord's broad shoulders as the boys led him across the room. She studied his thick black hair, unfashionably long where it fell to his shoulders. With a few braids, he would resemble exactly a barbarian chieftan of yore.

Could he have committed such savagery against a female? He appeared most capable. Or was the woman from some other time, an image from the distant past, or mayhap, the future?

Again she recalled the feel of the man as he'd lain atop her, his hearbeat pulsing through her body. She'd felt so protected.

Nay. She blinked. It could not have been a vision. She had seen the tapestries last night and been too busy ogling the naked Delamaure to note them. After that, her attention had been so focused on Nicolette, she'd noticed little more than the tub.

The dead woman was no more than a figment of her imagination, brought on by exhaustion and hunger. She would think on her no more.

"Sperville!" Delamaure roared as his sons drew up at the foot of the bed.

A dull thud issued from the wardrobe, followed by the chamberlain's appearance. "Your lordship?" He hurried forward.

Delamaure released his hold on his sons. Balling his hands into fists, he planted them on his hips. "I would hear your description of my attire."

Spindleshanks frowned and squinted, then his red-rimmed, sleep-deprived eyes rounded. His jaw worked, but no sound was forthcoming.

"I see you, too, are *speechless*," the baron gritted.

"Mi'lord, I—"

"The great Baron of Skyenvic," Delamaure mocked, sounding exactly like the chamberlain. "Poor blind bastard wanders about dressed like a court jester, yet the king continues to honor him with a fief. How charitable. What think you, Sperville? Will my appearance frighten away Vikings? Mayhap they will drown in gales of laughter."

Spindleshanks winced. "Forgive me, sir. There is no excuse for my lack of attention."

Guilt gnawed at Golde's inwit. Delamaure had done his best to dress himself. 'Twas no fault of his he could not see. "Mayhap Sir Sperville could arrange your garments in a manner that would not require sight," she suggested.

The baron turned in her direction, his nose wrinkled with distaste. "I need not direction from a woman who smells worse than dead fish. Mayhap Sir Sperville could arrange a bath for you."

Golde sucked in her breath. The baseborn mucker. And here she'd felt guilty for bringing his poor choice of garments to everyone's attention. Once again, she'd forgotten her vow to avoid emotional entanglements with her culls.

"My delicious aroma," she responded evenly, "is a result of confining myself to a steam-drenched bedchamber on your daughter's behalf. Doubtless, Satan has made similar heated arrangements on *your* behalf in anticipation of your demise."

Dropping his fists to his sides, Delamaure's jaw knotted. "Sperville, I will not tolerate this. You will get that magpie gone this instant."

Golde leveled an icy stare at the baron. She'd be strung up and gutted before she'd spend another moment in his company. And a pox on the senseless disappointment that crept over her promiscuous body at the thought of leaving. "I need not Spindleshanks' assistance to take leave. Indeed, I am capable—"

Abruptly the lord hooted. "Spindleshanks!"

Golde crossed her arms over her chest. "I fail to find amusement—"

"Spindleshanks!" he gasped, clutching a bedpost. "A more appropriate name I have never heard. Mayhap you were right, Sperville. I begin to see some merit in the woman."

At the indignant expression on the chamberlain's face, Golde was unable to keep a smile from her lips. Sir Sperville glared at her as if she'd just forced him to eat a toad.

Sniffing, the chamberlain spun about. Heels clomping on the wooden floor, he strode to the wardrobe, where he snapped his fingers over his head. "Roland. Fetch his lordship some suitable attire."

Listening to the sounds of the unseen Roland rummaging about in the anteroom, Golde struggled to contain her merriment. Unable to resist pricking the chamberlain further, she begged sweetly, "My apologies, Sir Sperville. I meant no insult. Your figure is most dashing."

"Your rude sobriquet does not disturb me in the least," he sniffed.

Golde pretended concern. "Come, sir, you appear much like a hen whose egg has been pronounced rotten."

The baron clutched his belly and doubled over while his sons giggled. Sperville cast a disdainful look in their direction, and raising his nose, disappeared into the wardrobe.

Without warning, Ronces screeched, "To arms!"

Golde near jumped from her skin. Grimacing, she watched the boys launch themselves atop the bed.

Faith! Was the baron deaf as well as blind? His demon sons made racket enough to raise the dead.

Her eyes widened. The brat and the bug were tunneling beneath the scarlet bedcover. Did none care that the boys were ruining such a beautiful piece of craftsmanship? The spread would be black by the time the little beasts were finished. Were they her children, she would . . .

She near choked. Heaven forbid! Death would be preferable to having such unruly offspring. 'Twas not hard to imagine their mother clinging to the ceiling by her fingernails and toenails from their unexpected outbursts. The unfortunate woman had doubtless gone to her premature death, gray and wrinkled.

Abruptly Golde chastised herself. 'Twas indecent to think irreverently of the dead.

Still, she wondered what had happened to the baron's wife. She must ask Sperville what he'd meant when he'd said the woman had died prematurely.

A dark-haired youth bearing noble raiment appeared from the wardrobe. Sporting a frown, the youth approached Sir Gavarnie, and Golde was distracted by the curious manner in which his hair was slicked to his scalp with oil. Was this some new hair fashion?

The squire waited for the baron's laughter to subside, then lowered his head. 'Twas as if he were presenting himself to the headsman for execution. "Mi'lord, I am to blame for your attire. When I served you in the hall this morn, I assumed you had reason for dressing thus."

"Nay, Roland." Delamaure grinned and raised his voice. "'Tis that fool *Spindleshanks'* fault. Were you not running errands at his direction, you would have been available to see me properly clothed."

A clattering crash issued from the wardrobe, and the

baron smiled broadly. "Sir Sperville! Have a care with my plate."

"Shall I see about him?" Roland queried, a confused, wary expression on his face. Judging from his look, he knew not whether he was about to be kicked or congratulated.

The lord chuckled and shook his head. "Methinks yon chamberlain needs to stew in his own piquant sauce for a spell."

Golde contemplated Delamaure's relaxed stance. At the moment, he did not appear forbidding. Indeed, he exuded a warmth that would thaw the deepest winter freeze; a humor that invited mischief.

What evil elf had made her think him capable of some woman's murder?

Again she was struck by the sensation of reassuring comfort he'd engendered in her earlier. And just now, he'd made certain of his daughter's welfare. So he was not the ogre he'd seemed last night.

The lord sidled away from the bedpost, and the squire hastily tossed the garments he carried to one arm. Clutching the baron's elbow, he made to steer him when, suddenly, Delamaure halted.

"I no longer need assistance to move about my own chamber." He removed the young man's hand from his arm. "Indeed, you may sleep outside the chamber door in future. However, I would that you make certain there are no impediments left lying about."

Pleased astonishment replaced the squire's discomfited look. "You may depend upon it, sir." Still, the youth hovered near the baron's side as the lord seated himself on the bed with slow consideration.

Roland carefully lay the black and gray garments next to him, then knelt at the lord's feet and tapped his knee.

Oblivious to his sons, who wallowed beneath the fine bedcover like two grunting piglets, Delamaure gave a booted foot to the squire. Then his eyes scanned the room in Golde's direction. "Now, silver-tongued angel. Let us discuss arrangements for your employ."

Golde's brows climbed her forehead. Silver-tongued angel! She'd been called many things, but never that. And 'twas foolish to derive such pleasure from the accolade.

Yet, unable to resist the annoying glow that settled over her, she found it impossible to inform the man she would be taking immediate leave. Instead, she queried, "At what task do you intend to engage my services? You have said naught can be done to restore your sight."

Delamaure nodded. "I am indeed convinced that such is the case."

Though he did his best to appear nonchalant, Golde detected a bitter undercurrent in his tone. He gave his other foot to Roland just as Alory extricated himself from the covers. Shrieking like a crazed hawk, the bug jumped up and down on the bed.

"I find, however," the lord fair shouted, "that my children are in great need of guidance. To my thinking, you are just the person for such a task."

He groped behind him until he caught the bug's leg and jerked it out from under him. Alory screamed his delight at the rough treatment, drawing forth Ronces from the tangled mass of quilting. Together the boys threw themselves at their father's back, grimy hands clutching at his neck in a bid to topple him.

Golde shook her head. 'Twas several moments before she trusted herself to reply in a tone that would not convey her horror. "I am ill prepared to care for children. My expertise lies in the healing arts."

Having removed both the lord's boots, Roland hustled to rescue the fine clothing from the bed. Gavarnie encircled both boys, one in each arm, and squeezed. Groaning and gasping mightily, they thrashed about until fear squirted through Golde. Could the man not tell he was hurting his children?

Then she saw their gleeful, wide-mouthed smiles, and her lip curled. Faith, she would be rich indeed had she the talent for fakery that the little mummers possessed.

"'Tis only until I can locate a nursemaid here on the isle," the baron continued over their moans. "What with the king's tourney at Atherbrook, I have not the time to look for anyone at present. If you would agree to stay 'til the tournament is past, I would reward you handsomely."

The boys pounded the lord with their small fists and Golde fidgeted, as if the breath were in fact being crushed from her. Was not coin the reason she'd journeyed to Skyenvic? But . . . a nursemaid?

"If you like," Sir Gavarnie offered, "you may try your hand at curing my blindness."

So captured was she with the little demons' display of agony, 'twas a moment before the import of his words struck her. Even then, she had to rethread both his statement and tone through her memory before she was certain.

Nay, she could not refute her first impression. The offhand manner in which he'd made the suggestion might have fooled her were it not for the quiet edge of desperation in his voice. The baron yearned to see again.

'Twas not difficult to imagine her dismay were she blind and dependent upon the whims of others for . . .

Nay, and nay. She would *not* feel empathy for the baron. Still, her feet would not obey her command to walk away.

She studied the squirming children. The little brutes should be locked away until they matured. They were worse than two evil sprites on the prowl for human marrow. And their sister, Nicolette, was no better. A cat would have been more amenable to the fever-cooling bathwater last night.

Golde's gaze shifted to Gavarnie's dark, distant-looking eyes. What had caused him to lose his sight?

Though the world was full of people blinded by ill humors, the lord could not be included among them. Vision slipped slowly from victims of such maladies, and their eyes dripped thickly and grew callused with a milk-colored film. Delamaure's eyes were clear as the star-glistened heavens on a moonless night.

Her brow furrowed. A blow to the head, then?

Mayhap he had foolishly gazed upon a glomung sun. Though 'twas well known that doing so caused blindness, there were e're vainglorious coxcombs who challenged the sun's power during its ecliptic daytime darkening.

But her bones told her Sir Gavarnie was not such a man.

"Well?" the baron prodded. "What say you?"

The boys were eyeing her with speculation. Doubtless, both were fomenting nefarious plots with which to entertain themselves at her expense. She shook her head until she realized the baron could not see her. "I have agreed to stay until Nicolette—"

"Pardon, your grace," a voice sounded from the doorway. Golde turned to find the fair-complexioned steward standing there. "De Warrenne has arrived."

A pox on Sir Nigel for interrupting before she could decline Delamaure's offer. Golde returned her attention to the baron, but at the look on his face, words deserted her. Where before his jovial spirits had rendered him most approachable, his features now appeared etched in pitted flint. One would have to be bold indeed to gainsay him at present.

She glanced at the children. Alory yet squirmed in his father's arm, though Ronces' visage had grown stony. Slipping from the baron's grasp, the brat moved to capture his brother. He whispered something in Alory's ear, and a troubled expression claimed the younger bug's sweet features. Both climbed from the great bed and moved to stand beside Roland, Alory clutching Ronces' hand.

'Twas as if the devil himself had just been announced, Golde thought. Who was this de Warrenne, that he could breed such ill will?

"Welcome de Warrenne on my behalf," the baron grumbled. "Serve him my finest wine and see he is fed. I shall attend him shortly."

Sir Nigel bowed and disappeared from the doorway. For a moment Sir Gavarnie sat motionless, and Golde was certain 'twas despair that tinged his hate-darkened features. Then a muscle twitched in his jaw and he rose from the bed. Immediately Roland began fumbling with the laces of his tunic.

"Sir Sperville!" the baron thundered.

The chamberlain's tone was yet disgruntled when he appeared from the wardrobe. "Mi'lord?"

Gavarnie sneered. "That whoreson, de Warrenne, has arrived."

Spindleshanks' petulant demeanor vanished and an icy mien settled over his thin features. "I can scarce credit the man's effrontery. That he would dare impose himself on your hospitality so long before the tourney begins."

The lord held up a hand. "He is shire reeve here and

needs time to collect taxes before the king arrives. However, I would that you . . ."

No wonder this de Warrenne aroused such hostility, Golde thought as Delamaure issued orders. King William was indeed clever, having empowered the old English office of shire reeve to care for all royal affairs in the shires. 'Twas a most effective check in controlling his e're rebellious barons, for one lord oft held the position of reeve in a shire that contained the estates of several other barons. In that way, they were kept busy fighting one another, instead of the king.

So caught up was she with her thinking, 'twas a moment before she realized Gavarnie's gaze was scanning the room in her direction. Roland still struggled with the knotted tunic laces, the tip of his tongue pressed to his upper lip.

"Mistress, uh . . ." the baron began.

"Golde," Spindleshanks supplied.

"Mistress Golde. If you would be good enough to see to the boys for a time."

'Twas not a question. 'Twas a dismissal.

Golde shook her head. "Mi'lord, I cannot—"

Gavarnie spoke before she could finish. "Admittedly, I have presented you with naught but my black temper. I am e're bedeviled with matters of state. However, I am much impressed with your treatment of my children. 'Tis a comfort to know they will never gut a person's buttocks, nor will they ever oppose their opponents."

Though his face held no trace of a smile, Golde's lips twitched at his humor.

"And 'tis a miracle that Nicolette—" He paused and raised an imperious black brow when Roland gave a vicious yank at the cords of his tunic.

"Your forgiveness, mi'lord," the squire begged, his face reddening.

Gavarnie nodded, and his gaze returned to Golde. "I would speak with you at length on your healing abilities at the first opportunity. Meanwhile, I would be in your debt if you would agree to take charge of Ronces and—Roland, do you seek to strangle me?"

"I cannot get the knots undone, sir." The squire's frustration was evident in his tone.

"Fetch a knife and have done with it, boy. De Warrenne is apt to steal the entire castle from under my feet before I am dressed."

Golde glanced at Spindleshanks. He bobbed nods at her and made ushering motions with his hands. Closing her eyes, she conjured an image of the baron's dark features, his alluring lips. Her thoughts skittered from the memory of his naked body as she'd seen him last night.

She took a deep breath, then gave her attention to the boys. Ronces eyed her with a graveness beyond his years. Alory lowered his head and avoided her gaze.

"Come along." Golde held her hands out, inviting the children to take hold.

Pulling Alory along, Ronces strode forward and walked past her, ignoring her kind gesture. The brat.

Golde swept from the room and caught him at the head of the stairs as he prepared to descend. "Where do you go?"

"Wherever I choose," Ronces sneered.

"Yea!" Alory seconded, grinning.

Golde raised a brow. "Then I suggest you choose the direction that will carry you to your sister's chamber."

"I am no babe to take orders from a nursemaid."

"And if you will recall, I am no nursemaid with whom you wish to cross swords."

Ronces stared at her with fullsome loathing. "Very well, hag. I will humor you this once because it suits me. But in future—"

His teeth snapped shut and he lost his hold on Alory as Golde grasped his shoulder and pushed him against the wall. "Call me hag again, boy," she affected her most evil voice, "and you will have no future."

Ronces gaped, his wide eyes unblinking. Golde decided he appeared much the way a fish looked upon discovering the bait it had fed upon was in fact a trap. 'Twas difficult to maintain an imposing facade when she desired nothing more than to giggle.

She released him and he sidled away, keeping his back to the wall until he was well beyond her reach. Then he grabbed Alory's hand and bolted for Nicolette's room.

Once they were out of sight, Golde grinned. The imp would think twice before challenging her authority again. She'd started forward when a wheezing sound distracted her. Laughter? Turning, she glimpsed Spindleshanks' thinning pate just before the baron's chamber door closed.

SEVEN

"**W**HY MUST WE STAY in this sticky, smelly room?" Ronces demanded.

Golde halted her pacing at the foot of Nicolette's bed and glared at the brat. Despite the midday hour, what little light the one narrow window provided scarce penetrated the gloom of the cramped room. Still, she could see sweat droplets, tiny crystalline balls, dangling from the tips of Ronces' short-cropped hair.

Pointing at him where he sat on the floor near the door, she shook a finger. "If you wake your sister again—"

"She is not our sister!" Ronces shrieked, his body rigid, his hands fisted in his lap.

"No, Ronces," Alory pleaded, covering his ears and squeezing his eyes shut.

Golde blinked. Good lack. What were the brats

about? She searched their features, unable to determine whether they were serious or pretending.

Nicolette stirred, and scowling, Golde moved quickly to settle her. Smoothing the ringlets around the girl's forehead, she studied the child's face. Truth tell, Nicolette did not at all resemble Alory or Ronces. Her hair was not black, but light brown, streaked blond in places. Despite the pale wash of her skin, 'twas obvious her complexion would tend more to pinkness than toward the boys' dark coloring. And the bones in her body were delicate and small-set as opposed to the brothers' sturdy, thickset frames.

Golde frowned as Nicolette quieted. 'Twould explain much if the girl were the baron's get of some serving wench.

She turned to inquire of Ronces what he'd meant when he'd said Nicolette wasn't their sister. But the question never got beyond her teeth.

The brat had drawn his knees to his chest and rested his head on them, his knuckles white where he clutched his ankles. Alory had scooted to a corner with his back to the room. His shoulders were shaking.

Nay. Surely the bug was not crying.

A sniffle answered her question and an uncomfortable feeling settled over her. Children were distressing at best. Crying children were enough to send her screaming for the nearest cliff from which to jump. What did one do with them?

She strode forward to tap Alory's shoulder. "You must not cry," she gently insisted.

He whimpered and did not turn around.

She reached down to clutch his upper arm and tried to draw him to his feet. But he locked his muscles and would not budge.

Straightening, she crossed her arms and admonished, "'Twill sour your belly."

A sniffle and a whimper.

"'Twill make your head ache," she added.

Silence at last. And it had not been difficult at all. she had not realized she possessed any gift for dealing with children. Relieved, she addressed the bug in her most sage tone. "There, now. Things are not so grim when looked at through clear, dry eyes."

A full-chested sob erupted, the discordant sound roiling through Golde like a tempest. Without thought, she swooped down and scooped the boy into her arms. "Hush, sweeting," she soothed, cradling his tense form. "All will be well."

Rather than calming him, her words seemed to make him cry harder, but she knew not what else to say. So much for her ability with children.

She looked to Ronces, hoping for assistance, only to find him peering at her from beneath lowered lashes. Tears tracked through the dirt on his face to wet his gray braies where he rested his chin on them.

What to do? Alory felt heavy as a boulder and she knew she could not long hold him. And it appeared Ronces' dam might burst any moment and drown them all.

She lumbered to the wall, and using it to support her back, lowered herself to the floor beside Ronces. Adjusting Alory in her lap, she wrapped an arm about Ronces' shoulders. Though he resisted at first, he finally allowed her to pull his trembling body close. Then he, too, dissolved in a weeping fit.

Golde felt like crying herself. Fine nursemaid she was. In less than an hour, she'd managed to transform two happy little monsters into wailing wrecks of despair. And the fault lay with their dimwitted father. He was to blame for charging her with their care. She had as much as told the baron she was incapable of keeping children. Had she any doubts, this proved her a dismal failure.

Absently she stroked the crown of each boy's head. Poor dearlings. She could smell the salt of their tears. The scent of their dewy, youth-laden breath reminded her of a puppy's, clean and unspoiled by the ripeness of age. Granted, Sir Gavarnie was blind, but could he not feel the anguish of his own children?

At last both boys snuffled, their bodies slack from their exertions. In the quiet that followed, Golde ventured, "Many children are born out of wedlock. Know you my meaning?"

Alory shook his head, but at Ronces' nod she continued. "'Tis no fault of yours if Nicolette is not your full blood. Nor is it hers. You still share the same father."

Ronces doggedly shook his head against her shoulder, obviously unconvinced Nicolette was not to blame.

Recalling the insults she'd suffered as a child, Golde chose her words carefully. "I am certain there are those who make sport of Nicolette."

Both boys nodded.

"When I was a girl, people teased me. Most did so because they were afraid of my unwholesome appearance. But the cruelest were those who were jealous, for I possessed something they lacked; a loving father who was not shy about extolling my virtues to any who would listen."

She'd intended to explain how their father loved them in the same manner, but was interrupted when Alory looked up, his puffy eyes filled with longing. "Did your mamma love you, too?"

Golde did her best to smile. "My mother died—"

Careful, she admonished herself. This was no time to speak of sad things. "I cannot remember my mother, though my father yet speaks of her with much devotion."

"Papa does not speak thus of our mother," Ronces grumbled.

"Ever'one says Papa kil't Mamma," Nicolette rasped.

Golde looked to see the girl sitting at the foot of the bed, dangling her legs over the edge.

"Cut her up in little pieces," the girl added, shivering.

"He did not!" Alory screeched, trying to scramble from Golde's lap. He grunted when she tightened her grip.

"I will hear no more of this foolish talk, Nicolette," Golde scolded. "You seek to do naught but upset . . ."

Her voice trailed away as the import of the girl's words struck her.

A chill curdled her flesh.

The dead woman in her vision. She was Gavarnic's wife?

"It was that bad man, de Warrenne!" Alory cried.

The bug's strident voice seemed to echo, and Golde trembled. Please, God, she prayed. She had no wish to see any more visions this day, or ever.

"De Warrenne killed Mamma," Alory shrilled. "He's going to take Papa from us, too. That's why he's here!"

Ronces pulled from her grasp so quickly, Golde had no time to catch him. Though he made no move to attack his sister, his tone when he addressed Nicolette was venomous. "A curse on you. Papa is not your father."

"Liar!" Nicolette rose on her knees atop the bed. "Papa would of tole me if that was twue."

"Why do you think he makes you call him 'sir'?" Ronces sneered.

Nicolette planted her small hands on her hips. "That is the way wadies talk."

"Then why is he so mean to you?" Ronces persisted.

A coughing fit seized Nicolette and she clutched her stomach. "He is not mean to me," she choked, her face red.

"Enough!" Golde spat.

'Twas as if the entire world were suddenly spinning widdershins, leaving her dizzy and sick. She eased Alory from her lap and forced herself to rise.

Grabbing Ronces by the scruff of his neck, she hissed, "You will sit beside your brother and shut your mouth." She shoved him down and turned her attention to Nicolette.

"Papa is not mean to me," the child gasped. "'Tis only 'cause I am not a boy that Papa tweats me diff'went. Hesper says so."

Golde moved to the bed and gently pushed on Nicolette's shoulders. "You need to lie down and rest."

Despite her small size and diminished health, Nicolette managed to resist Golde's efforts to force her down. "Papa will see. I am better than Wonces or Alowy."

❧ ❧

GAVARNIE SAT at the head of the table in the great hall. To his right sat his guests, Walther de Warrenne and his wife, Lady Gundrada.

The shouted challenges, boasts, and raucous jests of men-at-arms that filled the hall did not disturb Gavarnie in the least. Indeed, 'twas a welcome excuse to ignore the indefatigable chatter of Lady Gundrada.

Besides, he could think of naught but Golde. An interesting name, he mused, rubbing the polished surface of a dragon's head that ornamented the arm of his chair. Of course, he'd placed little faith in Sperville's—Spindleshanks', he reminded himself—glowing remarks on her striking looks.

He must admit, though, that the chamberlain had not done the wench justice in describing her as a sapling. Judging from the feel of her when he'd fallen atop her earlier, she more resembled the smooth sounding-wood of a finely crafted harp, curved to fit between the legs while resting against the chest and shoulder.

His groin had felt seared where it pressed her firm, rounded bottom. And when she'd scrambled from beneath him, he'd felt robbed. Had he his way, he would have lingered a while longer. Mayhap he would have brushed her breasts accidentally—while finding purchase to maneuver himself from her.

And what would the wench feel like unclothed? He imagined his hands roaming over naked flesh. Her hips, her belly, her nipples . . .

He caught himself before he winced, then shifted forward in the great chair. A pox on his lecherous thoughts. Never had he experienced the sense of touch so keenly as he had while lying atop Golde. He ran his hand over the linen-covered table, searching for his chalice while making certain the cloth's edge hung low enough to conceal his arousal.

"Roger de Breteuil has performed as lord at Chepstow beyond anyone's expectations," Lady Gundrada gushed, and he concentrated hard on her words. "Do you not agree, husband?"

At de Warrenne's grunt, she tittered, the cloying odor of the lavender she wore thick as syrup in the air. "'Tis a shame Fitz Osborne did not live to see his son's success. He would be pleasantly surprised."

Whore's gleet, Gavarnie thought. Was it not enough that he must entertain the Baron of Adurford? Nay, he must listen to the man's wife prattle on about the obsequious Roger de Breteuil. Though truth tell, between Lord and Lady de Warrenne, Gundrada was more clever by far.

She'd chosen well in taking the Baron of Adurford to husband, he reflected, doing his best to avoid the thoughts of Golde such musings suddenly evoked. De Warrenne was a bull of a man with a reputation for cruelty, so 'twas surprising how easily Gundrada manipulated him. But then, not only did her youth and beauty stand her in good stead, she was most adroit at inflating de Warrenne's opinion of himself—among other things, to be sure.

Against his will, Gavarnie's thoughts again wandered to Golde. How many men had she known? One? A dozen? Likely more than that, judging from the timbre of her voice.

No woman came naturally by such an alluring sound. It had to be practiced until it held just the right hint of languid huskiness. The type a self-assured woman knowledgeable in the fleshly arts would affect to manipulate a man's body against his reason.

Did not Gundrada use her vast experience with men to bend de Warrenne to her will? And de Warrenne, for all his power, was too dimwitted to see through the facade.

Crossing his legs, Gavarnie leaned back in his chair. No woman would ever bend him to her will using such methods. Take Golde, for example.

Aye, he would admit a rutting desire for her. However, he'd already determined she was no innocent maid. Her looks, regardless of Sperville's remarks, meant nothing to his blind eyes. Therefore, she would never be able use sweet words of guile upon him.

A small smile curved his lips. Not that she possessed any sweet words in her vocabulary. He certainly need never fear offending her with *his* sharp tongue.

And 'twas most entertaining to hear her outrageous remarks. Never gut a person's buttocks, indeed. A lesser man would e're be challenged to outwit her.

Again the feel of her backside commandeered his thoughts; the blossom of her hips below her slender waist.

"Your eldest son is of age to be fostered, is he not?" De Warrenne's coarse voice jarred him from his pleasurable musings.

Gavarnie commanded his features to remain blank as lustful thoughts of rounded bottoms deserted him.

What was the whoreson about with such a question?

'Twas de Warrenne who'd discovered him in his bedchamber the morning of Isabelle's death. He'd been the one who'd raised the hue and cry to King William, demanding Gavarnie be charged with murder.

Now, of a sudden, he was asking after Ronces? Would that Gavarnie could see the overfed bastard and know from his porcine eyes what scheme was mirrored there.

"What think you of pledging the boy to me?"

Gavarnie felt his face flush and he lowered his chalice to his lap, hoping to conceal his shaking hands. By the rood, de Warrenne's audacity knew no bounds.

"Ronces is already pledged unto Varin de Brionne." Despite his best effort, his tone was harsh enough to grind grain.

"For shame, husband," Gundrada piped. "You have made our host angry."

Gavarnie gritted his teeth. The soiled bitch was gloating over his discomfort. And whatever subterfuge the pair were about, 'twas likely Gundrada's idea. Anything that could not be beaten, bled, or tortured to submission was beyond de Warrenne.

"'Tis an offer made with the best of intentions," Gundrada continued. "Walther wished to mend the breach 'tween the two of you. 'Twas his thinking—"

Gavarnie interrupted. "I would hear Walther's thinking from his own mouth, if you please."

He almost smiled at the abrupt silence. Doubtless, Gundrada's overripe lips were pursed and her fair features sour as a fishwife's at day's end.

"Know you how many seek to place their children in my service?" de Warrenne blustered. "I am beseiged with requests until my household is overflowing. Yet I am willing to make a place for your boy. I believe the king would be content to know our differences are settled."

Gavarnie swallowed his distaste and forced a thoughtful expression. "Which of your sons will you give as surety?" he asked, though the question was moot. De Warrenne had four sons, and had a lost fifth whom he'd refused to ransom from an enemy baron several years past. He was hardly a man Gavarnie would trust with Ronces' life.

"Two already serve de Breteuil, but you may have your choice of the other two."

Faith. De Warrenne would never have made so bold a suggestion when Gavarnie could see, for he knew Gavarnie would take offense. That de Warrenne would now offer for Ronces bespoke his contempt.

Raw anger consumed Gavarnie. Did he appear so incapacitated by his loss of sight that de Warrenne believed him powerless? He drained the wine from his cup, then leaned forward and slammed it on the table.

"Think me a fool at your own risk," he warned hotly. "I yet have King William's ear when there is need."

"Perhaps before Isabelle's murder," de Warrenne responded flatly, "for which you should have been tried, despite her infidelities."

Gavarnie felt the blood drain from his face. If only he could see! De Warrenne would be cleaved in half where he sat. "Dare you repay my hospitality with scurrilous abuse?"

The bench beside him scraped against the wooden platform and he knew de Warrenne had risen. "'Tis I who should take offense," he spat. "I offer my house for your son, knowing full well you are no longer favored by the king—"

"Please, husband!" Lady Gundrada implored with honied falseness. "Lower your voice. You have everyone's ear."

At her mention of it, Gavarnie realized all discourse in the hall had ceased. Whore's gleet. Though de Warrenne's statement was a bold lie, it was more damaging than if he'd spoken the truth. Gavarnie could almost hear the disparaging thoughts of his liegemen that were present.

Poor blind bastard. Couldn't protect a lamb in the field, much less his possessions.

Were they ashamed of him?

His face felt as if it might crack with impotent rage. "I would have a care with my language and tone were I you. There comes a line beyond which no man will be pushed."

De Warrenne snorted. "You can ill afford a pitched battle under your roof. The king would never allow his shire reeve to be set upon with impunity. 'Twould set a far more dangerous precedent than the murder of an unfaithful wife."

'Twas a savage remark, and Gavarnie near choked on his ire. De Warrenne had drawn his last breath, and plague take the consequences. He would order Nigel to lop off the pig's head and deal with the king. . . .

A thread of reason wound itself through his anger. He inclined his head and forced a level tone. "Your insistence on referring to Isabelle's death wears thin. According to our king, adulterous offenses are punishable by death. You risk much to find fault with William's interpretation of the law."

He took a deep breath, pleased with the result of his control. De Warrenne would be brought to heel, not with deeds, but with words.

"Mi'lord, husband," Gundrada spoke quickly. "Let us not dwell on unpleasant memories. Not when there are other . . . matters to be considered."

Was it his imagination, or was there a note of warning in Gundrada's tone?

De Warrenne cleared his throat. "You are right, sweet wife. I wonder, Sir Gavarnie, why the king insisted upon billeting me here when I could as easily have lodged at Atherbrook? I confess, I cannot decide whether he desires a reconciliation between us or hopes one will kill the other. Fostering your son was my plan for avoiding the latter."

Gavarnie frowned, recalling his own dismay at being ordered to act as host to the Baron of Adurford.

De Warrenne continued, mirroring his thoughts. "I have no desire to become a pawn in our wily sovereign's games. Though William may have decided he cannot depend on a blind man to guard the Solent, I would never be so foolish as to underestimate you."

A robust cough sounded from below the dais, and Gavarnie recognized it as belonging to Fitz Simon, his barrel-chested castellan. Whore's gleet. The insinuation that the king could no longer depend on him to perform his duties would not be lost upon the castellan.

Again anger consumed him, only now it fed on the frost of fear. In his arrogant thinking, he had not once considered that King William might wish to rid himself of a baron whose sightless eyes were naught but a liability. He must assure everyone in the hall that de Warrenne's words were false.

"What brew have you been swilling, Walther?" he asked in a voice loud enough to carry. "Sit, before you collapse. 'Tis clear your head is muddled if you believe me to have fallen from William's favor. Even you will agree that did the king wish to rid his royal self of me, I would be keeping company with worms at present. I do not believe that is the case, is it?"

His congenial tone belied the true sentiment behind his last question, and he near laughed aloud when de Warrenne did not respond. 'Twas telling of the man's ignorance that he did not realize he'd just been compared to a worm.

But Gundrada understood. "Come, husband," she snapped. "Let us not abide where we are not wanted."

"You object to our sharing a drink?" Gavarnie asked innocently, convinced the entire discussion had been planned by the bitch. "Faith, mi'lady, you have grown shrewish to spoil your husband's pleasure."

The scrape of the bench told Gavarnie de Warrenne was seating himself again. "Either keep your tongue behind your teeth, wife, or take yourself off."

Gavarnie struggled to keep a grin from his lips. How

he would love to see Gundrada's face at the moment. Steam must be curling about her head.

He leaned back in the thronelike seat and introduced the subject of the war games that would be held at Atherbrook. At his lead, conversation resumed in the hall, and he congratulated himself on his restraint.

From whence had come his facile tongue? He'd never realized that words could be as effective as swords. Yet the evidence swirled about him. The tense silence that had pervaded the hall moments ago had been replaced with a cordial comaraderie.

Still, he was careful to avoid topics that might cause discord between him and the Baron of Adurford. And all the while, he thought on de Warrenne's comments concerning the king.

He needed time alone to sort through the maze of intrigue that was beginning to fester in his head.

EIGHT

❦❦❦

Golde wrapped a drying cloth about her shoulders. Padding to the scarlet-covered great bed in Lord Gavarnie's private chamber, she eyed her fresh clothing where Hesper had laid it out.

Strange that she should feel no discomfort here, where a dead woman had lain—if she were to believe her vision. Then again, she would not be surprised were Satan himself to walk up and tap her on the shoulder.

Indeed, after supping in the great hall, she would welcome a sight of the devil. Though the roast goose had been well prepared, it had been impossible to enjoy the fare where Golde had sat with the boys directly below the dais. Not with the rancorous stirrings that clamored in her belly.

'Twas bad enough that Nicolette thought Gavarnie had killed her mother. Worse was that the boys hated their sister, if in fact she was their sister. But all withered in comparison to the evil that emanated from Delamaure's two guests. "Lord and Lady de Warrenne," Alory had informed her.

There was an air about the Baron of Adurford and his wife that affected her like rancid, maggot-infested meat. Not that they smelled. Indeed, Lady de Warrenne applied lavender with such abandon that Golde could smell it despite her distance from the woman.

Nay. 'Twas not an odor. Rather, it was a putrid feeling that made her flesh crawl. Lord de Warrenne's small, close-set eyes and sweating, rotund countenance made her feel sick inside. His wife's avaricious blue eyes and blood-colored lips did naught but add to the feeling.

Chilled despite the hot bath she had just taken, Golde reached for her drawers and pulled them over her hips, tying the drawstring.

From her vantage point below the dais, it had been clear that Sir Gavarnie had not enjoyed his guests' company either. Yet the visiting lord appeared to savor the meal, as befitted his size, even though his wife, Lady Gundrada, had appeared sullen. She'd sat brooding while Gavarnie and her husband talked around and over her.

Golde frowned. 'Twas almost as if the baron and the woman had argued. A lover's spat?

Anger rose in her breast. 'Od rot the whoremonger. While he dallied with sluts, his children . . .

Good lack! She was doing it again. How often must she remind herself of her vow? She would not involve herself in the baron or his children's affairs. And that was that. The moment she was dressed, she would seek out the muckraking Sir Gavarnie and tell him she was taking immediate leave.

Pulling her chainse over her head, she inhaled its

scent of cedar and dried heather, which still clung from her storage chest. The smells suddenly reminded her of Mimskin.

She sighed, glancing out the narrow window near the bed to the orange-hued sunset. At this very moment, Mimskin would be mixing pounded leaves of green marche with white of egg for old man Ansel's gout. Even the stinging odor of verjuice that pervaded Mimskin's cluttered cottage during the salve's weekly preparation would be welcome.

Her throat grew constricted and she realized she was staring at her tunic. Compared to the shimmering, scarlet bedcover, her homespun green tunic appeared comfortably familiar. She plucked the drying cloth from the bed and rubbed her wet hair.

Mayhap she should set matters to rights concerning the baron's children before leaving Skyenvic.

She paused in drying her hair. Aye. Just this once, she would do something of which Mimskin could be proud. She would see to the welfare of those less fortunate than herself.

Aye. His lordship should be made accountable for the misery that racked his children's tender imaginings.

Abruptly the door to the chamber swung inward and she jerked the cloth to her chest.

"I cannot think how I will manage with that whoreson underfoot for an entire month," the baron grumbled as he entered the room assisted by Spindleshanks.

Before Golde could notify them of her presence, the chamberlain spotted her. His eyes grew round and he quickly reversed direction, drawing Sir Gavarnie with him.

"What—" Caught unaware, the lord stumbled over his feet as he was pulled backward.

"Come away," Sperville croaked, and steadied him.

The baron drew his sword, his eyes shifting in all directions as he backed toward the door. Golde raised a brow. Obviously, he believed himself endangered.

Sperville pulled the door shut and she grabbed her tunic. She'd just managed to settle the material down around her ankles when she heard the lord's indignant bellow.

"The witchwife!"

She snatched her corded belt from the bed and tied it about her hips as the door burst open. Dark-faced, the baron stalked into the room while Sperville hustled to keep pace.

"To what purpose do you skulk about my private chambers, wench?" the lord demanded. He drew to a halt and scanned the room, as if he would locate her position.

She waited for Spindleshanks to reply. After all, 'twas the chamberlain who'd procured the use of the baron's tub for her. When he did naught but level a disgusted look at her, she gave her attention back to the baron.

"Do you accuse me of thievery?"

His sightless gaze riveted on her, black and forbidding. "I can think of no other reason for your presence."

"Beg pardon, mi'lord highness." Her tone was syrupy. "Did you not suggest Sir Sperville might arrange a bath for me? And were he not so concerned with his own neck, he would tell you so."

Spindleshanks scowled. "The maid speaks the truth, though I had no inkling she would require the better part of an evening to bathe." He cast her a sour look before returning his attention to his master. "No harm has been done, and you have more immediate matters to attend to."

Delamaure's features grew impatient. "You are right.

Hie yourself off, wench, and keep yourself away unless I summon your presence."

Golde crossed her arms over her chest. "I will hie myself off, all right. But not before we have discussed your children's behavior."

For a moment it appeared he might strangle. "Chil— Behav—" He sucked air through clenched teeth and when next he spoke, 'twas with the succinctness of a scholar addressing a dull child. "As I told you earlier, I am much involved with more important affairs. I have not the time at present"—his tone grew angrier with each word he spoke—"to worry over trifles which have no bearing on aught but worthless social graces."

Golde clamped her teeth together and narrowed her eyes. Were all men consumed with such a sense of self-importance? Even Spindleshanks was eyeing her as if she were a bothersome gnat.

Spinning about, she marched to the tub and snatched up her shoes and dirty clothing. If his toadship couldn't bestir himself on his children's behalf, neither would she.

Still, she could not resist goading him with a parting remark. "'Tis no wonder your offspring are such maladjusts. They have been cursed with an officious, boot-licking halfwit for a father."

As the baron's jaw knotted, so did Spindleshanks' face pale. Golde smiled tightly and headed for the door. But she got no farther than two steps before the lord clutched her arm. The shoes and clothes slipped from her grasp as he jerked her back in front of him.

Her breath caught at her body's agitated response.

"'Tis you who is the maladjust, Mistress Dowd. Boys were not made to sit about stitching and simpering over the beauty of one another's needlework. Though their mischief-making can become tedious, my sons have oft been a source of great pleasure to me."

She now understood a cat's craving to be stroked. If her flesh had its way, she would rub herself up and down the length of the lord's body until he . . .

Plague take the bastard! What mean imaginings he inspired.

Horrified with the simile of cat to owner, she lashed out. "Alory scrambles to hide in corners while squalling like a babe to avoid his brother's foul innuendos. Ronces curses Nicolette and takes great satisfaction in telling her you are not her father. And Nicolette relates how you chopped their mother into tiny pieces."

She struggled to pull her arm from his grasp. "Maladjusted I may be, but my worst nightmares are naught compared to your children's thick-comings."

The baron's features grew ferocious. His nostrils flared like a maddened bull's, and his grip on her upper arm tightened until her fingertips tingled.

"Leave us," he hissed at Sperville.

Icy currents of fear coursed through Golde's veins. A pox on her wicked tongue. Staring into the venomous planes of Delamaure's face, she prayed for deliverance. How had she managed to convince herself of his benign nature? Not only did he appear capable of murder, he seemed bent upon the deed. She wrenched her arm frantically to free herself.

"Mayhap 'twould be best, sir—" Spindleshanks began.

"Gainsay me now," Gavarnie interrupted, his tone deadly, "and you risk your position with me."

The chamberlain backed toward the door, his features waxen before the yellow candlelight. Golde clawed at the baron's fingers with her free hand. "Sperville!" she pleaded, to no effect. The chamberlain continued his retreat.

She bent her head, prepared to sink her teeth in the lord's hand, but his hold was such that she couldn't reach. Panic seized her when the door closed behind Spindleshanks, and she kicked the baron's shin.

"Vicious bitch," he snarled, clutching his leg. His grasp loosened and she jerked against it with all her might. Just when she thought her escape assured, the brutal lord again tightened his grip. But instead of halting her movement, he was carried with her as she lost her balance.

She stumbled to the hard floor and the baron followed, landing beside her. Before she could roll away, he swung a leg over her hips.

Pinning her wrists above her head, he rose over her on his knees. "I have had measure in full of you, hellhag. You prey on the young and weak, stinging all with your waspish tongue that you may feed on their frailties."

His face was a scarce hand's span from hers and his breath fair scorched her cheek. Yet she could not look away. His black eyes held her gaze like a hangman's noose. In them she saw the ugly truth. Deny it all she'd like, she had indeed grown accustomed to belittling others.

He shifted his weight lower on her hips, and incredibly, a pulsing ache curled like smoke through her loins. 'Twas not to be believed. How could she respond thus when the man was about to kill her?

"If you wish to leave this island with your tongue intact, you will relate in a moderate tone all my children have said."

Golde winced. How was she to relate anything with her body demanding her attention like some wayward brat? It seemed she could feel each tiny point of contact between her body and his.

"Well?" he challenged when she made no immediate reply.

Recalling her chagrin at his critical insight regarding her waspish behavior, she licked her lips and started to apologize. But he would doubtless consider it a ploy, and she was not so certain it wasn't. He had managed to scatter her wits until she knew not her own thoughts.

Confused and angry at his ability to so unsettle her, she taunted, "What know you of moderation? If you would cease bellowing like a bull and threatening all in your path, you might hear what goes on about you."

Summoning all her strength, she bucked her hips in an attempt to dislodge him. But instead of falling sideways, he pitched forward. Her yelp of dismay was smothered when his chest landed against her face as he extended full-length atop her.

He raised himself on his elbows and drew his knees beneath him on either side of her ribs. Immediately she was aware of his groin where it pressed into the soft flesh just below her breasts.

In the same instant, the baron's breath caught. 'Twas as if lightning cracked between them, melting them together. His grasp on her wrists tightened and his muscles grew rigid.

For a moment she could not move, so intense was the heat that surged through her. It collected in fiery pools in her breasts and between her legs. Groaning, she squeezed her knees together.

Then she realized what she'd done.

Had the lord heard her? Could he feel her desire quicken?

No sooner had she posed the last question than Delamaure slid, slow and sure, down her body, dragging her wrists lower over her head. His male root came to rest against her woman's collop and she could not prevent the shudder that tore through her. The pressure his body provided was so exquisite, 'twas near painful.

His features held the look of a wolf circling a flock of sheep. Bold, yet cautious lest the shepherd discover his presence. His lips were parted, his eyes sharp as jet.

She had to stop this, and now. But how? A stinging comment? "If you would at least lick the drool from your slavering lips, mi'lord, that I will not be drowned."

He arched a brow, then gave her a cunning smile and did her bidding. Spellbound, she watched his tongue glide over his upper lip, leaving a faint, glistening wake of moisture. 'Twas as if he were licking every intimate spot on her body, and she squirmed against the unwelcome feelings.

He paused and smiled again, this time with satisfaction, and she realized she was holding her breath. Then he traced his bottom lip and sucked it.

By the raven! The man was enough to make a nun forsake her vows. She must escape before he snatched her wits completely. If she could trick him into releasing his hold.

"Mi'lord." She winced at the raspy timbre of her voice. She'd hoped to sound alluring. Clearing her throat, she hurried on. "Allow me to remove my clothing."

"Mmmm," he purred agreeably. But instead of letting her go, he lowered his head and pressed his lips to hers.

She had never imagined such torture. When he gently pulled her bottom lip between his teeth and sucked, she gasped. To her mortification, her hips curled upward, straining for contact with his body.

In response, he ground himself against her and slid

his tongue in her mouth. Far from appeasing the hungry ache that gnawed at her senses, his actions did naught but tease her woman's flesh until she feared she might perish from ravening need. She had to escape before she disgraced herself.

Tearing her lips from his, she panted, "Mi'lord. The bed. Let us adjourn. . . ."

All thought of tricking him into releasing his hold vanished as his lips traveled down her neck. She closed her eyes against the torrent of pleasure that seized her. She scarce managed to brush her throbbing core against him before he lifted his hips, just out of reach.

Frustration hissed through her clenched teeth. He was tormenting her a'purpose with his cat-and-mouse movements. She attempted to spread her legs that she might gain better access to his groin, but his knees wedged tightly against her thighs to preclude her intention.

Then he lowered his hips and raked her collop with indolent sureness. There was no mistaking his rutting desire. The knowledge that he wanted her inflamed her passion until she was naught but a quivering mass. Why did he not take her?

His lips captured hers again and she moaned into his mouth. Shifting his weight, he moved one leg between hers and she writhed against the thick muscles of his thigh. If she did not gain relief soon, she would burst.

His lips slid from her mouth to her ear and he whispered, "Ease your pace, sweet witch. I am near to spilling myself in my braies."

Her bid to comply with his wishes failed and she shook her head, afraid to speak lest her tongue betray her and beg him to end her suffering. He pulled his leg from between her thighs and she stifled a whimper as he stretched out beside her.

Switching his hold on her wrists, he grasped them in one hand while the other moved to her breasts. He kneaded the sensitive mounds, each in turn, while nibbling the lobe of her ear. His harsh, rhythmic breathing blew through her like white-hot quicksilver, and she bit her lip when he rolled a hard nipple between his thumb and forefinger.

"Have done," she pleaded at last, beyond caring how shameless she sounded. She would degrade herself further if need be. Anything to quench the fire that consumed her.

She felt the skirts of her tunic and chainse jerked upward, then the lord's hand slid between her thighs. Her legs trembled as he massaged the flesh there, his fingers working upward until they slipped beneath her drawers and reached the place that needed filling. She opened wide for him and bucked against his touch, silently urging him on.

For a moment he stroked her center, and she grew anxious at the relentless pressure building inside her. 'Twas as if her raging hunger had turned inward. Now, beyond her control, it was about to devour her.

Then the lord slipped a finger inside her. She squeezed her thighs around his hand, desperate to draw him deeper, when abruptly he pulled away.

"No!" she cried, and twisted her body in an attempt to mold herself to the front of him.

"Cease, greedy wench," he commanded, his tone stern.

She stilled and stared into his displeased, uncompromising features. He had found fault with her.

And what man would not? she berated herself. She'd

acted with less restraint than the lowest of whores. Tears of shame welled in her eyes and she pulled as far from him as his hold would allow.

"What is your age?" he demanded.

She squeezed her eyes shut as a sob billowed in her throat. When his fingers touched her face, she turned her head away.

"You are more prickly than a bramble bush," he groused. Capturing her jaw, he pulled her face back to him.

His fingers traced her chin and lips. Instinct told her that the musky scent on his hand was hers, lingering proof of her scandalous behavior. She swallowed hard, willing the ever looming sob to remain locked behind her clenched teeth. The pad of his thumb swept upward, roaming over her left cheekbone, until he reached her eye.

"Why do you cry?" he questioned sharply.

Unable to answer, she shook her head.

"My patience is near flown, wench, and your silence does naught for my temper."

She opened her eyes and glared at him. "Why do you not say you find me offensive and be done?" she choked. "There is little you can do to further humiliate me."

A light rap sounded at the door, but he ignored it.

"Offensive?" His look indicated he thought her an idiot. "I find you yet a maid. Were I a lesser man, my ears would presently be ringing with screeching accusations of how I'd taken you against your will."

The knock sounded louder. "My liege!" Spindleshanks' strident voice sounded from the other side of the door.

"Mi'lord, please," she entreated, fearing the door would open any moment. "I am near bare to the waist."

"A moment, Sperville," he bellowed, releasing her at last.

She scrambled to her feet and raced to the door, shaking her chainse and tunic down as she went.

"Golde!" Delamaure shouted, but she did not look back. Yanking the portal open, she dodged Spindleshanks and Sir Nigel where they stood in the corridor.

She flew to the head of the steps and took them two at a time, the sob finally erupting. Blinded by tears, she continued her rapid descent. Though she knew not exactly where she was going, she knew it would be as far from the Baron of Skyenvic as she could get.

NINE

GAVARNIE STOOD before a window in his chamber and inhaled the briny night air. Clangor from the kitchen below rose to bounce off the timber palisade behind the keep, echoing his disquiet.

The intrigue that had hovered over him earlier while listening to de Warrenne's insinuations had suddenly become a sticky web of deception. A pox on the parchment Nigel and Sperville had brought to his chamber.

Turning from the window, he clasped his hands behind his back. "Read it again, Nigel."

The steward's usual smooth tone was marred by a noticeable quaver. "Look to your own house for betrayal."

"There is no signature?"

"None, sir."

"There is no mark on the seal, either," Sperville added.

"And it was delivered by whom?" Gavarnie queried.

"A village boy left it with the gatekeeper." Nigel sounded as if he longed to take a whip to his own back. "Would that I had been present to receive it."

"You cannot sit at the gate day and night," Gavarnie allowed, though certainly Nigel should have prepared the gatekeeper for such eventualities.

Vowing to address the issue in future, Gavarnie changed the subject. "Is the handwriting familiar to either of you?"

He heard the rustle of parchment and steeled himself to patience. Sperville and Nigel were his most trusted advisors. Under the circumstance, 'twas fitting that he would consult them. Still, the longer they were present, the greater the chance that he would betray his fear. For at the moment, he felt as if he were standing upon the crumbling edge of an abyss.

"All writing looks the same," Sperville complained at last. "I cannot distinguish this from any other."

"Mayhap 'tis but a jest, mi'lord," Nigel offered.

"A jest!" Sperville squawked. "This can hardly be dismissed as a jest."

"I did not mean to dismiss it," Nigel returned hotly. "Rather, I would not have his lordship overly disturbed—"

"Our liege is not given to unwarranted fits of anxiety," Sperville interrupted. "'Tis he who will determine . . ."

Whore's gleet, Gavarnie thought as the chamberlain and steward argued on. They were worse than Ronces and Alory. He finally held up a hand to halt their yapping mouths. "Sperville, I would that you lock the missive in my silver chest. Meanwhile, Nigel, I would that you question the gatekeeper in depth."

"By your leave, sir," Nigel intoned.

"A moment, Nigel," Sperville huffed. "I would accompany you."

Nigel sighed heavily, and Sperville's bootheels clomped toward the wardrobe. Then both men's footsteps resounded as they tromped from the room, the click of the door latch signaling their complete departure.

In the quiet that followed, Gavarnie leaned against the wall. Though he would never admit such, it appeared de Warrenne was correct. Why had he not recognized it before? How could he expect King William to trust a blind man with guarding the Solent against invasion?

It suddenly felt as if iron chains were clamped about his muscles, strangling the life from his limbs. All along, he'd thought William's insistence on sending the royal physicians to heal his eyes a simple act of kindness. Now that the king realized his sight could not be restored . . .

Think! he ordered himself as panic threatened to overwhelm him. He had yet to fail in his duties. No Vikings or French had slipped past his watch. Not that the king could wait for such to occur. It could cost him England.

On the other hand, he had been a faithful vassal to William, had risked his life on William's behalf in numerous battles. For the king to reward such loyalty by relieving him of Skyenvic would hardly instill loyalty among William's other vassals. Indeed, the king's fractious barons might use it as a means to foment rebellion.

Nay. Better for William to quietly kill him and have done.

The idea sent a fresh awareness through him. If such were the case, whom had William chosen as his assassin? De Warrenne?

Gavarnie immediately discarded the possibility. To

murder him secretly would require great cunning. Though William had oft remarked on his faith in de Warrenne's abilities as a henchman, the king would never trust the man with any task that required subtlety.

So whom had the king selected?

Abruptly his eyes narrowed.

"Golde."

Her name erupted from low in his gut. What better person for the deed? Dangling the promise of restoring his vision while creating all manner of turmoil to distract him. With her knowledge of medicine, 'twould be easy for her to poison him once she'd gained his trust. Why else would she be so willing to lose her maidenhead?

Pushing himself from the wall, he slowly paced the floor. Aye, Golde was ready to sacrifice her virginity to gain his trust. Then when he least suspected, she would strike.

It would have to look like an accident. If she used poison, 'twould have to be slow-acting. Something that would steal his life gradually, as would any host of illnesses.

He turned and paced in the opposite direction. Had he known a short while ago what he knew now, he would have taken what the wench offered so freely. Doubtless, William had paid her handsomely to present him with such unholy temptation.

The thought of her heated body and passionate urgings yet had the power to stir his flesh. He winced and rubbed his shaft.

Lips, full and tender as ripe plums, nipples so hardened with desire he'd had no trouble locating them, despite the layers of material she wore. And the pouty flesh encircling her opening, slickened with lust.

Abruptly he collided with the bedpost.

"God be damned!" He clutched his forehead. The wench was stealing his reason.

Fingers splayed before him, he felt his way back toward the window with more caution. By the rood, she was most artful for a virgin. He'd lain with a host of practiced courtesans who possessed nowhere near the expertise he'd been plied with this eve.

His hand struck the wall and he edged sideways until he found the narrow window. Voices yet echoed outside as kitchen servants continued their evening chores.

His gaze searched the noisy black void. Was it possible Golde knew some secret for restoring her maidenhead? Though he'd heard of miraculous deeds performed by witchwives, he'd never heard of that particular accomplishment.

Still, 'twould be just like the conniving little hag. She doubtless had a bagful of tricks for every occasion.

Had she not incited his own children to bear testimony—

Whore's gleet. The children! How could he have forgotten?

He spun from the window and clambered for the door. His haste did naught but delay him, and by the time he located the handle, he felt wild with urgency.

"Roland!" he roared.

'Twas not the squire who responded. "My liege?"

Booted footsteps hurried toward him and he struggled to place the voice. "Eustace?"

"Aye, mi'lord. How may I serve—"

"Why are you on duty so early in the eve?" he demanded.

"Sir Sperville ordered it," the watch replied, a note of uncertainty in his tone. "Is all well?"

More footsteps sounded from the stairs, then

thumped on the landing. "Mi'lord, you called?" Roland asked, his voice winded.

"I want my sons." He paused to take a steadying breath. "And my daughter brought to me."

"But they are already abed," Roland puffed.

"Dare you question my command, boy?"

Before Roland could reply, he heard a door squeak down the corridor. Then Ronces spoke. "We are not asleep."

Gavarnie concentrated on wiping all trace of anger from his face before turning to his son. "Come." He held out his hands.

"You go," Alory whispered. "Papa is angry."

"Pigeonheart," Ronces hissed back. "Papa won't hurt you."

Even a deaf man would have heard the exchange. A knotted feeling clogged Gavarnie's chest. Alory feared him?

Eustace cleared his throat. "Is that all, my liege?"

Gavarnie nodded absently. 'Twas a moment until he felt a small hand clutch his. "Ronces?"

"Aye, Papa." The boy squeezed his hand.

"Where is Alory?" He yet held his other hand open.

"He is here."

Gavarnie nodded, determined not to reveal the bitter disappointment that threatened to squeeze the breath from him. "Mayhap Alory could lead the way to my bed," he coaxed.

At that, he felt his younger son take his hand, and he was slowly turned about.

"A moment." He halted. "Roland?"

"Aye, mi'lord." The squire's voice was filled with— was it pity?

At the thought, anger swept over him. "Fetch Nico—my daughter," he ordered harshly.

Ronce's hand stiffened in his, and Alory's trembled, as if they could not stomach Nicolette in their presence.

"The two of you have some objection?" His words seethed.

"Nay!" Ronces squeaked.

At the boy's frightened tone, his anger dissolved as if in a heap of dead ashes. It was not Nicolette who disturbed the boys. Rather, it was their fear of *him*. Unbidden, Golde's words rang accusingly in his head. *If you would cease bellowing like a bull, you might hear what goes on about you.*

"Your forgiveness for my sharp tongue," he apologized. It required no effort to sound sincere. "Alory, if you would, lead the way."

Did his sons move slowly to accommodate his blindness, he wondered as they shuffled forward; or did their feet drag with dread?

Within moments Ronces said in a subdued voice, "Here, Papa."

Gavarnie forced a smile and sat on the edge of the bed. "Come and join me," he invited, patting the covers to either side of him.

He felt the mattress give as the boys did his bidding, though neither said a word. The smell of dirt and sweat accompanied them.

In an attempt at levity, he waved the air in front of his nose. "Faith, have the two of you been mucking the sheep pens? When was the last time you bathed?"

"Bathing is for babes and girls," Alory declared, distracted from his silence by an issue to which he obviously attached great significance.

"It is not," Nicolette snapped from the direction of the door.

"Your . . . uh, Nicolette," Roland announced.

"Come, *daughter*," Gavarnie emphasized the word, motioning with his hand. "I would that you join us. Roland, close the door and await without until I summon you."

He paused for Nicolette to climb abed, and when she did not, he prompted, "I have asked you to join us."

"Thewe is no woom," the girl groused from near his feet.

He raised a brow. "Mayhap you would deign to sit on my lap, mistress."

"Papa!" Ronces' tone was disbelieving, and he felt the bed shift to his left.

"She is your sister as far as I'm concerned." Gavarnie measured his words as Nicolette settled herself in his lap.

"She is not," Alory huffed on his right.

"Who told you she is not?" Gavarnie demanded.

Silence.

Plague take his acid tongue. He must control his temper. He must.

Hoping to smooth the children's rift, he cleared his throat and concentrated on speaking evenly. "I learned some distressing news this eve. Mistress Golde tells me . . ."

His words trailed away. What was he to say? *I understand the three of you hate one another?*

His mouth grew dry. He knew not exactly what they'd said to Golde. He'd been too busy sampling her charms—which she'd so freely offered. The deceitful witch.

Still, as he recalled—*Alory scrambles to hide . . .*

Ronces curses Nicolette. . . . Nicolette relates how you chopped their mother—

"Golde tells me . . ." Again he paused.

Lackwit! he railed at himself. He should have thought the matter through before dragging his children before him.

"Why awe you shaking?" Nicolette broke into his frantic thoughts. "What did the bad witch say?"

'Twas all he could do to draw breath. "You hate one another," he wheezed. "I cut your mother—" He gasped for air.

For a long moments, no one spoke or moved. Then Nicolette rose on his lap to hug his neck. "She is lying. I tole you she was bad."

Gavarnie clutched the small body to his and rocked. Then Alory burrowed under his arm and Ronces patted his back.

What could he say to them? How could he possibly tell them—

Abruptly he stilled as Nicolette's words sank into his head.

Golde had lied?

She'd lied!

By all that was holy, she would pray for death before he was through.

TEN

❦❧

GOLDE WANDERED along the slick cobblestone quay in the village of New Market, her shoulders hunched against the early, cloud-chilled sea breeze. Would that she had returned to Nicolette's bedchamber this morn to fetch her cloak from her chest. But she had been too frightened.

Nay, she admitted, she'd been too embarrassed. She winced, recalling her lurid behavior last eve. That she had actually begged the baron to "have done." Heat stung her cheeks anew and she hugged her stomach. How sorceled she had been by his touch, his seeming acceptance of her. But of course, he couldn't see.

Grimacing, she glanced at the overcast sky. 'Twas difficult to believe the sun was more than a quarter of the way to its noon position. Indeed, dawn had never broken. For that reason, she had waited far too long to leave her

perch on the castle's wallwalk where she'd spent an uncomfortable night berating herself. By the time she'd
reached New Market, where she planned to secure passage across the Solent, she had already missed the fishing
fleet.

A half-dozen gulls clamoring over a bait scrap pulled
her from her brooding. The birds screeched at her approach, then flew away when she drew near. The slimy
object of their quarrel smelled even more rank than the
general fishy odor that permeated the quay, and she wrinkled her nose. Now she would have to await the fishing
fleet's return and hope she could persuade someone to
carry her to the mainland.

Her steps slowed and she gazed out over the gray
choppy water. Persuade them with what? Her wholesome
looks? What little coin she'd brought lay at the bottom of
her chest in Nicolette's chamber. She blinked against the
threat of tears. "Stupid girl," she grumbled. She'd thought
no further than escaping the castle earlier this morn.

Her stomach growled and she made a sour face as
another thought occurred to her. Not only did she lack
the means to purchase passage for herself, her belly would
needs go a'begging. Rubbing her arms against the cold,
she turned and retraced her steps along the cobblestones.

What was she to do? She'd never really needed
money. Even the coin she collected from her fortune-
telling would not be needed until her father grew too old
to work.

She halted and scanned the ramshackle, battered
buildings along the quay. That was it! An alehouse. All
ports provided a place for thirsty sailors. If she could convince a proprietor to allow her use of a corner in his
establishment, she could cast fortunes.

A raindrop struck her head and she swiped at it. Aye.

She'd have to share a portion of the profits with the alekeeper in exchange for a table. But even so, she'd have enough money by nightfall to pay for her own fleet.

She strode briskly across the quay to an open-air booth where a fishwife was cleaning wooden bins in preparation for the day's catch. The woman directed her to a weather-grayed, two-story building.

As she neared the windowless alehouse, she saw that both stories sagged in the middle. Just when she would have knocked on the splintered door, it was jerked inward. She jumped aside as a heavy, ruddy-complexioned woman flung a pile of refuse into the lane.

Realizing she'd just missed heaping the stinking filth on Golde, the woman snapped, "Them that ar'nt got sense to stay clear o' doorways in the morn deserves wot they gets."

Golde raised an imperious brow at the mean-tempered shrew. "I would speak to the owner of this establishment."

The woman tilted her head back and laughed, a harsh, strangled sound, which erupted into a coughing fit that bent her double. Straightening, she poked her face nearer to Golde's. "Speak, me lackwitted dearie. Ye've got me ear."

Golde took a backward step. The woman's breath smelled rancid with onion, and her oily, gray-brown hair likely hosted numerous vermin. "You are the owner?"

The dowd squinted at her. "Ye ar'nt from 'round here if ye've not heard o' Maid Sigi's alehouse. Off with ye, girlie." She turned and waddled back inside.

Golde followed and caught the door when the woman would have slammed it shut. "You are Maid Sigi?"

The dowd turned and looked up at Golde, not the least impressed with her height or her eyes. "Ye are worse than a pesky flea. Wot is it ye want? I ar'nt got all day to stand about gossipin'."

'Twas not an auspicious beginning, and Golde bobbed her head in an attempt to appear humble. "I would present you with a proposition, mi'lady."

"Mi'lady!" Maid Sigi slapped her leg and hooted, then her eyes narrowed. "If ye've come to charm me money from me, have done. I ar'nt dull of wit and I'll wager I been plied with ever' scheme ye can think of."

Golde stifled a grin. Here was a woman she could come to like very well if given a chance. "'Tis not my wish to part you from your coin, but to add to it. I am a seeress and have need of a table to cast fortunes."

Maid Sigi gave her a hard look. "Don't allows witchery in me place. I gots me regulars wot don't take well ta' sorcelry."

Golde glanced at the lopsided tables, the soot-blackened walls, the dirt floors littered with fish bones. There was little to give her any indication of Maid Sigi's life, other than a tattered gray sail tacked to one wall.

"Very well, Widow Sigrid." She affected a mysterious tone, praying the sail belonged to the woman's departed husband, and that Sigi was short for Sigrid. At the woman's startled look, she continued. "There are other alehouses I could have approached. I knew not why I was directed here until this very moment."

When she paused, Maid Sigi grew impatient. "Go on."

'Twas so simple to cozen even the most shrewd of persons. Once the initial facts were established, there were naught but three things left to foretell. Health, wealth, and love.

"Your departed husband, the fisherman." At Maid Sigi's nod, she clasped the woman's roughened hand and closed her eyes. "He wishes, foremost, to say that though you had many quarrels"—that was true for everyone—"he loved you deeply. He has sent me to you, knowing you are in need of funds to repair your household." That was obvious from the dilapidated condition of the building. Now came the difficult part. "He is jealous, though," she intoned, and cracked one eyelid to see how Maid Sigi was taking everything.

At the alekeeper's round eyes, she knew she'd guessed a'right. There was not a woman living who did not secretly cherish a man other than her spouse. "The man whom you have grown fond of . . ." She paused to be certain.

"Shipmaster Argul!" Sigi gasped.

Golde closed her eye. "That is the one. Your husband does not care for him, but he understands your longing for a mate now that he is gone. And since he knows you have a long life ahead of you, he will bide quietly until you meet in the hereafter."

She took a deep breath and shuddered for effect, then opened her eyes.

"Ye are indeed possessed of the all-seeing eye," Sigi breathed reverently. "'Twas truly me dear Orlaf speaking through ye."

Golde nodded. "If you will allow me a table, I will split my earnings, one-third to you and two-thirds to me."

Abruptly Maid Sigi sobered, and a cunning look crossed her features. "'Twill be half to me and half for ye."

Golde studied Sigi's determined, square jaw. She could not afford to miss the opportunity. Looking heavenward, she sighed. "Orlaf told me you would drive a hard bargain."

By midmorn the clouds had opened to spill their rain-filled bellies. Due to the inclement weather, the fishing fleet had returned earlier than usual, and the men had sought refuge in Maid Sigi's alehouse. Though it had at first appeared no one would avail himself of her second sight, Sigi herself had sworn to Golde's abilities. The room had grown silent when she'd forecast her first cull's fortune, and after that, more and more people came forward.

By noon she was doing a brisk trade, and the ale-loosened tongues of those present grew raucous. The place was packed with unwashed bodies until Golde felt certain her nose would never recover from the odor of fish. Some of the men had run home and fetched their wives and children to come witness the spectacle. No sooner did one person vacate the chair across the table from her than another filled it.

The room was smothering with smoke from the hearth, and Golde cast a bleary-eyed smile at her most recent cull as he rose and thanked her. Tired beyond measure, her voice fast growing hoarse, she was ill prepared for the grime-encrusted, ragged boy who next sat in the empty chair.

Inexplicably, the child, no more than ten, annoyed her. Still, she could not have others believe her unkind, so she forced a gentle tone. "Off with you, little fellow. There are those with pressing needs and you steal their time."

The boy gave her a sullen, gray-eyed look. "I gots a silver piece, same as ever'one else." He opened his be-grimed hand to reveal a shiny coin, along with several fish scales that clung to his thumb.

'Twas not his looks so much as his manner that reminded her of Ronces. She stared at his pinched little face as several drunken adults in the room snickered.

"Look at 'im," she heard a woman say. "Dull Lull. Think he'd know by now 'is fancy sire ar'nt comin' to fetch 'im."

Golde bristled at the cruel words and held out her hand. "Well, Sir Lull, let us see what your future holds."

The boy dropped the coins in her palm, his stony features near to crumbling after the insulting remark.

Golde deposited the silver in a cup, and reaching across the table, clutched both the boy's hands. His small fingers were chapped and cold. Closing her eyes, she prepared to spin a fantastic tale that would wipe the look of misery from his face. But before she could speak, the same blinding light that had savaged her senses in Skyenvic's hall tore through her body.

Her head jerked and she gasped against the searing pain. She tried to open her eyes, but 'twas as if they were permanently sealed.

Abruptly the light dispersed into a host of blinking stars and she found herself on a deserted, windswept moor. The smell of damp gorse and heather rose from the ground, and the wind blended into a rhythmic pattern until she recognized it as breathing. She didn't walk; rather, she drifted toward the sound with no effort.

Wait for me, a man's husky voice whispered. *Swear it.*

Squinting, Golde saw two shadowed figures entwined below her, but the starlight was not bright enough to see them clearly. Still, she felt a strong bond between them and knew she witnessed more than fleshly desire.

By my mother's soul, a woman whispered. *I will wait for you.*

Golde knew the woman lied, but 'twas without malicious intent. Before she could determine the purpose of the falsehood, the woman's belly glowed as if a host of candles burned within her. In that moment Golde saw the man's lean, powerful face. A lord. And the woman.

Though her features were twisted with the fierceness of her love, Golde recognized beauty in her face.

Then they melted away as the sun rose over the barren moor, its light growing more intense with each moment. Colors changed from mauve to pink to yellow, and Golde gritted her teeth against the pain that stabbed her more deeply with every change in hue. Her hands shook. She bent her head, trying to escape the piercing brilliance she knew was near upon her. Just before the fiery light consumed her, she saw the lord's silhouette and heard his agonized cry of rage.

She flung the boy's hands from her and clutched her eyes. Her heart hammered in her chest and she sucked air as if each breath might be her last. 'Twas no easy task to remain in her seat. Dizzy, she longed for nothing more than to curl in a ball on the dirt floor.

She forced her eyes open to stare at Lull. His features appeared anxious and drawn. The room had grown silent and she looked beyond the boy to find everyone's gaze fixed on her, speculation mixed with fear. Had she spoken aloud? Did they know what she'd seen?

She gave her attention back to Lull. He would never understand the implications of her vision. "Fetch your mother," she directed. "I will tell her—"

"Me mum's dead."

"And so she is," a snag-toothed woman squawked, coming to the fore of the crowd. "Now, wot did ye see?"

Golde leveled a frosty glare upon the overbearing hag. "Were I you," her tone carried low and menacing, "I would have a care with my tongue. Though I know little of the boy's mother, his father is a lord of the moors. And the man loved his mother true and sure."

A round of gasps rippled through the assembly, followed by a wave of whispers. When she looked back at

Lull, his gray eyes shone, not with the smugness of victory, but with the comfort of peace. Whatever demons he'd wrestled with, they'd been laid to rest.

"Here, now." Sigi elbowed her way to Golde from the corner of the room to thrust a large mug of ale into her hand. Grabbing the cup that held the coins, she announced, "The seeress needs a bit o' rest. She'll be returnin' forthwith."

Sigi pulled her from the chair and escorted her past a black drape that covered an opening in the back of the room. Golde glanced at a huge tub overflowing with dirty dishes, and surmised she was in the kitchen. A great pot hung on rungs over the hearth in the middle of the earthen floor and a small, lopsided table was positioned near it. Sigi led her to a stool at the table and seated her.

Golde gulped the brew in the mug, uncaring that it was watered down.

"What ye jest done . . ." Sigi drew her attention, and Golde looked to see the alewife's head cocked where she stood beside the table. "'Twas true sight, weren't it?"

Golde opened her mouth to tell her 'twas no more true than the vision she'd had of Orlaf, but at the knowing look in Sigi's sharp eyes, she bowed her head and nodded. Then she looked up. "If you knew I was a fake, why did you allow me in your establishment?"

Sigi snorted. "Ye passed me test with that Orlaf business. I knows a moneymaking scheme when I hears one. The way I sees it, this time next week I'll be swimmin' in silver."

Golde shook her head. "I cannot stay. I but need enough coin to secure passage to the mainland." She inclined her head at the money cup Sigi held. "I believe I already have funds a'plenty."

Sigi gave her a doleful look. "Ye don't wish to stay? We'd be rich in less than a fortnight."

"Would that I could, if only for the kindness you have shown me." At Sigi's disconsolate pout, she offered, "You are welcome to my portion of the profits from the rest of the day."

Sigi sighed. "We would o' made a great pair. 'Specially seein' as how yer so quick to give in to me greedy nature." She winked. "The rest o' the day's profits, ye say?"

Golde couldn't help smiling. An avaricious woman who made no bones about it. Sigi reminded her of herself.

"The rest of the day's profits," Golde repeated, then added, "You had best fetch me another mug of ale, and not that watery slop you serve your patrons. I am in need of the real thing, lest I collapse from fatigue."

Sigi frowned. "Ye do look a bit pale. Mayhap ye should lay down upstairs. I don't be needin' money that bad."

Golde held out the empty mug. "Let me finish the afternoon to pay for a bed. I'll need one come nightfall."

Sigi squinted, then took the mug. "If ye insists."

Watching her depart, Golde frowned as she recalled Lull's glowing gray eyes. The boy might be happy with what she'd seen, but she felt dismal. Of what help had she been? His mother was dead and she'd been unable to tell him who his father was. And the village seafolk yet appeared most hostile toward him.

Sigi came back through the curtain and Golde asked, "Why does everyone dislike this Lull?"

Sigi handed her the mug. "They are by and large jealous fools. Lull's mum e're treated him like a prince, makin' him speak proper and teachin' him manners and such. Though his mum labored at all manner of mean tasks, takin' in laundry and mendin' clothes, she kept to herself."

Sigi shrugged. "Ye knows how folks is. Wot they don't knows, they don't trusts. And wot they don't trusts, they fears. Didn't take long for 'em to start tauntin' her, 'specially after she turned down three proposals of marriage."

"So what will become of Lull now?"

"He's managin' jest fine. Goes out with the fleet and all. Rents a room from old man Ragenhere. He's a smart boy, so don't waste yer time feelin' sorry fer him."

Golde grew silent and sipped the ale, enjoying its bite. Mayhap she could take Lull home with her. After all, eventually her father would need help in the fields. And he'd never have a son-in-law, courtesy of her cursed eyes.

She lowered the mug abruptly and slapped a hand on her forehead. When would she learn? She must distance herself from her culls. Had she stuck to her vow with the baron, she would not have come to this wretched pass.

Home. She concentrated on the thought, savoring the word like a delicious sweetmeat. Away from Skyenvic. Away from the swarthy Gavarnie Delamaure who brewed unspeakable, all-consuming passions in her.

She stared into the mug. What was it about him that so fascinated her? He was far from pretty, though she would admit there was a rough handsomeness to his face. His smile was appealing, not due to its warmth, but rather its dark cynicism that so matched her own. The bitterness she'd seen claim his features on occasion bespoke great adversity, yet his deeds and mannerisms indicated a strength of character that would withstand any tempest.

She almost choked on the ale. Faith, she sounded like a simpering, love-struck girl. The baron had not refuted her insinuation that Nicolette was not his. Nor had he denied murdering his wife.

Nay. Instead of responding to her accusations, he'd chosen to lure her into a pit of rutting lust, despite the fact he knew nothing of her. Indeed, he knew not how she looked. Yet his seduction had been bold and sure.

Why?

She took a deep swig of ale. He'd wielded her body's desires against her like a depraved demon. Like a man—

She shifted on the stool as a horrible thought took seed. Having spent the majority of her life in Mimskin's company while her father toiled in the fields, she'd learned a great deal about human nature. There were men a'plenty who despised women; who took perverse pleasure in humiliating females to prove their superiority.

Was the baron one of those men?

An image of the mutilated blond-haired woman from her swevyn assailed her. 'Twas not difficult to envision the half-clothed, dark-fleshed lord standing over the lady, a dripping blade in his hand. Had he killed his wife not only for her infidelity, but to satisfy some sick bloodlust?

Maid Sigi interrupted her chilling thoughts. "Are ye all right, girlie? Yer lookin' paler by the moment."

Golde blinked, concentrating on connecting the two Sigi's that swam before her eyes. "Faith, 'tis a potent brew you've served me. I can scarce see."

"Made it meself," Sigi crowed, then frowned. "But it don't look like it's set well wi' ye. Mayhap ye should lay down after all."

Golde shook her head, anxious to avoid being alone with her thoughts at the moment. "Nonsense. Never felt better. We have a bargain and I intend to fulfill it."

She drained the remainder of the ale and sauntered

back to the front room, Sigi guiding her by the elbow. It appeared more crowded and noisy than ever, and she didn't see Lull anywhere. *Ah well.* She shrugged and took her seat.

A pleasant, fuzzy glow encircled the oil lamps that hung on the walls, melting her troubled spirits. She smiled at the red-bearded man who came to sit across from her. He handed her his coin and she flipped it into the money cup that Sigi set beside her. Clasping his hands, she drew a deep breath and began with his health.

The afternoon dragged on. Sigi continued to bring her ale until all the fortunes grew jumbled in her head. By the time dusk settled, she was having difficulty recalling what she'd told to whom. 'Twould be most unseemly to tell the same thing to more than one person. She giggled, then covered her mouth when she hiccuped. Her next cull had trouble understanding her, and she had to repeat herself with increasing frequency for the dunderwit.

Well, she conceded, her tongue had grown a bit thick.

"Enough," Sigi barked at last. "The poor dearie is too tired to continue."

"A moment, Maid Sigi," a raw-edged voice called from the entrance of the alehouse.

Golde swiveled her gaze in the door's direction. It sounded just like his toadship, Sir Gavarnie. She squinted, but could see naught for the bodies that blocked her line of sight.

"There is one more fortune to tell," the voice continued.

A path parted in the midst of the patrons where Sir Nigel led the baron toward Golde. Her lip curled heartily as she anticipated the fortune she was about to tell. Delamaure would learn here and now that to play with fire was to be burned. The steward seated him at the table, then stood to one side, avoiding her gaze.

"So, mistress of darkness," the baron challenged. "Say me my fortune."

ELEVEN

OTHER THAN THE SOUND of shuffling feet as the peasants made way for several men-at-arms, the alehouse had grown silent. Golde smiled grimly.

"I have seen your fushure." She frowned. Though her pitch was loud enough to carry through the room, which was as she desired, her tongue was being uncooperative. She slowed her delivery and concentrated on speaking clearly. "'Tis a red tail and horns that await you."

Ha! she congratulated herself as murmurs wafted through the crowd. *Take that, mi'lord lecher.* Before she was finished, he would appear more dim than an empty oil lamp.

Instead of scowling, as she expected, he smiled. Leaning his elbows on the table, he rested his chin atop his hands. "I already possess horns and a tail. I have a forked tongue and fangs as well, if you will recall."

Indeed, she could attest to his venomous bite, and the carnal poison it contained. A hiccup threatened, and though she managed to prevent its escaping her mouth, her head bobbed. Marshaling her thoughts, she pointed out, "Vipers have weak moments, particularly after they have fed."

"None would know better than you."

Golde narrowed an eye. Was he remarking on the fact he'd fed upon her, or did he insinuate she was the viper?

Before she could decide, he continued. "Let us have done with this banality. You tell me naught which I do not already know."

His black eyes held a challenging glint, and his smooth lips . . .

Nay. She would not fall in that trap again. Another hiccup assailed her and she clamped her teeth together as her head jerked. Faith. It felt as if her eyes might float from her head. Praise God the man could not see, else he would know she'd overindulged.

She blinked until Delamaure became focused in her vision. "Very well, mi'lord. Do you wish to hear of the blond woman whose blood soaks your bed?"

A chorus of gasps resounded from the crowd. The lord lowered his hands to the tabletop and leaned forward, his eyes suddenly barren as a frozen wasteland. "Maid Sigi, tell the fortune-caster of my wife's precipitate demise."

Golde glanced at the alewife. Sigi's florid complexion had paled and she was shaking her head. "Now why would ye want me to be sayin' tales 'bout that, yer lordship? Ever'one knows—"

"Precisely my point, Sigi." The baron's tone was chilling in its flatness. "Everyone knows I murdered my wife when she confessed her infidelities. I would have murdered her lover, too, only the skulking bastard managed to get himself sent to Northumbria, where he took a Scotsman's spear in his chest and died."

The numbing ale-haze that clouded Golde's senses cleared, and its warmth seeped away. That he would boldly admit to such an atrocity. And far from feeling remorse, 'twas as if he dared anyone to gainsay him.

"The law makes allowance for the murder of an unfaithful wife," he said in an even tone, "as it does for those who use fraud to part hardworking folk from their coin."

His nostrils flared, and Golde's breath caught at the deadly glint in his eyes.

"Now, great seeress, if indeed such is the case, I would hear my fortune. And it had best be sound, lest you find yourself charged with thievery."

A disgruntled buzz rose from the assembled seafolk. Glancing about, Golde saw a number of hostile looks directed at her. 'Od rot the baron's twisted soul. She shivered as fear fluttered in her breast. Was it his intention to see her hanged?

Why?

She had done nothing to him. 'Twas he who'd spurned her. She stared at his hard features. Her eyes rounded as she recalled her earlier thoughts concerning woman-haters. Mayhap the baron's particular obsession was to rid the world of all loose women.

There had been just such a man who'd lived in Cyning during Mimskin's youth. He'd lured young girls to lie with him, promising to wed them. The moment they gave themselves to him, he pronounced them Satan's spawn. Four had been murdered before one managed to escape and the man had been caught.

A sharp elbow to her back startled her and she glanced up to see Sigi give her a pointed look. "Have another mug of ale, dearie. It may be yer last."

At least Sigi's intent was clear, Golde reflected dismally. Though the alewife wished her no ill, she would not defend Golde if it meant endangering herself.

Golde picked up the mug and drained its contents. The bitter taste mirrored her thoughts, and she wiped her mouth with the back of her hand. Why had she ever come to this wretched isle?

"Your time grows short, wench," the baron prodded.

Gooseflesh rippled over her body as she recalled the savage vision of the dead blonde. His wife, she amended. Could she withstand another such experience?

She gritted her teeth. She could ill afford not to. Summoning her courage, she set the mug on the table, then reached over and placed her fingertips atop the baron's where they rested on the scarred, wooden surface.

His flesh felt hot beneath her frozen touch, its color darkly robust compared to the purplish tint of her own. Though her hands would never be considered small, his dwarfed them.

She shifted in her seat as heat from his fingers curled its way up her arms and slid down her body to settle in the crutch where her thighs met. Her gaze jerked to his unyielding face and she cursed her hands for trembling. Like the evening before, she wondered how she could feel thus, knowing his rancorous intent.

She squeezed her eyes shut, unable to bear the ruthless appearance of his features. A vision. The pain and fear of second sight would be a welcome release from the baron's black hold over her body. She focused her thoughts and waited for the soul-piercing light. In the silence that surrounded her, she listened for the stirring of wind.

Nothing.

Desperate to feel something, she tilted her head from side to side, hoping to unbalance her senses and thus foster the proper atmosphere. She sighed gratefully at the faint dizziness that touched her. But it was not enough, and she leaned farther and farther . . .

Abruptly the chair tipped. Her eyes flew open and she clutched at the baron's hands, to no effect. She toppled sideways, grunting when she hit the ground. Ribald laughter scalded her ears.

'Twas as if she were an ugly little girl again and the village children were ridiculing her. Scrambling to her feet, she edged around the table, then bolted for the door.

"Stop 'er!" a woman shrieked.

Angry shouts erupted around her, and clawing hands grabbed at her tunic and arms. The odor of fish combined with ale-soaked breath and rotten teeth until she thought she would be sick.

She fought against the grasping clutches, kicking with her booted feet. If only she could reach the door. She bit an arm and heard a howl of pain above the din.

Just as a fist came flying at her face, her legs became entangled in her skirts. She stumbled to her knees and the intended blow sailed over her head, barely grazing her hair.

Before she could rise, someone placed a wooden-soled shoe to her backside and shoved. She snarled as the force pitched her forward to land on her hands.

"Don't look like no sage now, do she?" a man jeered.

"Looks like the cur she is," a woman cackled.

Golde fought to gain her feet, but everyone within reach began pummeling her. It felt as if her arms and legs were being hammered. One boot caught her beneath the chin, snapping her head backward.

Stars danced before her eyes. She swayed.

A shin slammed into her ribs and she dropped on her side. Covering her head with her arms, she curled in a ball.

The enraged mob was going to kill her. She wanted to scream, to curse them all before her breath deserted her. Most of all, she longed to plunge a dagger in the baron's chest. To have the satisfaction of seeing his life seep from him.

A ragged sob burst from her mouth.

"Enough!" the baron roared from somewhere near her feet.

Instantly the clamor abated. Feet scuffled away until the room grew still. Hope flared in her breast. Mayhap she would live after all. At least long enough to slit Delamaure's gullet.

Cautiously she lowered her arms from her head. The movement aggravated every bruise on her body, and she clenched her teeth. Cracking an eye, she surveyed her immediate surroundings. One of the baron's liegemen stood directly in front of her, brandishing a sword. The baron himself stood an arm's length from her feet, another liegeman guarding his back.

Golde squinted, puzzled. Sir Gavarnie's blade was drawn, his features savage. What had he to be angry over? Had he not wished her dead? She rose to sit, that she might have a better view, thinking surely her eyes had deceived her.

She was scarce upright before burning pain tore through her ribs. Her gasp added fuel to the fiery agony and she held her breath, praying for surcease. Were her ribs broken? She leaked the pent breath from her mouth, and gradually the pain lessened.

"Disperse yourselves," the baron ordered.

"Wot abouts our money?" a man demanded.

Delamaure snarled. "Your coin is forfeit to me, in exchange for the illicit sport you have enjoyed this night." His blind gaze burned as it swept the onlookers. "Now get yourselves gone, for the next person who dares question my command will forfeit his life."

Golde winced with each shallow breath she took. The baron's actions were a mystery. First he threw her to the wolves, then became enraged when they mauled her. To what purpose had he rescued her?

TWELVE

GAVARNIE AWAITED his groomsman's assistance to mount his destrier, Rime. Though the rain had ceased, the smell of wet horse and leather lay thick in the humid air. Somewhere down the quay, an argument erupted between a man and a woman, their voices tinny and distant above the clop of horses' hooves against cobblestones.

The sound reminded Gavarnie of the cracked, angry voice he'd heard above the commotion in the alehouse. It had seemed to come from nowhere. Who had been the speaker, he wondered? Like the argument down the quay, he'd not been able to distinguish actual words. Yet the meaning had been clear. *Fool!* the tone accused. *Golde will die at your instigation.*

"Here, mi'lord," the groomsman, Trelle, broke into his musings.

Gavarnie reached out until he felt Rime's damp saddle. Grasping the pommel, he placed a foot in Trelle's cupped hands and swung up.

Like as not, it had been his own inwit he'd heard, Gavarnie decided while adjusting his seat. Indeed, he had been a fool.

An agent of the king. He snorted. Golde was no more than a fake soothsayer, a woman who preyed on others' hopes and dreams for the coin it could bring her. Doubtless, her great passion for him was but a ploy to fleece him out of a few silver pieces. Not that he could excuse his actions. She had not deserved the beating he'd incited.

Settled in the saddle, he commanded, "Henri, you will carry the witchwife and ride on my right. Lund, on my left."

Guilt prickled his flesh at Golde's groan. "Christ's blood, Henri. Have a care with the wench."

"I'm doing my best, mi'lord."

Gavarnie hunched his shoulders. Despite her dishonest nature, regardless of her acid tongue, he could think of naught but Golde's good deeds. Had she not saved Nicolette's life? Mayhap she *could* restore his sight. And what of her wit? Spindleshanks, of all things! When had he last laughed with such complete abandon?

Chagrined, he directed his attention to the matter at hand. "Nigel?"

"Aye, mi'lord," the steward answered from near Rime's left flank.

"You will take the lead. Stephan and Bogo, the rear."

Boots scraped against cobblestones as his men moved to do his bidding. He lowered his head, unable to staunch the flow of his thoughts.

Not only was he a fool, he was a spineless worm. How

soothing it had been to believe Nicolette's claim that Golde had lied; much simpler to torture Golde into admitting she'd concocted the entire story.

It took no great intellect to see Golde had spoken the truth. His children's furtive actions were proof.

He rubbed the back of his neck. Would that he'd had the courage to consider such before tearing into New Market like a demon from hell. But, as always, he'd allowed rage to rule his reason. And his rash conduct could have cost Golde her life.

As it had Isabelle's.

He winced. Judging from Golde's responses to his questions, her ribs were severely bruised, mayhap cracked. 'Twas imperative he get her to the keep where she could be properly cared for. Once she was healed, he would send her on her way, with a stern reproach for her false practices.

Saddle leather creaked, drawing his attention, and he surmised his men were mounted. He motioned with his left hand for the groomsman to mount behind him. "Come, Trelle."

"Beg pardon, mi'lord," Stephan spoke. "Mayhap Trelle would best serve seated in front since 'tis dark."

He gritted his teeth. *Witless get of an idiot.* His men must think him an imbecile to not realize it was night. 'Twould be difficult for Trelle to direct him, as the groomsman had earlier when it was daylight.

Yet he'd be butchered before he'd ride double behind Trelle. 'Twas unseemly.

He rubbed the damp, slick reins between his fingers. "Trelle, you will ride behind and I will pass the reins about my waist."

While the groom mounted, he turned his attention to Henri. "The wench. She is settled?"

"As well as possible, sir."

"A pox," Golde panted, "on you . . . son of a . . ."

He interrupted before she could finish, his flagging spirits raised by her display of anger. "If you would shut your flapping mouth, you would feel less discomfort."

Her heated little hiss further improved his humor. Knowing her wounds had not destroyed her sour tongue was of great relief, though God knew anyone else would be most content to hear naught but silence from her.

"Ahead," he ordered Nigel.

He gripped the pommel and raised his elbows so Trelle could hold the reins closer. The groomsman spurred Rime's flanks and the horse pranced forward, anxious to reach Skyenvic's stables and a bin of oats.

Golde moaned, and Gavarnie opened his mouth again to admonish Henri, then decided against it. There was nothing the liegeman could do to make the trip more comfortable for the wench.

Within a short time, the cobblestone clatter was replaced by the duller sound of earth. Muddy earth, judging from the sucking noises made by Rime's hooves. New Market had been left behind for the lane that ran through the forest surrounding Skyenvic.

Rime dipped beneath Gavarnie, and uneasiness crept into his head. He could fair smell the ink of darkness, could feel the crowded closeness of the trees that lined the lane. He clutched the pommel more tightly. 'Twas foolhardy to be riding at night, no matter the urgency. 'Twas doubly so, considering de Warrenne's presence at Skyenvic, and the message warning of betrayal.

He grimaced. "Henri, did someone think to bring a lamp?"

"Aye. Sir Nigel and Bogo each have one."

Gavarnie clamped his legs about Rime as the horse

swayed. The oil lamps would provide no more than feeble light and were of little comfort. The lane was rutted and he would never remain seated if Rime stumbled.

Why had he not listened to Sperville? The chamberlain had implored him to send someone else after Golde. But nay. Gavarnie gritted his teeth. After searching for her half the night and all morn, he'd near been frothing at the mouth. When he'd heard reports of her activities in the village, he'd greatly anticipated fetching her himself.

"At least ride a mount less spirited than Rime," the chamberlain had persisted.

"I could hold your reins," Nigel had offered.

His lip curled. Did both men think he'd allow himself to be led before the village like some doddering old man? He silently congratulated himself for having solved the problem. It had been his idea to have Trelle ride double behind him and tell him where to guide his mount.

Still, he wished he'd taken Sperville's advice and worn a hauberk instead of the simple leather coat he sported.

He was pulled from his thoughts as Rime's gait grew choppy. "Have a care, Trelle. You go too fast. Henri will be unable to keep pace."

"Your forgiveness, my liege, but Sir Nigel—" He bumped Gavarnie's back. "He is outstripping us."

"Why did you not say something, man? Nigel! Hold."

Trelle slammed against his back, near unseating him. "God's blood!"

Gavarnie started to yell at Nigel again when the groomsman clutched his waist and hauled him sideways.

"The light!" Stephan's panicked voice crawled over his flesh.

Even as Trelle pulled him from Rime, a vast icy emptiness consumed Gavarnie. They were under attack! In the same instant he hit the ground, he heard a masculine scream of pain, then a thud. One of the men behind him had fallen.

"On your feet," he commanded Trelle, who sprawled half atop him.

When the groom did not respond, he shook his shoulder. "Tre—"

His hand met a shaft, then another, and he slid his hand upward to the feathered end of an arrow.

The groomsman was dead.

Shoving the limp body aside, Gavarnie drew his sword and clambered to his feet.

How would he die? An arrow to the breast? Gutted by a sword? At this very moment, someone could be aiming a mace at his head.

The thought turned his insides to slush. He was naught but a hindrance to his liegemen. Men who would fight to the death on his behalf. Men who'd been led, at his direction, to their doom.

And what of Golde? She, too, would likely die.

From nowhere, a disgruntled voice hissed, *She had best not, boy.*

Gavarnie spun about. 'Twas the same voice he'd heard at the alehouse.

A wisp of mist darted in the corner of his vision. He turned toward it, but all he could see was Rime's . . .

His heart skipped, stealing his breath. He blinked.

Was that the vague outline of Rime's flank?

"Sir Gavarnie!" Henri's frantic cry jolted him.

His heart began to pound with a vengeance. He jerked his gaze heavenward.

Stars. Glittering jewels in the sky.

By the Blessed Virgin. He could see.

He could see!

He adjusted his grip on the sword. Let the attackers come. Let them come in droves. By all that was holy, none would take his life this night.

He could see!

✿✿✿

"SIR GAVARNIE!" Henri bellowed again, and fair threw Golde from his horse. 'Twas a miracle she landed on her feet.

"Henri!" a man shouted to Golde's left. "The baron—"

"My liege!" Henri shouted a third time.

An ache welled in Golde's chest that had naught to do with her injuries. She'd seen the two arrows protruding from the groomsman's back; had seen the baron go down. Then the lights had been extinguished.

Sir Gavarnie was dead, else he would have answered. The empty ache swelled and she choked for breath. To never see his dark face again, to never hear his rumbling voice, to never feel his touch. Though he'd admitted to killing his wife, Golde knew better. She could feel it in her bones. He had not done it, and—

"Form up."

Her heart paused, then hammered at Gavarnie's sharp-honed command in the darkness. Her knees near buckled, so great was her relief.

She gulped air, then bent double, clutching her ribs. Why had he not answered sooner? The great oaf. She should have known no arrow would be sharp enough to pierce his thick hide.

The ground vibrated and she smelled horse, heard the sound of mud sucking at hooves, the blowing breath of the animal. If she did not move quickly, she would be trampled. She staggered forward, widening her eyes in a effort to see.

"Call off," Sir Gavarnie ordered, and she followed the sound of his voice.

"Lund," a man reported. "Henri," the liegeman who'd been charged with her care snapped. "Bogo."

When no other names were offered, Henri urged, "Mount up behind me, mi'lord. Let us begone."

"Silence," Sir Gavarnie hissed.

His voice sounded near, and Golde made straight for it. The thought of an arrow sinking between her shoulder blades lent her impetus. Abruptly she bounced off a horse's rump and her feet slipped. Gasping, she stumbled sideways and crumpled to her knees. She'd scarce hit the ground before a hand bumped her forehead, then slipped to grasp the neckline of her tunic. Cold steel pressed against her throat.

"Nay," she pleaded, trying to shield her neck with her hands.

The grip on her tunic loosened and the sword was withdrawn. "Quiet," the liegeman Lund whispered.

Praise God it was one of the baron's men. She started to stand, but Lund's hand stayed her. Wet, grainy mud had already seeped through her tunic and chainse to her knees. Now it began leaking into her boots.

She clamped her teeth together as a shiver produced tearing pain in her ribs. Yet the wretched ache was preferable to being skewered by an arrow.

Unable to see, she strained to hear any sound that might indicate their attackers yet lurked about. Crickets whirred, but other than that, all was still. No brush rustled, no twigs snapped. The air did not stir.

She felt like a blind insect wrapped in a giant co-

coon. No wonder the baron was so often dark of spirit. 'Twas maddening to have no sight.

"'Twould appear we are safe for the moment," Sir Gavarnie said at last. "What became of Nigel and Stephan?"

When Lund made no attempt to help her up, Golde clutched his forearm and pulled herself to her feet.

"Stephan went down at the same time as Trelle," Bogo intoned.

"Nigel was a good space ahead of us," Henri offered.

Lund moved away from her as he spoke. "I saw Nigel look back and extinguish his lamp."

"Bogo, a light," Sir Gavarnie ordered.

"Are you certain, my liege?"

"I'll not leave our dead lying about. Dismount and hold the lamp low, that none can draw a bead on you."

Sparks flew as a flint was struck and a small pool of yellow light flickered to life. Golde's gaze immediately latched onto the baron where he stood encircled by horses and the remaining liegemen.

Her heart leapt upward to clog her throat. Sword drawn and legs braced, it appeared he looked directly at her. A lusty, pagan barbarian. A savage who would enjoy a contest between himself and the devil. A powerful chieftan of yore who would embrace her unholy eyes as a sign of good fortune, not evil.

His gaze shifted away . . .

She sighed, ignoring her discomfort at the slight exhale. Would that the baron could see, and that his fearless heated look was meant for her.

THIRTEEN

GAVARNIE LEANED over the small bed, holding a rushlight nearer Ronces' and Alory's sleeping forms. What changes three months had wrought. Ronces had thinned considerably. Gone was the child he remembered, replaced by a boy on his way to manhood.

Alory, on the other hand, appeared to have gained every bit of weight that Ronces had lost. And he was sucking his thumb, a habit Gavarnie had thought long dead. With his chubby body and his thumb in his mouth, Alory appeared to have regressed from boy to babe.

Gavarnie smiled wistfully. Would that his sons were yet infants and he could hold them, to once again see their innocent toothless grins while he played with them. To blow on their soft, rounded bellies 'til they squealed with laughter.

He fought a sudden urge to reach out and touch

them, if only to smooth the hair from their brows. But he dared not. Were the boys to wake, they might guess he could see, a secret they would be hard-pressed to keep.

And he wanted none to know he'd regained his sight. Better to let his enemies think him incapacitated. Mayhap they would grow careless and, perchance, reveal themselves.

His thoughts ran to Golde as he straightened. *Look to your own house for betrayal.*

He'd been right yestereve. Golde was the betrayer in his house. After tempting him beyond endurance with her body, she had known he would follow her to the village. 'Twas she who'd lured him from Skyenvic's protection, that he could be killed.

Turning, he crept to the boys' chamber door, which he'd left ajar. Though he'd devised orders that would carry everyone away from the upstairs corridor, he made certain it was empty before stepping into the hallway. Then he hurried toward Nicolette's chamber at the opposite end of the hall. Once inside, he tiptoed to the girl's bed, where he studied her features.

Light brown hair, curly where it wasn't matted, a square little jaw beneath a stubby nose; though her coloring was yet shaded by her recent illness, 'twas more pink than pale.

He frowned. Whatever had made him think Nicolette looked like Isabelle? In no way did the child resemble his wife's sleek, Nordic appearance.

The girl coughed, startling Gavarnie. He'd best return the rushlight to its sconce before he was discovered. 'Twould be difficult to explain why a blind man had need of a light.

No sooner had he closed Nicolette's door behind him and replaced the light in its holder than his bedchamber door swung inward. Hesper appeared, a troubled crease in her brow. She glanced in his direction.

"Mi'lord, ye are alone?"

"Eustace is making his rounds," he grumbled, masking his features with blankness. "I would see to mistress's comfort before I retire. What is the delay?"

Hesper winced and kneaded her back. "Yer forgiveness, sir. The poor dearling cannot get herself from the tub, and I am not much help. I'll fetch Eustace and have her a'bed a'fore ye can blink."

The woman shuffled toward the stairs, and Gavarnie scowled. Despite the fact that Golde should be put to the whip for her treachery, he could think of naught but the sights Eustace would see.

Her breasts, her thighs—

"A moment," he called after Hesper. "I would not have you disturb Eustace."

The servant turned back toward him and he looked at a rushlight behind her, careful to keep his gaze unfocused. "I will help with the maid."

From the corner of his eye, he could see Hesper's features cloud. "Mi'lord! 'Tis not yer place to be fishin' women from yer tub."

Again he thought of Eustace viewing Golde. She of the night-and-day eyes, of raven-black hair, of smooth virgin flesh. Sperville's description of her "striking" looks was an understatement of immense proportion. 'Twas like calling a diamond a clear piece of stone. Never had he beheld such beauty as that he'd witnessed in the lane when Bogo had lit the lamp.

Gavarnie beckoned to Hesper, who was eyeing him with no little puzzlement. "I'll not have my liegeman disturbed in his duties. I am to blame for mistress's condition. 'Tis my obligation to see to the matter."

Hesper frowned. "If ye insists, sir."

She hustled back to him. Touching her fingertips to his elbow, she led him toward the bedchamber.

'Twas not just his lust that prompted his actions, he assured himself. Had he not planned this show of concern by insisting Golde recover in his comfortable chamber? Was it not his intent to pretend affection for Golde that she would relax and grow careless? Then he would learn who had masterminded the ambush.

Upon crossing the threshold, Hesper paused to close the door.

Gavarnie's gaze flew to the tub, where the curtains were drawn away. Candlelight haloed the area. It reflected off Golde's wet, black hair where she sat with her back to him. He inhaled deeply. The room was fragrant as the forest after a summer rain.

All his fine reasoning deserted him as excitement curled through his loins. Did the wench look as good as she'd felt last eve? He strode forward.

"Mi'lord?" Hesper questioned, a note of curiosity in her tone.

At her query, Golde's head swiveled in his direction, a grimace contorting her features. He halted and fixed his gaze on one of the candles at the foot of the tub.

Lackwit, he chided himself. Doubtless, Hesper was wondering at his abilities, as was Golde. "'Tis all right. I am quite familiar with my chamber. The tub is there." He pointed in the general direction.

"More this way," Hesper directed, again taking his elbow.

"Nay," Golde rasped.

Hesper faltered, but Gavarnie continued on, unassisted. He let his knees bump the bath before he stopped. "How do you fare, mistress?"

"Take yourself off," she hissed.

He allowed his gaze to drift toward her voice. Bold lips pouted at him, full of challenge. 'Twas amazing that such pink sweetmeats could spew such venom. His gaze slid lower, following the trail of thick, wet tresses. Inviting swaths of moist skin peeped from beneath the black mass.

He eyed the exposed flesh. 'Twas shimmery, like the glowing pink color found in oyster shells. Soft and smooth, yet durable enough to withstand all but the most insistent of predators.

It required no effort to produce a warm tone. "'Tis my understanding you are unable to get yourself from the tub."

Her lip curled, and he just managed to prevent himself from remarking on the dirt she'd missed on her chin. In fact, it appeared the green eye was ringed with it.

"I would sooner drown than be assisted by you."

The little witch. She could not be unaware of her appealing appearance. Had doubtless practiced the sultry look until her lips held just the right fullness, her eyes the perfect come-hither sparkle.

He cleared his throat. "I have apologized for the distress I have brought upon you. I will be sleeping on the floor while you repair in my bed. Despite my exhaustion, I have waited up half the night to be certain of your comfort."

He crossed his arms over his chest. "'Twas my thinking you would prefer the service of a blind man to help you from your bath. Since you obviously have no objections to presenting your unclothed body to anyone, I shall summon Eustace forthwith. You have my wishes for a speedy recovery."

Pretending to grope for balance, he turned. Hesper

was eyeing the proceedings with a good deal of interest from where she stood near the bed. He took slow, deliberate steps toward the door.

Insolent daughter of a hellhound. How had he managed to find appeal in her tart tongue, to enjoy her stinging humor?

What lowly Saxon wench would dare instruct a lord's son on the proper manner of gutting a person? Who would dare chastise a lord of the realm for bellowing like a bull? What brazen miscreant would dare demean a baron's chamberlain with a name like Spindleshanks?

That Sperville remained fond of the wench gave him pause. Strange. The chamberlain was not given to lightly regarding such insults.

Unwelcome thoughts on her advice to Ronces claimed his head. *Never underestimate your opponent.* 'Twas a lesson Ronces would not soon forget. Indeed, it might someday save his life.

Very well, then. The wench had spirit. He would not begrudge her that. Still, 'twas a shame such a clever woman should be so corrupt. Though why he should feel disappointment over it was beyond him.

"A moment, mi'lord," Golde entreated just as he reached the door, her voice hardly more than a whisper.

He glanced over his shoulder in her direction, careful to keep his gaze above her head.

"Your forgiveness. If you would assist me?"

He turned back. Though he felt like crowing, he made sure no hint of triumph registered on his face. "As you wish."

He shuffled forward and again let his knees bump the bath, then ran a hand along the tub's rim. Upon reaching her upper arm, he felt his way to her shoulder. Her cold wet hair contrasted sharply with the soft warmth that radiated from her damp flesh. *Lean in the way of woodland creatures*, he recalled Spindleshanks' description.

Fit she was, he would concede. But more in the way of a sly, sylvan nymph, not some innocent woodland creature. Indeed, it felt as if her skin were growing hotter beneath his touch. She shivered when his fingertips touched her collarbone.

He placed his other hand on her. Leaning closer, he smoothed his palms over her shoulders. He even managed a part in the curtain of hair where it fell over her breasts.

"You need not grope my entire body," she groused.

He stilled, staring over her shoulder at her chest. Whore's gleet. Another moment, and he might have glimpsed something worthwhile about her person.

He blinked as another thought occurred. Mayhap she knew he was looking at her. That he could see.

"How am I to find purchase to lift you when I cannot see?" he snapped, intent on disguising his lecherous fondling. "All I can feel is hair. Mayhap you could assist by guiding my hands."

Her muscles tensed and she emitted a harsh little croak. Before she could say anything, Hesper appeared at his side.

"There, dearie." The old woman patted Golde's shoulder with nervous, birdlike movements. Then she gathered the hair at Golde's nape and pulled it back.

Gavarnie near strangled. He could see, all right. By the Blessed Virgin, he could see. Breasts. Round, water-slickened flesh. Ripe, berry-red nipples, stiffened by cold. Were they as succulent as they appeared?

"If ye bend a bit more, yer lordship," Hesper instructed, "and lean forward."

Faith, if he leaned any farther he'd fall face-first in the bath.

"That's it," Hesper encouraged. "Now, Mistress Golde, wrap yer arms 'bout his neck."

Golde's low groan registered in Gavarnie's head as she did Hesper's bidding. Pain? The sound was more guttural than the moans of pleasure he'd heard last night. Still, he dared not look to see her expression.

Cradling her neck with one arm, he dipped the other in the tepid water and slid his hand beneath her bottom to her knees. At her sharp intake of breath, he asked, "I have hurt you?"

She shook her head where it leaned against his chest. Faith, how could flesh be so soft, yet so firm? And the scent that surrounded her; morning flowers and dew. Where had she come by such a fragrance? He lifted her from the water, anxious to lay her on the bed, that he might inspect her more closely.

He scowled when he turned to find Hesper right in front of him, a drying linen in her hands. Whore's gleet. The old woman was too efficient by far. Marshaling his features, he strode forward as if he hadn't seen her.

"Hold, yer lordship," Hesper squawked, and began rubbing at Golde's body.

"Hesper," she gasped. "Have a care."

"I'm doin' me best, dearie. Wouldn't want you catchin' cold." Hesper patted the cloth around, then draped it over Golde. "There, mi'lord." She took his elbow and guided him to the bed. "Here we are."

Hesper threw the covers back and he squelched the urge to dismiss her. "Nice and gentle, now," she admonished. "There ar'nt a place on her poor body that ar'nt black and blue."

He lay Golde on the bed and forced himself to pull his hands from beneath her, though he did manage to drag the drying linen from atop her. Straightening, he glanced down. Her face was twisted in an agonized grimace, and he could not look away.

By the blood of Christ. Hesper's words were no idle claim. What he'd thought was dirt around her eye and chin was in fact bruised flesh. His gaze swept lower. Indeed, her ribs and legs sported dark purple lesions, one on her thigh the exact shape of a round shoe-toe.

He clenched his teeth to keep his temper from erupting. By all that was holy, the churlish villagers would pay for their cruelty. He would . . .

Hesper moved to apply the drying cloth, and he unfocused his gaze. He would what? Hang the entire village?

Golde was the enemy, he reminded himself sternly. She'd got no more than she deserved.

"If that is all, Hesper?" He forced a neutral tone.

"We're quite right now, yer lordship."

He turned and headed toward the door.

"Mi'lord," Golde rasped, halting him. "What became of Sir Nigel?"

Gavarnie didn't look back. That she dared to ask after the steward, as if she cared. 'Twas difficult to separate his jaws to speak, so great was his anger. "Sir Nigel is well. He returned to the castle to raise the hue and cry."

She mumbled something as he started forward again. He didn't ask her to repeat herself. If he did not remove himself from the room, he was like to kill her.

To think he'd felt guilt over his treatment of her at Sigi's; was ready to believe the tales she'd spun about his children.

And what of Trelle and Stephan? His words of comfort had done nothing to ease the grief their families felt.

Two good men who would be hard to replace. Two good men who'd given their last breath to protect him. Two good men, dead because of Golde's treachery.

FOURTEEN

"M E APOLOGIES for me tardiness, mistress."
Hesper bustled into the bedchamber carrying clean linen.
"Wot with preparin' for all them guests that'll soon be
arrivin', a body ar'nt got time to spit, much less care for
sick folk."

She kicked the door shut and moved to dump the
pile of laundry on the foot of the bed. "How are ye feelin'
this afternoon?"

Golde leaned forward where she sat propped against a
host of pillows. "Afternoon already?" she gritted, unable
to keep the drip of sarcasm from her tone. "I can scarce
believe time's fleetness."

She stilled while Hesper tied her hair back. Would
the pain in her ribs never cease? Though five days had
passed since the attack, she had yet to draw a breath that
did not hurt.

Hesper patted her hair. "There ye be, mistress." The serving woman drew the covers away and shook her head as her gaze scanned Golde's nude body. "I can't sees how these hot soaks is doin' ye any good. All this gettin' up and down when ye can scarce sit. And yer still black and blue. Ye ought to be restin'. Won't hurt none for ye to miss one day's bath."

Golde gingerly slid her legs over the edge of the bed. "Nonsense." She dug her nails into the sheets and waited for the pain to relent. "Look how improved I am. Lord Gavarnie will be pleased that I can reach the tub without his assistance."

Hesper rolled her eyes. "There's some folks wot's too stubborn for their own good."

Golde cast her a vicious look, but apparently the woman had become immune to such after five days in her company. All she did was cluck her tongue.

Curling her lip, Golde peered down at the floor. It seemed a furlong distant, so high was the bed. Praise the saints she was tall. She grimaced. It was now or never. The pain had eased as much as it would. She let herself slip down the bedside, and her breath caught when her feet reached the floor. Iron tongs of pain, white-hot, clamped about her ribs.

She clutched Hesper's hand and waited for the tongs' pressure to fade.

"Please, mistress. Let me fetch his lordship."

Golde shook her head, then shuffled forward, bent at the waist like an old crone. Steam rose from the bath, and she used Hesper's arm for leverage once she reached the tub. Heat stung her flesh and she panted while lowering herself into the bath. Then she sighed as the water began working its magic.

She soaked for the better part of half an hour while

Hesper busied herself folding laundry and tidying the room. When she rose at last, she truly felt some relief. The pain in her ribs had subsided to a dull ache, and she waved Hesper's hand away when she stepped from the tub. For the first time in days, she stood fully erect. Still, she allowed Hesper to dry her, anxious to do nothing that might aggravate her condition.

Clothing required more effort than it was worth, and she climbed back into bed wearing naught. Settling herself against the pillows, she posed the question that had plagued her for several days. "Who has been caring for the children?"

Hesper drew a bedsheet over her. "Sir Sperville, Roland, and me been sharing turns, but his lordship keeps them with him most of the day. 'Tis such a pleasure ta' see the four of them together."

"The four of them?"

"Aye. Nicolette goes right along with the boys."

Golde frowned. "But I thought Gav—er—the baron spent most of the day practicing with his sword and bow."

"Well, whose eyes do ye s'pose he uses?" Hesper beamed. "His lordship is a clever man. He lets the children tell him where to strike and makes a merry game of it all. 'Tis amazin' to see how he hits the target when he takes to his bow and arrows. Dead center ever' time. And with only the children tellin' him where to aim."

A knock sounded at the door and Hesper hurried to answer it.

Golde pursed her lips. Gavarnie and the children? Each day, after the noon meal, he came to carry her to and from the tub. Each eve he came to bathe the sweat from his body after working his muscles all day.

He e're took gentle care with her person and entertained her with tales of this lord, or that lady. But not once had he mentioned the children.

She was distracted from her thoughts when Hesper swung the door wide and two shaggy serving boys—Dirt and Grime, as she'd come to think of them—entered the room.

Whispering between themselves, their eyes darting in all directions, they scrambled to the bath. Dirt unstoppered the tub, which would drain through pipes into the Solent. Grime tugged on the rope at the drawing point where water buckets were passed from floor to floor.

"I'm off to the kitchens," Hesper called from the door. "His lordship will be up forthwith to bathe."

Golde glanced at the window. Judging from the sun's light, there were yet a good four hours left to the day. "Why does he come so early?" she queried, turning back to Hesper. But the woman was already gone.

A lever squeaked over the drawing point and Grime grabbed a bucket as it came through the hole in the floor. "'urry up, pea-pate," he snapped at Dirt while holding the pail.

"Can't make it go no faster, dunghead," Dirt replied, waiting for the water to drain.

Golde snatched at the tie that held her hair and dragged her fingers through the tangled mess. A pox on Hesper for leaving before seeing to her appearance. She must look . . .

Witless girl. What difference whether she glowed with beauty or oozed pus? She dropped her hands to her lap. Gavarnie could not see.

Water splashed as Grime emptied a pail in the bath, and she glared at the huge posts at the foot of the mattress. Faith, she was sick unto death of lying abed. She plucked at the bed linen and wiggled her toes. The easing of pain had done naught to improve her spirits. Rather, she was anxious to be up and about.

The sound of boots thumping in the corridor drew her attention and she stilled, eyeing the open door. A moment later, Gavarnie gusted into the room, half dragging Roland, who clung to his elbow in an attempt to guide him.

"My gray tunic, boy, and be quick."

The squire hurried to the wardrobe while Gavarnie strode toward the tub, stripping a sweat-ringed, brown short-shirt over his head.

His shoulder muscles bunched as he tossed the shirt to the floor, and Golde stared at his back. 'Twas strong and weathered—thick—pebbled with holes as if it had been struck by hail. A back that would never break, no matter the load it carried.

Abruptly Gavarnie's gaze swept in her direction and she lowered her head as heat stung her cheeks. By the raven! He was appealing, with his dark looks and hard features. A swarthy demon come to steal her soul.

Memories of his touch when he'd carried her to and from the bath each day caressed her flesh. His hands e're seemed to linger on the twitchiest of places.

"Mistress." His voice was like a burr rubbed against sensitive skin.

She raised her head enough to see him bow.

"My, uh . . . my apologies for my haste." He felt for the tub's edge without taking his gaze from her direction. "I . . ." He cleared his throat. "I have ordered a feast prepared for this eve, as more of my guests have arrived."

What was he dithering over? She frowned and looked him full in the face. Since the attack, his eyes always appeared unfocused, not sharp like they had before.

Mayhap the fall from his horse had injured him more than he let on.

She licked her lips as worry nettled about in her head. "Mi'lord, are you—"

"How goes it?" he asked before she could finish.

"I am truly improved. Indeed, you will be pleased to know I have already bathed."

"So I se—er—smell," he stammered, then added quickly, "Those fragrances you add to the water are most pleasing."

"Yer tub is ready, yer lordship," Grime announced.

Gavarnie tugged at a boot. "'Tis a shame you cannot attend the festivities this eve."

Golde pushed herself to sit up straighter. "Oh, but I could. I would need some assistance up and down the—"

Abruptly Gavarnie's eyes crossed and a deep-chested coughing fit seized him. Before Golde could rise to give aid, Roland hurried from the wardrobe.

The squire threw Gavarnie's clothing on the bed. "Mi'lord, you are ill?"

Gavarnie gasped, his eyes watering. "Something," he pointed at his throat, "in the air." Patting his chest, he straightened. "Fetch me something to drink."

His eyes shifted toward Dirt and Grime, and his tone grew agitated. "You two, hie yourselves to the kitchens."

Both boys made a clattering dash for the door while Roland darted to the water stand, upon which sat a pitcher.

Golde studied Gavarnie. His behavior was most strange. Did she not know better, she would think him about to have a fit of vapors. Perplexed, she crossed her arms over her chest.

Christ's blood!

She looked down and her jaw dropped. At some

point the bed linen had slipped, baring her breasts for all
to see. Snatching the sheet to her neck, she slouched
back against the pillows as heat spread from her chest, up
her neck, and across her face.

An insidious thought snaked through her head. Her
gaze whipped to Gavarnie, who stood rubbing his eyes
with a thumb and forefinger. The cunning bastard. Was it
possible he could see?

"Mi'lord." Roland thrust a cup of water in his hand.

He drained it, then groused, "At your leisure, Roland. I could have strangled ere now, and I have but a
half-legion of lords and ladies awaiting my presence."

Roland bent to remove his remaining boot, and
Gavarnie grasped the youth's head for balance. Abruptly
his brows swooped down, while his nose drew up in a
pucker. "You are putting fat in your hair again?"

"It's too curly," Roland mumbled, his face reddening
as he rose to unlace Gavarnie's braies.

"I look like a girl," Gavarnie whined, then his tone
became exasperated. "I tell you, boy, the ladies are most
fond of curly locks. You do yourself a disservice by slick-
ing them thus. Ask yon maid." He gestured in Golde's
direction.

She relaxed. Gavarnie would hardly be discussing
Roland's hair if he'd caught her in such a compromising
position. He'd yet be ogling her charms.

That he was not was unaccountably disappointing.

Without warning, Roland pushed his master's braies
downward, and Golde found a sudden interest in the
rough, wood-beamed ceiling. Faith, the squire was so rattled, he'd forgot to draw the tub curtains.

Before she could say aught, Gavarnie prodded,
"What say you, mistress? Do you not find curly-haired
men pleasing to the eye?"

Was it her imagination, or was the last question spoken with a hint of . . . what? Challenge? Nay. 'Twas more like trickery. She glanced at him, hoping to determine his intent by his countenance.

Her eyes rounded and she jerked her gaze back to the ceiling. He was facing her direction with his hands on his hips. Had anyone asked what his chest or legs looked like, she could not have said. Her gaze had been drawn squarely to his—

'Od rot! She could no longer even think straight. Had she not seen men a'plenty with nothing on? In fact, she had seen Gavarnie nude her first night at Skyenvic.

Golde opened her mouth, prepared to inform Gavarnie that the curtains hadn't been drawn. Just as quickly, she clamped her jaws shut. The dunderwit would likely tease her for noticing.

"Well," he persisted with the curly-hair issue. "Have you suddenly been rendered speechless?"

She would not look upon his unclothed form again, despite the devilish little voice that urged her to do so. "'Tis well known amongst females that curly-haired men make the best lovers." *Take that, mi'lord straight-hair.* "They are more considerate than other men and make the best husbands."

"Truth tell?" Roland asked.

She covered her heart with her hand. "On my honor."

"There, you see?" Gavarnie demanded, his voice suddenly churlish. "Just have a care that all these females do not coax you to the altar with sweet words of praise. Now, are my clothes laid out?"

"They are on the bed," Roland answered cheerfully. "Then fetch the children from Spin—uh, Sir

Sperville, and care for them that he may attend my guests until I arrive."

"Who will attend you?" Roland asked.

"I can tend to myself."

"But who will—"

"Begone, boy. Mistress can assist me if need be."

A plopping sound in the water told Golde that Gavarnie had stepped into the tub. Then water swished, and she knew he'd immersed himself.

Her gaze wavered from the ceiling, then trailed to where he'd settled with his back to her. Had he truly wished Roland to fetch the children? Or did he wish to be alone with her? The thought warmed her with happiness.

'Twas a moment before she noticed Roland's beseeching look. He gestured at her with upturned hands, silently asking if she would care for Gavarnie's needs. Immediately, doubt replaced the flush of joy that had settled over her.

Gavarnie had spent much time with her these five days past. Far from being a woman-hater, as her disturbed imaginings had portrayed him that evening at Sigi's, he was most courteous and respectful. Indeed, he was charming. And therein lay the problem. She was fast coming to find him irresistible.

Roland repeated his hand gesture, only, now a frown puckered his forehead. If she shook her head, would he stay?

Nay, she was being foolish. She nodded emphatically and made a shooing motion with one hand while maintaining a solid grip on the sheet with the other. The squire's countenance cleared and, bowing, he took his leave.

"'Twas kind of you to reassure the boy," Gavarnie

remarked the moment the door closed behind Roland. "He e're worries over his hair."

His thoughtful tone pricked Golde's inwit. That he would compliment her when her intent had been to put a tuck in his tail. "Youth is an awkward time," she commented, low-voiced. "Roland is fortunate to have an understanding lord."

Her gaze followed his hand as he slowly dragged a lump of soap over his shoulder. "If I am understanding, 'tis because I am familiar with Roland's plight."

"How is that?"

He shrugged. "I was oft concerned with my blemished appearance as a youth."

"But look how handsomely you have matured."

The muscles in his shoulders grew rigid. "Handsomely?"

She winced. The statement had leapt from her lips before she'd thought.

"Pockmarks suit you."

He shot an angry glance over his shoulder. "Do you imply I am flawed inside as well as out?"

"Nay!" God, she was fuddling the matter. "I mean that you are the type of man who . . . is more attractive . . . that is, the scars lend a sense of . . . strength to your countenance."

Scowling, he turned away, and several moments passed before he spoke again. "I was unaware women preferred curly-haired men."

At any other time, his disgruntled tone would have been laughable. But she sensed a rawness in his feelings that near wrung her heart. "I lied."

His head swiveled in her direction. "You gave your word of honor," he accused childishly.

For the first time since the attack, it appeared he was

looking directly at her. "Have you not heard," she queried, staring into his black eyes. "Women have no
honor."

A look of concentration settled over his features.
"That is so. Yet your words eased Roland's discomfort,
thus your intent was honorable."

As he spoke, her gaze slid to his lips. She recalled
vividly the crippling pleasure they had wrought the night
she'd taunted him with his children's thick-comings.
How she longed to feel them trail fire down her neck
again, to feel them pressed against other secret places.

"There was nothing honorable in my intent." She
looked away. "I sought only to hurt you."

Silence followed her words, and she kept her gaze
latched on the bedposts. Though her admission left her
feeling like the lowest of worms, it had the effect she'd
hoped for. No longer did her body rage with desire.

"Your reasoning eludes me," he said at last, his tone
patient. "I cannot see how you thought to distress me
with what you said."

Was the man serious? She glanced over to find him
yet peering at her.

"Your hair is straight, is it not?" she asked.

For a moment he appeared puzzled. Then one black
brow soared heavenward. "You will have to do better
than that, mistress, to pierce my thick hide. Mayhap you
should tell me why you wished to hurt me. Surely it is due
to some terrible deformity in my nature."

Golde grinned, relieved he had not taken offense.
"Truth tell, the more I am in your company, the less fault
I can find." She sat up straighter, dragging the sheet with
her. "'Tis most annoying to discover a person whose
perfection so nearly matches my own."

"Such modesty." Chuckling, he turned away to soap himself vigorously.

Golde sobered, anxious to settle matters while he was in good spirits. "Mi'lord, now that I am on the mend, I would discuss arrangements for my return home."

He stilled for a moment, then felt for a pitcher that sat on the rim of the tub. Dousing his hair, he scrubbed and rinsed it, making her wait for his reply. Finally he groped for the drying cloth Roland had left on a stool beside the bath. "Hesper says you are yet badly bruised and can scarce walk."

"I thought . . ." She hesitated, then cleared her throat. "I thought you might be glad to rid yourself of me."

Slowly he rose from the tub, presenting her with his buttocks. The thickwitted oaf. He had not asked her to stay, as she'd hoped. Indeed, as she'd prayed. Her throat convulsed and she swallowed hard. She would miss the miserable cur.

He dragged the drying cloth over his shoulders and back, then turned to face her, running it over his chest.

"I am in no hurry to be rid of you."

His voice sounded lazy and her eyes followed the towel as he rubbed lower. She winced. It had been foolish to imagine he might want her to remain at—

Her gaze flew to his face. "What?"

"I find I have grown most fond of your presence, mistress. I am in no hurry to see you gone. As well, there has been a great dearth of nursemaids knocking at my door, anxious to care for my sweet children. 'Twould be comforting to know you might be interested in caring for them on a more permanent basis. Once you are healed, of course."

He wrapped the cloth about his waist and stepped

from the tub, but not before her lecherous eyes had glimpsed his engorged shaft. Even now, its tip was clearly defined beneath the white linen.

He wanted her. The knowledge made her long to hug her knees to her chest, but she didn't dare. Instead, she crossed her legs beneath the sheets, squeezing her thighs together.

"I do not believe your sweet children would be thrilled to think of me as their nursemaid on a permanent basis."

"It matters not what they think. I am their father and know what is best for them. And that is you, mistress."

Golde felt that her heart might float from her chest. That he would pay her such a compliment.

He approached the bed with cautious deliberation. "Where has Roland laid my clothes?"

"At the foot of the mattress," she directed, eyeing his progress with no little interest. Each step he took parted the drying cloth to expose a goodly portion of his right thigh. Faith! but it appeared rock-hewn, just like his buttocks.

He ran a hand along the sheets until he located his apparel, then looked in her direction. "I trust you will tell me if I am not properly dressed."

His eyes held the black magic of a glomung sun and his hair glistened like star-studded jet. He dropped the drying linen.

By the Blessed Virgin! The man could not be unaware of his arousal. It rose thickly from a dark matting of hair, as if in challenge.

She licked her lips. Was that his intent? To challenge her? 'Twas a battle she would lose, she thought. His lips had sucked every bit of denial from her during those few moments of passion that one night.

He bent to feel about for his clothing, and she summoned a cool tone. "Have a care, mi'lord."

He stilled, and his gaze seemed to bore into her. "Have a care?"

"That you do not poke yourself in the eye."

His features hardened. "Poke myself in the eye?"

Inexplicably, she felt uncomfortable. His tone was almost accusing. Clearly, he had no idea to what she referred.

"Your shaft is so stiff, I fear you may do yourself injury."

'Twas a moment before a smile overtook his lips. "Never have I been laid so low."

He affected an effeminate voice and tossed his head, running his fingers through his hair. "Here I have given you full leisure to view my charms and you do naught but make jests."

Golde giggled, clutching her ribs. "I beg you, do not make me laugh."

He finally located his braies. "'Tis the least you deserve. I can only assume much has changed since I lost my sight. In times past, women could not keep their hands from me. They used to fight one another to sit at my feet, so great was their adoration."

His braies secured, he wrapped a silver belt about his waist. A good hand's span in width, the belt was studded with huge rubies. "Indeed, 'tis a miracle I am yet in one piece."

Grabbing a pair of silver-buckled boots, he sat on the bed. "Poke myself in the eye," he muttered as he yanked the boots over his feet.

He rose and swept a robe over one shoulder, then turned to pose for her. Licking the tip of one pinky finger, he ran it over his brows. "Hmph!" He planted a hand on one hip and headed for the door, hips rolling.

"To think I considered submitting myself to the curling tongs, knowing your fondness for curly-haired men. 'Twill not happen now, ungrateful wench."

He yanked the door open and sallied forth, slamming it behind him.

Golde stared after him. She would never have believed he could be so handsome. Dressed in silver-shot, gray finery, he approached the blinding beauty of a god.

'Twas some time before his absurd imitation of femininity struck her. Grabbing her ribs, she gasped between bursts of merriment. A pox on the odious fool.

FIFTEEN

THE SWEET SCENT of honey roused Golde from sleep to consciousness. It smelled delicious. Doubtless, Hesper had delivered warm bread to go with it. 'Twas a morning routine that had evolved during her recovery these two weeks past.

Rolling to her side, Golde tried to open her eyes, expecting to find a tray of food at the bedside. Instead, her eyelashes felt glued together.

She frowned and ran her fingertips over her lashes. Her fingers came away gooey.

Had she caught some dread disease? Her heart flopped sickly in her chest. Prying at her lids, she rose to sit.

Hair clung to her arms and breasts in clumps. She swiped at it, only to have it stick to her hands. What the devil?

Abruptly she stilled.

'Twas no devil, but three evil sprites. They'd poured honey over her head!

Plague take the brats! Her vision blurry, she scrambled from the bed to light a candle against the early morning shadows. Then she marched to locate her clothing in the wardrobe. It, too, was drenched with honey. Her hands shook with rage as she struggled to don the sticky apparel.

Yestermorn she'd awakened to hopping toads beneath the sheets. At the time, she'd thought it best to ignore the childish prank. Her anger might only encourage the little beasts. But this—she yanked at the tunic where it was stuck to her chainse—this was more than she would tolerate.

Just wait until Gavarnie returned from the king's reception. She'd roast his ears with the foul deeds his children had committed during his absence.

The hems of her chainse and tunic wrapped about her calves, she spied her boots to one side of the wardrobe. Were they full of honey as well?

She dropped them a scant moment after picking them up. 'Twas not honey they held, but worse; cow dung, judging from the odor.

The little monsters had breathed their last, she swore. She would not await Gavarnie's return on the morrow. Nay, she would kill his children today.

"Mistress Golde?" Hesper's call interrupted her thoughts.

Tromping from the wardrobe, she found the serving maid at the bedside, a breakfast tray in her hands.

"My, but ye are up and about . . ." Hesper's words trailed away and her brows rose.

"Where are they?" Golde demanded.

Hesper blinked. "Who?"

"The children!"

"Yer clothes . . . and yer hair," Hesper gasped.

"They poured honey on me while I slept, and my shoes are filled with dung."

Rather than frown with disgust, the older woman smiled benevolently. "Ah. The little dearlings."

Golde stared. "Little dearlings! You are more daft than their father. He will doubtless congratulate them for their ingenuity."

Hesper's features softened, as did her tone. "Can ye not see? The children are jealous of the attention his lordship pays ye."

"Jealous!" Golde crossed her arms over her chest and glared at the serving maid. Then she frowned. "Jealous?"

Truth tell, Gavarnie had made her feel like a Celtic princess with the attention he'd lavished on her these weeks past. Fashioning a sling-type chair, he'd placed it before the window, that she might enjoy the sunset. On eves when he could escape the lords and ladies who now camped about Skyenvic, he would join her there. The tales he'd spun of Hindward the Horrible, a knight who e're did everything backward, were worthy of any bard.

Later, once she'd healed enough to move about, he'd carried her downstairs, that she might enjoy the banqueting festivities. Despite the crush of important guests who dined at his table, he'd always made space for her, seating her directly on his right.

Indeed, his manner toward her was so courtly that Lady Gundrada had waspishly inquired if there were a match in the making. 'Twas then that Golde had felt an undercurrent pass between Gavarnie and the woman. Clearly the two shared some secret—likely an illicit liaison.

Golde swallowed the anger that rose like bile in her breast. She would think no more on Lady Gundrada. Instead, she concentrated on the matter of Gavarnie's children.

Gavarnie had forbidden them to come near her. "I will not have them disturbing you until you are well," he'd said.

Golde lowered her gaze to study the floor. Aye. The children were jealous, and who could blame them? 'Twas easy to imagine her disgust had her father entertained another woman during her youth. Indeed, she might not be overpleased were such to occur now.

She winced. How could she have been so dullwitted? Not once had she given Gavarnie's children a second thought. 'Twould now be doubly difficult to reestablish herself as their nursemaid. They probably hated her.

She clenched her teeth and raised her head. Dolt. What was she thinking? Since when had it mattered what others felt toward her, especially children? Selfish little miscreants. Did they think they owned their father?

The sound of pounding feet on the stairs suddenly invaded the room. What now?

The footsteps raced past the closed bedchamber door in the direction of the boys' room. Then a door slammed, and all grew silent.

Golde's lip curled. "I believe the little dearlings have returned to roost. If you would, Hesper, have a bath prepared for me, and remove this bed linen. I shall return shortly."

An anxious look settled over the woman's features. "Why not let Sir Nigel handle the matter? Give yer temper a spell to cool."

Golde pulled a sour face and made for the door. Give

her temper a spell to cool, indeed. She intended to blow fire at the little demons, and watch them cook.

Marching down the corridor, she threw open the boys' door. Three pairs of rounded eyes riveted on her where she halted.

She planted her hands on her hips. "Know you what evil befalls children who dare to test my temper? I skin them alive and boil their bones for pottage."

Alory shrieked and dove for the opposite side of the bed, Nicolette fast on his heels. Only Ronces remained where he stood, the stubborn little mule.

Golde raised her hands and crooked her fingers into talons, determined to frighten him. "You will be first, boy," she crowed.

Ronces started, as if he might flee, but he checked himself. Then his jaws worked.

Without warning, he launched himself at her. "Go ahead, crone. Kill me!"

"Nay!" Alory and Nicolette screamed in unison.

Golde fought to contain the boy's thrashing fists. That he would dare to attack her. Grabbing his wrists, she wrestled him to the floor. He would learn here and now . . .

The children are jealous of the attention his lordship pays ye. Hesper's words whispered in her head, giving her pause.

Nay. It should not matter what the children felt toward her. But it did. Just like it had mattered, more than anyone could imagine, when she'd been an ugly, lonely little girl.

"Cease, foolish child. I did but jest. Your father would have my hide if I did aught to harm you."

A tear slid down Ronces' temple where he lay on his

back beneath her. "Papa will thank you for killing me. I deserve to die."

His breath caught on a sob, and Golde winced. *Please, God, not another crying spell.* "Silly boy. Of what do you speak? Your father loves you."

Ronces closed his eyes. "Papa will hate me when he returns."

"He shot one of the swineherd's pwize pigs," Nicolette intoned, peeping over the edge of the mattress.

"He didn't mean to," Alory added, his head popping up beside Nicolette's.

Golde returned her attention to Ronces, whose eyes were squeezed shut. Releasing his wrists, she smoothed a tear from his temple. "Accidents cannot be helped. You are yet young and cannot expect your aim to be accurate at all times."

His dark eyes, so like Gavarnie's, opened to focus on her. They reflected no hatred or anger, only misery. "I am forbidden to use a bow unless Papa is with me."

"Wonces is not all to blame. Me and Alowy dared him to shoot—the awwow, not the pig."

Golde drew a deep breath. Realizing she yet pinned Ronces, she quickly moved to sit beside him. Though the boy should be taken to task for disobeying his father—indeed, she should be punishing Ronces for the tricks he'd played on her—she could not do it.

"I once stole a spell from my great-grandmother against her wishes," she said instead. "Well do I know how you feel."

Ronces rose to sit, hugging his knees. "Did you shoot a prize pig, too?"

Golde sighed bitterly. "Nay. I only killed an innocent toad, but it haunts me to this day."

Tears again pooled in Ronces eyes. "Did the toad die quickly?"

Golde nodded, unable to speak.

"Would that the pig were dead," he mumbled, resting his forehead on his knees. "It yet squeals."

"Could you make it bettew?" Nicolette pleaded from where she'd crawled atop the bed. "You awe a witch, aftew all."

"The pig still lives?"

Ronces swiped at his eyes and gave her a hopeful look. "'Tis a sow."

"Where is it shot?"

"In its hindquarter."

Golde shook her head. "I don't know. Sows are foul-tempered at best. An arrow in their hind will make them no sweeter."

"Oh, pwease, mistwess," Nicolette begged.

"Couldn't you just try?" Alory asked.

Golde eyed the three expectant faces. Only a fool would tend a wounded sow. Yet . . .

"Faith," she grumbled as she rose. "Never have I met children whom trouble seems to stalk with such tenacity. If I am gored by tusks, I will make the three of you wait on me hand and foot."

Ronces scrambled to his feet and hugged her waist, only to pull back. Wiping his hands on the front of his tunic, he gave her a sheepish look. "I am sorry for the honey."

"We all awe sowwy." Nicolette grabbed Golde's hand and pulled her into the corridor.

"I cannot go like this." Golde halted. "I don't even have on shoes."

Alory studied the floor and shuffled his feet, while Nicolette fair glowed with innocence. "You look vewy pwetty for a witch. And you do not need shoes. They will only get diwty in the stye."

Golde raised a brow. "I cannot imagine how much filthier they could get, considering they are filled with dung."

The girl winced, then glared at the boys. "I tole you we shouldn't do that."

"We will clean them for you," Alory offered.

"But we must huwwy now." Nicolette fair danced with urgency. "The pig is huwting. She might awweady be dead."

Golde glanced heavenward and sighed. "Very well. First we must collect my salves from my chest."

After rooting through her stores and gathering what she needed, Golde followed the children through the empty great hall and into the bailey. Sir Nigel was nowhere in evidence, praise the saints.

As they approached the pig stye, a rotund man stomped from around the back of a pen, shooing at several servants who idled at the railing.

Upon spying the children, he shook a fist at them. "Take yerselves off, lest I give ye the beatin' ye deserves."

Golde strode forward, the children close behind her, carrying her jars and flagons. "I have come to see if I can be of help."

"Wot!" The man backed away at her approach, his face red. "Can't let no witch-woman in me pens. Look at ye, drippin' all manner of goo. Yer person might poison the whole stye."

"Foowish man," Nicolette chided, coming to stand beside Golde. "Witches awe not . . ." She paused, her small brow furrowed with concentration.

Abruptly her features cleared. "Witches awe naught but the 'maginings of simpletons."

Golde pursed her lips. Clearly, the child was reciting something she'd heard.

The man crossed himself, and spit in his palm. "Arn't nothin' to be done fer the sow."

Golde crossed her arms over her chest. "Why do you not slaughter her now so she won't suffer?"

The man snarled. "If she weren't about to litter, I would. As 'tis, I'll be waitin' 'til she dies to slit her belly. Mayhap I can save some of the piglets. His lordship will charge me, ye knows. Not only for the sow, but fer what dies of the litter."

"Then step aside," she affected a sweet tone, "and let me see what can be done."

Ronces strode forward and cleared his throat. "I will take responsibility for my actions, as well as Mistress Golde's."

"Me, too." Alory moved to stand beside his brother.

Warmth curled around Golde's heart like a furry kitten's tail. That Ronces and Alory would pledge themselves on her behalf. And Nicolette. From whom had she heard the saying about witches?

The swineherd trundled forward. "We shall see what Sir Nigel has to say about this."

"A moment," Golde commanded, separating herself from the children.

"You will say nothing, lest I place a curse on you," she hissed in his face. "Your seed will dry up, and your shaft will wither, until you have naught to piss with."

The swineherd backed away, jowels quivering. "Do wot ye will."

Spitting in his palm again, the swineherd took himself off, and Golde followed the children to peer over a thick, slatted railing. The wounded sow lay opposite from the pen's gate, her small black eyes half-closed, Ronces' arrow yet embedded in her hind. Her sides heaved and she grunted with each breath she took.

Golde wrinkled her nose at the stench, and eyed the flies swarming above the filth-strewn ground.

"The three of you go 'round to the other side of the pen." She gestured at the children. "As I need things, you can hand them to me through the slats. Stay well back of the railing until I call for you, and under no circumstances are any of you to enter the pen. Understood?"

Three heads bobbed in unison, then the children moved off to do her bidding, as several people halted to watch the proceedings.

Grasping the latch, Golde opened the gate and stepped inside. Slime gushed between her toes, but she paid it no heed. The sow's eyes had snapped open, and never had Golde seen a more suspicious look.

"Easy, mi'lady," she soothed.

The sow snorted and Golde stilled. "'Tis quite a nasty wound you have there."

She eased to a squat and waddled forward, balancing on the balls of her feet. "How brave you must be, mi'lady. And very pretty, too. 'Twould be a shame for such a fine pig to die."

The sow wallowed to sit, her grunts more guttural and threatening. Again, Golde stilled until the pig's grunts subsided, then waddled closer. "I mean you no harm."

Abruptly the sow tried to rise. Gasps issued from the onlookers, and it took all of Golde's will not to jump up and run.

But the pig only squealed its misery, then collapsed on its side, its body trembling.

'Twas now or never. Golde quickly closed the gap

between herself and the pig before it could regain any strength.

Its eyes rolled in its great head and its tongue hung panting from its mouth. Short tusks peeked from its jaws.

"All is well." Golde babbled as she reached out to stroke the sow's ears. "All is well."

She glanced at the arrow. It appeared to have sunk the length of a man's hand. Golde pursed her lips. The animal would have to be rendered unconscious to remove the arrow. Which was a problem unto itself.

How much tonic would be necessary to make the pig sleep without disturbing the litter she carried?

"There, there," she crooned, and continued to pet the animal. "We'll soon have you back on your hooves."

As the sow's grunts eased, so did its flat, round nose begin to twitch. Before Golde realized what it was about, the pig's tongue had captured her sleeve.

The honey! It was after the honey that soaked her garments.

Golde worked quickly. Leaning her head to one side, she scraped her hair across her shoulder to obscure the pig's vision so it would be less frightened. "Ronces, I need the black flagon."

She reached through the slats with one hand while stroking the pig with the other. Uncorking the bottle with her teeth, she dribbled a small amount on her sleeve.

The pig suckled a bit more, then her tongue moved to lap at Golde's hair.

God's teeth, she thought. She felt like a contortionist. The muscles in her neck, arms, and legs were screaming for relief. Meanwhile, it felt as if her toes might cramp any moment from the way she was squatting on the balls of her feet.

For what seemed an eternity, she dripped tonic in the area where the animal licked, waiting to gauge its effect before dribbling more.

The sow's breathing slowly grew deeper and more even, until finally its tongue lolled to the ground.

Hushed voices whispered from the assembled castlefolk as Golde rose. "Ronces, the rope."

Grabbing the cord, she tied the animal's feet, then again directed the boys. "The knife, Ronces. Alory, the cloth."

The boys' hands shook as they handed the items to her. "Be careful," Alory urged.

Golde knelt beside the pig. Holding her breath, she cut the arrow shaft away, and placed the blade's sharp tip to the sow's punctured flesh. She then gave the knife a hard thrust until it scraped against the embedded tip of the arrow.

Sweat trickled down her forehead as she set to work, cutting a core around the arrow. Faith, 'twas like trying to cut a wheel of cheese that was composed of nothing but rind. Once finished, she used the knife for leverage. Steeling herself, she gave a mighty yank on the arrow while pulling up on the blade. The arrow came free cleanly.

And not a moment too soon. Already the sow's breathing was growing lighter and less even.

"Ronces . . ." She looked at her hands. They were covered with blood and gore.

For a moment she swayed, certain she was going to sick. A snort from the sow sent fear to her rescue. Sick or no, she'd best finish quickly.

"Ronces. You and Alory will have to light the taper."

Ronces fumbled with a flint until Nicolette jerked it away. While he held the tinder, the sure-handed girl struck the flint. Once the tinder caught, Alory held the candle to it.

Another snort issued from the sow as Golde held the knife above the flame. "Hurry, hurry," she muttered.

The blade grew black, then ashen. Kneeling beside the sow one last time, Golde sunk the knife in its bloody hide.

In the same instant that the blade hissed, she heard Ronces shout, "Papa!"

Golde dared not look away from the pig. The animal's body writhed as it tried to wake, but Golde held. The knife needed a few moments to cauterize the wound.

Abruptly a mail-clad arm wrapped about her waist.

"Leave go," she snapped, leaning all her weight forward and locking her muscles.

"Witless get of an idiot!" Gavarnie hissed in her ear. "You will get yourself killed."

The pig began to grunt with ferocity, and its hooves flailed.

"Mistress!" Sperville croaked, prying at her hand where she held the knife.

'Twas more than she could withstand. In the same instant the blade came free, Gavarnie jerked her backward. Her momentum carried them both to the ground, where she landed in his lap.

Sixteen

GAVARNIE SCREECHED. There was no
other word for the high-pitched wail that erupted all the
way from his *coillons*, where his plate armor had pinched
him.

Pinched him? Nay.

Shoving Golde from his lap, he clutched himself between the legs and rolled to his side. He'd been torn
asunder. His body quivered with the pain. He squeezed
his eyes shut against scalding tears of agony, and curled in
a ball.

As if it understood his misery perfectly, the sow began to squeal.

"Lund!" Sperville called. "Have your blade to ready
lest the pig breaks its bonds."

"Nay!" Nicolette wailed.

"Mi'lord." Sperville touched Gavarnie's shoulder, and he flinched. "What—"

"The witch did it," the swineherd accused.

"She did not," Alory cried. "She was only trying to help."

Gavarnie's heart pounded thickly in his chest. Dear God, he could not look. How much blood would there be?

"He is having a fit," Lund remarked anxiously. "See how he shakes?"

Instantly a thumb was prying his eyelid open, and he saw Golde's apprehensive features peering at him. Groaning, he rocked away from her touch.

Castrated. Emasculated.

"What spell have you cast upon him, hellhag?" Henri demanded from nearby.

His eyes squeezed shut, Gavarnie heard scuffling sounds to the tune of the sow's grunts and snorts.

"Unhand me, fool," Golde huffed. "'Tis no fit. Can you not see he is in great pain?"

Soft, warm fingers brushed the hair from his forehead. "Mi'lord, tell me where you are hurt."

He shook his head. Death was preferable to discussing his malady with her, or anyone.

Sir Shaft le Mort, Baron of Gelding. He could hear it now.

"Sperville, what became of the knife I held?" Golde sounded frantic. "Mi'lord, did I stab you?"

Mud squished, then the chamberlain replied, "'Tis here."

Gavarnie ground his teeth. Opening his eyes to slits, he found Golde kneeling beside him, her hair stuck to her face and clothing in black clumps. Beyond her, Lund held his sword at the ready, prepared to kill the sow if she attacked. Henri stood beside Lund, his features drawn. And inexplicably, an overpowering scent of honey permeated the air.

"It is his stomach," Golde concluded aloud, tugging at his wrists. "Mi'lord, let me see. 'Tis not safe to move you until we determine the extent of your injuries, and this is no place to tarry."

As if to underscore her words, the pig loosed another round of howling squeals.

"Leave go," he gritted, locking his muscles in place.

"I swear I will not hurt you," she cajoled, pulling harder.

The pain was beginning to ease, and he wished only for privacy. "Get thee gone, wench. Sperville, disperse this crowd. Then you, Lund, and Henri, remove yourselves to the hall."

Golde's eyes jerked upward, her worried gaze directed behind him at Sperville. She pursed her lips.

"I cannot leave you thus," the chamberlain declined, "not with an angry sow. Let Golde look at you. Then we will know how best to proceed."

The throbbing rapidly diminished, leaving a numb sensation in its wake. Doubtless because there was nothing left to feel pain. He grimaced.

"For once, Sperville, you will do my bidding without argument. You will take yourself off, or by all that is holy, I will crush that stubborn head of yours."

"But sir—"

"I tell you, my complaints are naught to concern yourself with. Begone!"

It seemed the sow agreed with his sentiments, for it grunted heartily.

"He is out of his head," Golde pronounced solemnly.

"Lund, Henri, you will have to help Sperville hold him if I am to find the source of his ailment."

Plague take the wench, Gavarnie swore to himself. She would badger him to the grave. Even now, Lund and Henri were moving toward him, the louts.

"The first person who lays hands on me will die," he blustered.

Lund and Henri halted to exchange wary glances.

"Papa, pwease, let her help you!" Nicolette cried from outside the pen.

"He will remember naught of this once he is recovered," Golde persisted. "Indeed, he will understand your good intentions and be grateful."

"I will not," he vowed.

"Come," Sperville addressed the two liegemen. "Would you truly consider leaving our liege in a pig stye?"

The simpering bastard. Rage blew through Gavarnie like a hell-borne gale. To be forevermore pitied and scorned. But the devil would take him before he'd be physically restrained while the buzzards ogled him.

He scrambled to his feet. "There!" He backed toward the gate. "Are you satisfied?"

He spread his arms and legs wide. "Does it please you to see a man so foully disfigured?"

A hush fell over the stye. Even the pig stilled and grew silent. Lund glanced at Henri, though there was no horror on their faces. Sperville was peering at him with a puzzled tilt to his brows. Finally Golde rose from her bent position.

"Calm yourself, mi'lord," she soothed. "I know it appears dire to you, but I have treated such wounds often. A few cobwebs and bee tails and you will be fine."

He frowned at her. What in God's name was she

talking about? He glanced at his hands, then jerked his head down.

No blood. No half-hinged appendages dangled beneath the hem of his mail tunic.

Giving the buzzards his back, he spun to face a deserted corner of the stye. He yanked up the chain mail tunic that covered the armor plate on his thighs, then snatched at the drawstring of his braies. Closing one eye, he peeked inside. Everything appeared normal. He opened his eye and pulled the material farther away from his belly. Nothing. He eased his hand in for a closer inspection.

He flinched.

Then he sighed gratefully. Though the area was most tender, all was intact. He felt like jumping for joy. Well, mayhap not jumping, but—

"Mi'lord?" Golde's husky voice invaded his good cheer.

So, that was what the wench was about with her talk of cobwebs and bee tails. She believed him daft and sought to humor him.

Of all the arrogance, the conceit. That she would think she knew more of his person than he. Turning, he glared at her.

"You dare to presume much which does not exist. Cobwebs and bee tails. There is naught wrong with my head, Mistress Know-All. My armor pinched . . ."

Words deserted him. Everyone was looking at him, nonplussed. He stabbed Golde with a hateful look and lowered his voice that the entire castle would not hear.

"When you landed in my lap, my plate caught . . ."

Faith, were they not all so stupid, he would not have to be so explicit. "I thought I'd been—that is, it felt as if . . . Well, you can imagine my horror."

Abruptly Henri and Lund grew interested in the ground. Sperville turned his head to study the pen's railing. Only Golde continued to look at him, her lips trembling as if she were holding back tears.

Good, he thought. The hellhag deserved to humiliate herself by weeping before the assembled castlefolk. With luck, the humbling experience would improve her nature. In future, mayhap she would not be so quick to insert her overblown opinions where they were not welcome.

He hitched up his braies, then smoothed the mail tunic over them.

Golde's shoulders quivered. Her nostrils flared. Her mouth opened.

His brows swooped down abruptly, and he narrowed his eyes. 'Twas not a cry of regret that issued forth.

'Twas laughter! Bubbling peals of mirth. Gut-wracking, tear-dripping gusts of merriment.

"Only a woman," he snapped, "filled with sick whimsy, would find humor in such a lamentable state of affairs."

His comment did naught but make her laugh harder.

"You do not hear—"

He clamped his jaw shut. He'd meant to say how no one else was laughing, but the point was disproved before he could make it. A chortle here, a snort there, those present acted like a bunch of giggling virgins at the first sight of a naked man. Even the pig seemed to be snickering.

Of a sudden, Golde sobered. "Hold, Ronces. We are coming out."

Gavarnie looked to see the boy straddling the rail. By all that was holy, if aught befell his son—

"Come, mi'lord," Golde clutched his elbow.

Whore's gleet, Gavarnie swore to himself as she

steered him toward the gate. He'd forgotten his supposed blindness. But apparently he'd not given himself away, due no doubt to the chaos in the stye.

Plague take the hellbag. 'Twas all her fault. "What are you doing here?" he demanded, exiting the pen.

"She was helping the pig," Nicolette proclaimed, racing to greet him.

"The sow caught a splinter in her hindquarter." Golde's voice carried loud as Alory and Ronces approached.

Was it his imagination, or did the wench's tone carry a hint of threat as well? He glanced at her to find her gaze leveled on Ronces.

Abruptly worry settled in his head. What went on here? His son's thin features reflected great distress.

"Was it your plan to let the sow kill my children?"

"Nay, Papa." Ronces voice was scarce more than a whisper. "She—"

Golde stalled him with a slight shake of her head before he could finish. "I could not carry all my medicines, and ordered the children to help me."

Something was amiss, and he would know what it was, by God. Though how he would go about finding out was another matter. If he were truly blind, he would never have realized the undercurrents that waxed beneath his very nose. But to say aught of what he'd witnessed would expose him.

"Mi'lord." Sperville came to stand beside him before he could determine a solution. "Let us get you and mistress to the bathing barrels. 'Tis only midmorn, and already the day grows short."

At the double meaning behind the chamberlain's words, Gavarnie's hand swept to his chest. Beneath the chain mail and undertunic, he could feel the pouch that hung from his neck. It contained another message warning him of danger.

He'd found the missive stuffed in his chalice yester-eve at the king's reception. 'Twas the reason he'd returned from Atherbrook a day early.

It took all his will not to stare accusingly at Golde. Gone was the unreasoning terror that had gripped him upon discovering Golde in the pig pen. Gone was the fear for her life.

Instead, anger fed on his belly. He'd forbidden his children to go near Golde, using her convalescence as an excuse. Not that she didn't appear healthy as a bear at the moment.

But he'd reissued his command to Nigel before leaving for Atherbrook. Under no circumstances were his children to be allowed near Golde. And though the steward did not know his suspicions regarding the wench, an order was an order. Yet here were his children with Golde, and Nigel was nowhere about.

Scowling, he turned his attention to his oldest son. "Ronces, take your brother and sister to your chamber. Stay there until I send Roland for you."

❧❦❧

SEPARATED BY WOODEN SCREENS, a half-dozen public bathing barrels were housed beside the laundry. Despite the heat of the stall where Gavarnie sat upon a stool, chills gripped his flesh.

Not that he was sick. Rather, 'twas an icy wasting of his soul, until all the sun in the world could not warm him.

He had decisions to make. Decisions that would see him live and prosper, or see him dead.

That the king intended to kill him, he no longer doubted. He and Sperville had purposly been seated at the table farthest from William's throughout the royal reception. Meanwhile, William had surrounded himself with those most royally favored at the moment, including de Warrenne and Gundrada.

Betweenwhiles, in the two days since Gavarnie had left Skyenvic, it appeared Golde had managed to ingratiate herself to his children.

She was only trying to help. Alory's words to the swineherd in Golde's defense. *Please, Papa, let her help you.* Nicolette's words. Since when had either child trusted Golde?

And what was Ronces about? The boy had silently reached out to touch Golde's hand, casting her a grateful look, before leading Alory and Nicolette away from the stye.

Gavarnie's lip curled. 'Twas well and good he'd returned home when he had. Another day, and the wench would likely convince his own children to murder him.

No sooner had he completed the thought than he heard Golde's voice as she entered the bath house.

". . . is the only other tunic I brought with me, Hesper. Until I can afford another, I can hardly dispose of this one."

"Just so's ye knows," Hesper puffed, "I don't think I'll be able to get rid of all the stains."

"Hmph," Gavarnie snorted. Doubtless, the deceitful wench would buy an entire new wardrobe with the coin William would pay her for killing him.

Footsteps entered the bathing stall next to his, and he crossed his arms over his chest. While he sat unattended, Golde had her own personal servant. Sperville was out hunting Nigel, and Roland was taking his leisure in fetching him clean clothing from the wardrobe. His water would be long cold before he stepped into the barrel.

"Yech," Golde muttered to the swish of wet material.

Hesper tsked. "'Twould not be so difficult had the chil—"

The serving maid's words ended abruptly, followed by several moments of silence.

Then Golde inquired in an overloud voice, "Where is his lordship?"

Gavarnie gritted his teeth. Did the wench think to fool him with her innocent facade? Whatever trickery she was about, she'd enlisted Hesper's aid. Just wait until he got hold of the older woman.

"I am here," he snarled, unable to keep his anger at bay.

More silence, and Gavarnie stared at a small knot of wood in the screen that separated him from Golde. There wasn't a man, woman, or child in the castle who didn't know the knot had once been removable, after the milk-maid had caught a stableboy peeping at her and near poked his eye out.

But it appeared the screen had not been repaired, as he'd ordered. And though he would never stoop to such methods only for self-gratification, 'twould serve him well if he could see the deceitful goings on in the next stall right now.

"My apologies for the trouble you went to on my behalf," Golde said at last.

Water splattered, and he surmised Hesper had just poured a bucket over her. Using the noise for cover, he eased from the stool, then nearly slipped. Though it required only two steps to pluck the knot from the screen, the floorboards were slick as seaweed.

"You should speak to Spindleshanks about his squeamishness," Golde continued, as he closed one eye and peered through the hole. "Doubtless, 'twas he who insisted you come to my rescue. If you could see, you would have known I had matters well to hand."

Gavarnie sucked in a breath. If he could see any better, his eyes would fall from his head. Instead of sitting on a stool, Golde was standing. Indeed, were she not moving, she would appear to be a precious piece of metalwork. Light from the opening between the outside wall and ceiling sprinkled over her like silver dust.

But move she did, soaping and scrubbing her hair. Below her raised arms, her breasts danced like juicy, ripe melons in the hands of an experienced juggler.

Gavarnie licked his lips, then winced as pain lanced through his loins. How long since he'd had a woman? Of its own volition, his gaze lowered to the crutch where Golde's thighs met.

He scowled. Must that, too, sparkle with invitation? Indeed, the black curls there seemed to wink at him teasingly.

Cease, he ordered his lecherous thoughts. 'Twas no more than sunlight striking beads of water. Tonight he would avail himself of . . .

Breta? Nay. She was too skinny.

Enid, then? He wrinkled his nose. She was overripe.

He envisioned every woman he knew who would be more than eager to share his bed, but all were lacking in one feature or another.

Hesper's voice intruded on his musings. "If ye would sit on yon stool, mistress, I would do yer hair."

Whore's gleet. If the old woman ruined his viewing pleasure, he would—

"My rear is the only thing that has not been exposed to filth this day. I would rather rinse before I sit."

Gavarnie loosed his pent breath and rubbed his shaft. Praise God for Golde's practical nature; or praise the devil. At the moment it mattered not who held Golde's soul, so long as she continued to scrub her hair . . .

Or run soap over her breasts and belly. His mouth opened as her hands slid lower.

". . . mi'lord?"

'Twas a moment before he realized Golde was speaking to him.

"What?" His voice bounced in his face and he leapt backward. Immediately his feet slipped, and he barely caught himself on the barrel's rim to avoid a fall.

"I say, why are you returned so early from Atherbrook? We did not expect you until tomorrow."

He straightened, praying she'd not noticed how near the screen his voice had sounded. "I—I . . ."

Sweat broke on his brow as he cast about for a lie. "I returned early to make certain of preparations for my guests."

Aye, that was it. Tomorrow the lords and ladies billeted at Skyenvic would return from the king's reception. None would question his decision to ensure their continued comfort.

"But you are arrived so early in the day." Abruptly her tone grew anxious. "You took no chances riding through the forest at night, did you?"

Her concern was affected, he told himself, though why he should feel disappointed with the knowledge was a mystery.

"No one knew I was leaving," he groused. "Indeed, my own liegemen knew nothing until they were wakened in the dead of night."

He blew a sigh of relief. That much was fact. After he'd discovered the second message, he could not abide at Atherbrook. And while he knew not who was sending the missives, he had not questioned the warning. Not after the attack in the lane.

At the sound of more splashing water, he scuttled back to the peephole. 'Twas only to see Golde's face, he assured himself, to gauge her true feelings by the look in her eyes.

Which he never saw.

He flattened his hands against the screen to steady himself.

Bent at the waist, the wench had turned her backside to him while Hesper poured clean water over her hair.

Her bottom seemed to pout at him, as if it had been denied his attention.

And so it had, he sighed gustily. A full fortnight had passed since he'd last carried her from his tub. Longer still since the night he'd felt her slick lust for him; since she had begged him to have done.

He fair stroked the flesh from his shaft while eyeing the pink bud that peeped at him from the center of her core. To taste its musky sweetness, to bury himself—

"Uh-hmm."

Sperville's discreet cough startled him. His feet slipped as he jumped from the peephole, and he thudded to the floor, a water bucket clattering where he struck it.

"Mi'lord?" Golde called.

He gave the chamberlain an I'll-slit-your-throat-if-say-aught look, and forced a casual reply. "'Tis naught but the squeamish Spindleshanks, come at last to assist me."

Sperville cast a withering look upon him and helped him from the floor to the stool. Then the chamberlain grabbed a bucket and dipped it in the barrel.

"Were Sir Varin and Arnulf present at the reception?" Golde asked, just as Sperville doused him.

"Nay," the chamberlain answered while Gavarnie blew water from his nose. "His wife was recently delivered of a babe, and he is not expected for several days."

The sneaky bastard, Gavarnie thought, clearing his throat. Sperville had deliberately thrown the water in his face. He swiped back his hair and cast the chamberlain a vicious look.

"Speaking of babes," Golde grumbled, "you could at least try to control your temper around your children, mi'lord."

Gavarnie's anger suddenly blossomed to full rage. "I need not your advice on how to raise my offspring."

"Stupid man! Your children performed a good deed this morn, and their thanks is your foul tongue. I suppose you beat them for attending mass."

'Twas the last straw. Gavarnie shot upward, determined to break down the screen and strangle the wench.

And he would have, too, had his cursed feet not slipped from beneath him again. By the time Sperville had helped him up, Golde had stomped from the bath house.

SEVENTEEN

GOLDE GRIMACED upon entering the wardrobe. Hesper had already removed the soiled bed linen, and without the smell of honey, the small anteroom reeked from the dung the children had placed in her boots. Scooping them up, she strode from the dark little room.

Gavarnie would doubtless complain were he to find such filth in the wardrobe. And while she would claim that her boots were filled with dung from the pig stye, he would yet wonder why she'd brought them upstairs without first having them cleaned. Indeed, he might take Hesper to task for not cleaning them, under which circumstance Hesper was liable to crumble and tell him the truth about her boots.

Golde rolled her eyes. Easier to avoid the entire issue by removing her boots from the wardrobe before

Gavarnie arrived. Besides, she had no desire to speak with his toadship at the moment. She'd already explained to Sperville that she'd accidentally spilled honey on herself while treating the pig.

The sound of footsteps halted her midchamber.

"Where have you been?" Gavarnie demanded, his voice echoing from the corridor.

"I was called into New Market to resolve a dispute," Sir Nigel responded. "I had no idea you'd returned."

Golde spun and hurried back to the wardrobe.

"Could you not leave notice of your whereabouts?" Sperville complained. "It has taken me half the morn to locate you."

"Your forgiveness, my liege," the steward apologized, his voice losing its distant sound. Clearly, the men had entered Gavarnie's chamber. "What is it you wish to discuss?"

Golde heard the chamber door close and her spirits sank. Unless she wanted Gavarnie to know she was here, along with her boots, she was stranded.

"I received another message at the king's reception." Gavarnie spoke in a low tone, then paused.

Another message? Golde wondered.

Of a sudden, Gavarnie asked, "Why does my chamber smell of bull's wind?"

Golde held her breath.

"'Tis probably pig's wind," Sperville sniffed. "Roland must have brought the odor with him when he fetched your clothing."

"Pig's wind?" Nigel queried.

"It matters not." Sperville sounded annoyed. "I, for one, am most interested to know how and when his lordship regained his sight."

Golde near dropped the boots. Gavarnie could see?

For a moment she felt numb. Then a lump clogged her throat.

He could see! The numbness was quickly replaced by a tingling sensation.

God had wrought a miracle!

"Y-y-you can see?" Nigel spluttered.

Golde hugged the boots to her chest and raised her face to the ceiling. Praise be to God. 'Twas wonderful!

". . . scarce had a chance to explain before leaving Atherbrook," Gavarnie was saying. "Nor did I wish to discuss anything in front of the men during the ride home. For all I know, one of them could be party to the plot."

Golde jerked her head down from where she yet stared heavenward. What plot? And what messages?

Abruptly the stench from her boots invaded her nostrils and she realized where she was holding them. Scowling, she stuck the offensive boots out at arm's length.

"But . . . you can see?" The steward yet sounded wonderstruck.

"He has already said as much," Sperville snapped. "Cease interrupting, that our lord may tell us how and when."

"'Twas the night of the attack." Now Gavarnie sounded irritated. "'Tis of no consequence. What matters is whether or not I inform the king."

"Why would you not?" Sperville asked the question, even as Golde thought it.

"'Tis the king who is trying to kill me."

Golde clutched the boots tighter again, lest they fall from her fingers. The king was trying to kill Gavarnie? Surely, he was mistaken.

"You have lost your wits," Sperville finally pronounced. "'Twould serve you well to avail yourself of Golde's magical cures."

"Golde's magic," Gavarnie ground. "She is the king's agent in the affair."

Golde suddenly felt as if the floor were spinning beneath her feet. She blinked hard against the dizziness. Had she understood correctly? Did Gavarnie think she was trying to kill him?

"However did you reach such a conclusion?" Sperville's tone mirrored her own horror.

"Would you deny the attack on my person in the lane?"

"Of course not. But—"

"Consider, my dullwitted man, who lured me to the village that eve."

"Golde? How could she know you would come after her?"

"She knew," Gavarnie spat. "The conniving slut."

Abruptly Golde felt as if a cinch were being drawn about her chest, choking the breath from her. She lowered her arms, uncaring that the boots dangled against her only clean tunic.

A conniving slut. Gavarnie's words echoed in her head. But of course. What else would a man think of a woman who offered herself to him with such ease? She winced as embarrassment, raw and hot, prickled her flesh.

"The wench let it be known far and wide that she was casting fortunes at Sigi's that day," Sir Nigel mused. "It seems too neat for coincidence."

"It is not possible," Sperville declared. "'Twas I who approached Golde to come to Skyenvic not the other way around. Indeed, 'twas her great-grandmother's services I sought."

"Truth tell?" Gavarnie's tone was mocking. "And how did you learn of Golde's great-grandmother?

"Sir Varin—"

"Precisely," Gavarnie hissed. "I'll wager Sir Varin contacted you with the news he'd found someone to heal my eyes."

"Allow me to finish" Spindleshanks snapped. "Sir Varin and I first visited Golde's great-grandmother, a more crotchety old crone than I have e'er met. She was most displeased with her great-granddaughter's 'thimble-rigging,' as she put it. She agreed to heal your eyes if I would bring Golde here, that the old woman could teach her a lesson."

Golde's breath knotted in her chest. *Mimskin?*

Mimskin had discussed her dishonest practices with Sperville? And now the magpie was confirming for Gavarnie that she was a fake, just as Gavarnie had thought that night at Sigi's.

Her embarrassment intensified until she thought the entire wardrobe would glow red.

". . . proves nothing," Nigel was saying. "Indeed, Sperville, it sounds to me as if you were tricked into bringing the wench here. Unless you, too, are part of the scheme."

"How dare you accuse me of such! His lordship can see, can he not? Meanwhile, who turned turned tail and ran the night his lordship was attacked?"

"Turned tail?" The steward's voice shook. "I risked my neck riding full speed to raise the hue and cry."

"Cease!" Gavarnie commanded. "Someone is trying to kill me. If it is not Golde, then who?"

"There is de Warrenne," Sperville huffed. "His greed knows no bounds."

Gavarnie scoffed. "De Warrenne has not the intelligence to piss with the wind. William would never trust him with such a deed. Nay. 'Tis that worthless Varin de Brionne."

Golde's belly felt so overfull, she feared she would be sick. To think Gavarnie had made her feel like a Celtic princess while she recovered from the beating at Maid Sigi's. The memory drove knives in her heart.

"But Sir Varin has yet to arrive," Sperville reasoned.

"All the better," Nigel said. "He could scarce be convicted of a crime he wasn't present to commit."

"Think what you are saying," Sperville implored. "The king has made a covenant with Sir Varin to have you killed? William could easily have rid himself of you upon Isabelle's death by convicting you of murder."

"Aye. But at the time, William thought my sight would return. Now he has recognized my blindness as more of a liability than he can support."

"You do not know that for certain. Indeed, for all we know, it could be the king sending the warnings."

"Pff. If that were the case, why would not William just tell me?"

"Aye, Sperville," Nigel sneered. "Your reasoning strays beyond the limits of believability."

In the pause that followed, Golde hugged herself. It felt as if her insides were being clawed and pecked by a host of black crows. 'Twas an effort to draw breath. Would that she could lie down and die where she now stood.

"Let us put Golde to the whip until she confesses all she knows," Sperville finally suggested.

"Flog her?" Gavarnie sounded incredulous.

"Why not?" Sperville persisted. "She languishes in your bed while you sleep on the floor like a commoner. And all the while, she plots your demise. Indeed, once she confesses, you should stake her bleeding hide in the Solent that her death will be slow and tormented."

Golde frowned. She should be frightened unto death, should be cursing Sperville's evil nature. But somehow she knew. Strange, but she knew the chamberlain meant her no harm. She would wager her life on it. So what did he hope to accomplish with such talk?

"Wha . . . wha . . ." Gavarnie managed to stutter at last. "Are you daft? The wench is stubborn as a mule. Likely she would ply me with naught but curses to her dying breath."

"I have yet to see a man refuse to spill his guts under the lash. She is but a woman. Give her unto Fitz Simon. She will talk."

"The idea has merit," Sir Nigel seconded.

Golde narrowed her eyes. Unlike the chamberlain, the steward was more than willing to promote her death. She would bet her life on that, as well.

"I cannot allow Fitz Simon to question her," Gavarnie snapped. "For all I know, my castellan is part of the plot."

"Very well, mi'lord. You wield the whip and I shall see to the rest," Sperville offered.

"Nay!" Gavarnie fair shouted.

There was another pause, and she imagined Sperville drawing himself to his full height, an insulted expression on his face. "I do not understand your reluctance to spill a little blood. Forgive me for saying so, but you sound squeamish as a maid."

"Whore's gleet. What if the wench is innocent?"

"You have just spent half the day convincing me of her duplicity. What matter if she is innocent? Are you willing to take such a chance with your life? 'Tis not as if she is royalty. None will ever know what became of her."

"Sperville's point is well made, mi'lord," Nigel agreed.

Golde heard Gavarnie's fist slam against the bedpost. "I will hear no more of this. Let us get to the business at hand. There are but two options for me. I can tell the king I have regained my sight, or . . ."

"Or what?" Nigel asked.

"Do not say it." Sperville's tone was disgusted, as if he knew what Gavarnie was about to say.

Gavarnie's voice grew harsh. "Would you have me serve a master who has plotted my death? After all I have done for him?"

Sperville blew an exasperated breath. "The Danes have not the leader or the means at present to take England from William. You have said so yourself on many occasions."

"Better to die like a man than lie docile with an adder."

A keen sense of urgency roiled through Golde's veins at Gavarnie's words. Did he imply he would foment rebellion with the Danes rather than serve a king who'd tried to kill him?

She shuddered at the thought. Gavarnie could not hope to pit himself against William's might.

"Whatever you decide"—Sperville's tone was one of defeat—"I will remain your man."

"As will I," Nigel declared. "Doubtless, every man here will follow you, once they learn you have regained your sight. I confess, I was beginning to worry there might be those liegemen whose loyalty would waver."

"You have heard whisperings of discontent?" Gavarnie asked.

"Nay. But I feared de Warrenne's reasoning might

poison the entire castle. Of course, now that you can see—"

"You will tell no one at present," Gavarnie ordered. "Not until I have made my decision concerning the Danes. Meanwhile, I would have an accounting of my men and their armor."

"Of course, your lordship." Nigel sounded excited. "By your leave."

Once the steward's footsteps had receded and the door closed behind him, Sperville made a final appeal. "You are wrong, mi'lord. William has no designs on your life. Nor does Golde."

"You will cease this whining," Gavarnie snarled. "I would have an accounting of my coin, lest I have need of it."

The heavy fall of Gavarnie's footsteps followed the exchange.

"Where are you going, mi'lord?" Sperville asked, his tone disillusioned.

"I go to find Hesper. Golde practices trickery with my children, and the old woman knows the reason."

Even after the chamber door slammed behind Gavarnie, Golde remained rooted to the spot. If she dared move, she would surely crumble into countless broken pieces.

She must return home. Yet the only place she knew to catch a ship was in New Market. And she dare not go there. The villagers would long remember her as a thief.

Caught up in despair, it did not occur to her that Gavarnie's coin was kept locked in the wardrobe where she hid. At Sperville's unexpected appearance, she started. The chamberlain jumped back, and they both gasped in the same instance.

Sperville recovered first. "Mistress! What do you here?" He wrinkled his nose. "And what is that smell?"

Shaken, Golde seated herself on a chest before she collapsed. "I came to fetch these." She held out the boots in a lame gesture, as if that would explain all.

The chamberlain moved swiftly to sit beside her. Easing the boots from her fingers, he hurled them beyond the wardrobe into the bedchamber.

"Do not fret." He patted the back of her hand. "Gavarnie is no fool. He will soon find the error in his thinking."

Golde shook her head and stared at the floor. "Is it possible the king truly intends to kill him?"

"Pff! 'Twas de Warrenne who lured his thoughts in that direction. And it is de Warrenne who is trying to kill him. I'd wager my life on it."

Golde glanced up. "Mayhap the Baron of Adurford has good reason to murder Gavarnie."

Abruptly the chamberlain withdrew his hand, and his tone grew cold. "You have every right to be angry, mistress. But de Warrenne's only reason for killing Gavarnie would be that he could gain control of Skyenvic."

"Come, Sperville. I have supped with Gavarnie enough to know. There is much hostility between him and de Warrenne's wife. Indeed, were you not present the eve Gundrada grew jealous over the attention Gavarnie paid me? When she peevishly demanded if there were a match in the making?"

The chamberlain stared at her as if she were a two-headed toad. "Gavarnie and Gundrada? Surely you jest."

Golde felt her face warm. Had she drawn the wrong conclusion? "Why else would Gavarnie feel so bitter toward the woman?"

Sperville's features puckered until it appeared they might be sucked inside his head. "I tell you, Gavarnie would sooner bed an eel."

"She *is* comely," Golde snapped, "both in face and figure. She *is* of the nobility. She *is* witty, and other lords and ladies seem to enjoy her presence."

"Aye. She is witty. Witty like the Serpent of Eden. Her nobility springs not from Norman loins, but from Saxon. And her beauty can, and has been, bought. Gavarnie has never felt anything other than loathing for the woman. But while he respects her cunning, he feels naught but contempt for her husband, an arrogant sentiment that is about to get him killed."

Golde winced and help up a hand. She could stand no more. "You must do something."

"Indeed, I intend to."

Golde eyed the chamberlain's crafty features. "What are you thinking?"

"I'm thinking what his lordship needs is a swift and hard kick. And I'm thinking you should be the person to dispense it."

Golde shook her head. "I cannot remain at Skyenvic. Not now."

"Exactly." The chamberlain smiled.

❧❧❧

BY THE TIME Gavarnie located Hesper at the laundry, he was seething, and the heat of the afternoon sun did little to cool him. Without Sperville or Roland, who was busy cleaning his armor, he'd been forced enlist Eustace as his guide.

'Twas galling to continue to be led about when he

could see. Nor did he want the guard listening while he questioned Hesper. 'Twas none of the liegeman's affair.

"Hesper can help me back. You need your rest." He dismissed Eustace, who bowed and took himself off.

At his words, the old woman rose from where she bent over a tub. "Mi'lord, 'tis good—"

"I would know what deceit you and your mistress are about," he snarled.

Hesper glanced about. "Are ye speakin' to me?"

Gavarnie planted his hands on his hips. "Do you see anyone else about?"

The serving maid rubbed her hands nervously on her frayed apron. "What did ye say?"

"Do you think I did not hear your words in the bath house? You will tell me what goes on between Golde and my children."

Hesper's gaze again darted about. "Golde and yer children?"

Gavarnie's body trembled, so great was his rage. "Test my temper, and I will have you locked in stocks."

Fear clouded the old woman's eyes and her head began to shake. "Mi'lord, I don't know what yer askin' about!"

Gavarnie's hands fisted on his hips. It took no little effort to not reach out and shake the serving maid until her secrets tumbled from her mouth.

"When you first entered the stall next to mine, you said it would not have been so difficult had my children . . ."

Hesper leaned forward, her gaze fastened on his mouth, her brows raised expectantly. "Had yer children what?"

Gavarnie felt like tearing his hair from his head.

"That is what I am asking you! Your mistress interrupted before you could finish speaking."

Abruptly Golde's angry voice rang behind him. "Had your children not poured honey all over my garments and my person, the tunic would not have been so difficult to remove."

He spun to face her where she'd drawn to a halt, Sperville at her side.

"Why do you not go find some hapless dog to kick, and leave poor Hesper alone?" she queried sourly.

His mouth worked, but the only word he could produce was, "Honey?"

"Aye. The children agreed to help me with the pig in exchange for my silence, that I would not tell you of their mischief. Meanwhile, Hesper has worked her fingers to the bone, scrubbing your sheets and my tunic."

He glanced back to the serving maid, who was wringing her apron. "Me apologies, yer lordship."

"'Tis no fault of yours," Gavarnie muttered, fighting the sudden urge to slink away. "'Tis mistress who decided to keep the information from me, despite the fact that I have a right to know what goes on with my children."

"Truth tell." Golde's tone reflected contempt, as Gavarnie's had earlier when he used the same expression. "I suppose it matters not that the children resolved their problems on their own. Nor does it matter that they worked at a low task to pay for their deeds. Nay. You are duty-bound to demean them, because anything that cannot be beaten to submission is beyond you."

With that, she turned and strode away.

The little hag. Who did she think she was, speaking to him thus, and in front of a servant?

He started forward, intent on teaching her some manners, when Sperville clutched his arm.

"Allow me to assist you, mi'lord." The chamberlain's tone was filled with double meaning. "The ground here is most uneven and I would not have you fall."

Immediately Gavarnie halted. Whore's gleet. How he would love to declare his sight returned, and the consequences be damned. But he dare not until he'd made his decision on what he would do.

"At your leisure," he grumbled to the chamberlain.

As he was led forward, Golde's words tumbled through his head. *Anything that could not be beaten to submission . . .*

His anger ebbed with each step he took. And as his anger ebbed, so did his discomfort grow.

Anything that could not be tortured, beaten, or bled—his thoughts concerning de Warrenne. He eyed Golde's back where she walked a good space ahead. Was it possible that she truly possessed the all-seeing eye? That she knew his thinking almost word for word, and had used it against him?

Would that it were so, for the only other explanation dug at him like a burrowing flesh-mite. Had he sunk so low as to exhibit the same traits as a man like de Warrenne?

EIGHTEEN

GOLDE LAY FULLY CLOTHED beneath the sheets in Gavarnie's chamber. The lecherous oaf had insisted she continue to sleep in his bed—that he could continue to ogle her charms, no doubt.

"Hmph."

Again and over, his toadship's conversation with Sperville and Nigel had wound through her head—Gavarnie's suspicions, her lurid behavior the night she'd begged him to have done, Sperville's knowledge of her thimblerigging.

Tormented by mortification, it was not until several hours later that she recalled the portion of discourse when Gavarnie had spoken of regaining his sight.

The night of the attack.

Rage coursed through her blood anew. The times he had carried her to and from the tub. His coughing fit the day the sheet had accidentally slipped below her breasts. The moments she'd surreptitiously regarded his body— with him watching her.

And he had the gall to call her deceitful?

"Pff."

Pulling the covers to her chin, she rolled to her side. She could scarce wait to undertake Sperville's plan for getting her to Atherbrook. Once there, Sir Varin would see to her needs, and she would return home with him after the tourney.

"Hmph."

The morn would find her well rested and ready for the journey, she vowed. She would not lie wide-eyed all night, longing for what would never be. She would not remember how special Gavarnie had made her feel. She most certainly would not recall their passionate encounter . . . the searing fire he'd lit in her . . .

The ravenous hunger he'd aroused.

Undeterred by her furious avowals, a tear slipped over the bridge of her nose. She clamped her teeth together against the sob that boiled in her throat.

How could she have been so stupid, so naive? That she'd actually believed Gavarnie cared about her. Indeed, on one occasion, she'd dared to dream what it would be like if he loved her.

Embarrassment flashed hotly over her face. How could she have thought herself worthy of any man? Was she not ugly to look upon? Was she not tall and ungainly? *Grendelskin. Dragon-hag.*

Gavarnie could have his pick of women. He had admitted as much the afternoon she'd teased him about poking himself in the eye. Why would he choose her?

She squeezed her eyes shut to hold her tears at bay. Would the bereft ache that now fed on her heart remain with her all her days? Never would she feel toward another the way she felt about Gavarnie.

Her lips twisted in a bitter smile. How ironic. No sooner did she find a man who did not fear her cursed eyes, than fate snatched him from her.

Abruptly the bedchamber door creaked, intruding on her thoughts. She willed her face to stillness as footsteps moved toward the bed. The darkness behind her lids grew brighter as a candle or lamp was held near her face.

'Twas Gavarnie. She could smell him. His scent beckoned to her like some wild, sweet night-fest in a secret grove.

She struggled to maintain a serene countenance. Despite the fact he was spying on her, despite his unholy feelings toward her, she longed, body and soul, to be held in his embrace.

To feel the safe protection of his strength, the steady rhythm of his heart, the calm ease of his breathing.

Was there not some way she could convince him of her innocence?

❧❦❧

GAVARNIE CLOSED his bedchamber door behind him and strode down the corridor toward Ronces and Alory's chamber. He'd almost wakened Golde to apologize for his rude behavior, but then changed his mind.

Nay, he admitted. 'Twas more than that. He wished nothing more at the moment than to hear her soothing tone. To lay his weary head on a pillow beside her and drown in the husky timbre of her voice.

Upon entering the boys' chamber, he paused, his desire for peace further strained. Ronces and Alory were not in their bed, but sleeping on Gavarnie's pallet on the floor. Nicolette had returned to her own bedchamber.

His shoulders slumped and he crossed to the bed. Not once in the past two weeks had his sons offered him such comfort as they did now. He'd been forced to share the small pallet with Nicolette, who hogged what little space there was.

That his children would be so gracious this night was like a slap in the face. He needed their warmth and affection, their bickering and endless fidgeting, not the cold spaciousness of a lonely bed.

Anything that cannot be beaten to submission is beyond you. Golde's words returned to accuse him as he undressed.

Had his mean disposition beaten his children into submitting their bed for his use?

He winced, and doused the lamp. 'Twas time and past he approached Golde to discover what his children knew of their mother's demise. He had let the matter slide since the attack, foremost because he had little faith in Golde. He'd also been preoccupied with his thoughts on assassination.

Climbing into bed, he flopped on his back.

Truth tell, he'd been so overjoyed to see his children again, so overcome with the changes wrought in their features in three short months, he had wished to do nothing that might spoil his pleasure.

Now that he thought on it, though, were not Ronces' dark eyes tinged with a brittleness he'd never seen before? Was Alory's smile a little less carefree? And what of Nicolette? She seemed much older than her five years.

He could avoid the evidence no longer. As careful as he had been to conceal the truth from his children, he'd been a fool to think they would not hear rumors in a castle filled with gossip.

He grimaced. What was he to say to them? *Yea, I murdered your mother, but though I despised her, 'twas not done a'purpose.*

Or, *My apologies, dearlings, but your mother was a slut and richly deserved her fate.*

He scowled. 'Od rot his soul to hell. When said thus, it did not sound as if Isabelle were at fault. It sounded as if he were the murderer he was.

He gritted his teeth. Why had he not sent Isabelle away those two years ago when she'd confessed that Nicolette was not his?

Because, he answered himself, he'd enjoyed punishing her. Aye, it had been balm to his battered pride to make her suffer.

How inconsequential her infidelity seemed now, compared to the misery he'd heaped on his children. He'd never loved Isabelle, nor she him. They'd been married for purposes of familial alliance. Isabelle was not the first woman to follow her heart outside the marriage bed, as he well knew. Had he not taken advantage of a host of dissatisfied wives during his days at court?

And what of Golde?

Sperville's insistance on torturing her had accomplished in one stroke what endless argument could never have achieved. It had made him think there was a possibility that Golde was not a part of the king's plan to have him assassinated.

Would that it were so. After all, he had been completely wrong in his suspicions of Golde where his children were concerned.

Locking his fingers together, he moved his hands behind his head and stared toward the ceiling. Indeed,

Golde's actions were most peculiar at times for an assassin.

What were those heated looks she cast his way each day when he came to bathe? She did not know he could see, yet it was as if she could not take her eyes from him. And that nonsense of how pockmarks suited him . . . 'twas absurd. To listen to her, one would think she found him attractive.

Nay. He dashed his hopes before they could bear fruit. Golde's remarks on his looks were meant only to flatter, to lull him into a false sense of security.

Because God knew, in all other matters, she was incapable of doing aught but bedeviling him. Indeed, the wench would drive a saint to do . . .

Murder.

The thought chilled his very bones.

Hands locked behind his head, he brought his elbows up and pressed the insides of his forearms against his temples.

He'd kept the blood-weltering memory at bay for so long . . .

Aye. He'd murdered Isabelle.

It had been during the late spring tourney at Atherbrook. Then, as now, Skyenvic had hosted the guests that could not be accommodated there.

What had he and Isabelle quarreled over that eve? Had it been something of eminent import? Or had Isabelle nettled him over something as insignificant as the length of his toenails?

His throat grew constricted. He would never know.

One moment he'd been sitting in the hall pouring mead down his gullet. The next, he'd awoken in bed beside her mutilated corpse.

He'd stumbled from the bed then, desperate to escape

the blood that smeared Isabelle, the blood that soaked the sheets, the blood that covered his hands.

At the memory, bile rose to scald his throat. He dragged his hands from behind his head and ground his fists against his temples. He must not think of it.

He must not . . .

By the Blessed Virgin, how could he have done such a thing? In all his years on the battlefield, never had he smelled the stench of death so strongly as he had in his bed that morn. Its sticky sweetness had oozed into his nostrils like yellow pus.

Despite the innumerable times he'd seen men torn limb from limb and heads split wide, never had he witnessed such carnage as that he had wrought on Isabelle.

His heart tumbled sickly in his chest as his inward eye traveled over every wound.

He'd stumbled from the bed all right. But in his haste, he'd slipped and cracked his head against a bedpost.

Lights had sparked before his eyes, and he'd squeezed them shut. Then there'd been a pounding at the door. Only, when he'd opened his eyes to answer it, he could no longer see.

Abruptly he jerked himself to sit upright. Golde. For no reason, her image flashed before him, her raven hair swirling about her all-knowing eyes. The night-soft hush of her voice whispered in his head.

Was it reckoning he heard in her husky murmur, or redemption?

Unable to bear his thoughts, he rose and dressed, then quietly let himself from the room.

He would confront Golde now with his suspicions of her. Determine once and for all . . .

Anything that cannot be beaten to submission is beyond you.

His hand stilled on the door latch outside his bedchamber.

Though his suspicions of Golde were not unfounded, considering what she knew of him would she not view his murder with some sense of justification?

If the king were to command him to kill a man who'd murdered his wife, and appeared to be a threat to his own children—never mind that he was also a threat to England—Gavarnie knew he would have few qualms about carrying out the order. More the better if William were to reward him handsomely for the deed.

Removing his hand from the latch, he stared at his shadow where it played on the door from the rushlight behind him.

When considered thus, Golde did not seem at all deceitful. Rather, for a woman to brave the perils of dealing with such a man seemed courageous.

And if he were to describe Golde, courageous would be foremost among his praises. Along with clever.

In a world where women were completely dependent upon men, she depended on none. Should blindness afflict her, doubtless it would never get the best of her. Indeed, the pale priest of death likely dreaded the day he would have to fetch her.

But while only God could bestow such blessings as courage and cleverness upon a woman, 'twas only the devil who could make her so desirable.

Tugging at the crotch of his braies, he adjusted his *coillons*. Faith, but he'd never suffered such constant torment from unslaked lust. Spying on Golde during her bath earlier had been but a continuation of torture for him. How many days had he carried her to and from the tub in his chamber while her ribs healed? Four?

Four days of warm, moist flesh. Four days of long, sleek legs and tender bottom. Four days of piquant breasts that begged to be tasted. He'd forgotten the beauty of dusky-hued nipples.

Licking his lips, he grasped the latch again.

Nineteen

At the dull tread of boots ascending the stairs, Gavarnie jerked his hand from the latch and turned.

"Mi'lord?" Roland queried as he reached the landing. "Is there aught that you require?"

A pox on the squire for disturbing him. He scowled and stepped back from the door. "Why are you yet awake?"

"I have only just finished cleaning your armor, sir."

The youth's words pricked his inwit. He had not given a thought to the difficulty of scrubbing pig slop from the small threads of chain mail.

He cleared his throat. "Take your ease, Roland. I was just going to bed."

Turning, he made his way back to the boys' chamber, where he again undressed and lay down on his back.

'Twas a fitful sleep that finally claimed him, filled with friends who turned to enemies on crimson battle-fields.

❧❦❧❦

ARISING TO THE GRAY LIGHT of dawn did little to cheer him, though he could see no help for what he must do.

Until he spoke with Golde concerning what the children had said about Isabelle's death, he would know no peace.

Dressing quickly, he crept from the boys' chamber to wake Roland where the squire slept outside the door.

"I shall breakfast with mistress," he informed the yawning squire. "Have a meal brought up for us."

The youth scurried off, and Gavarnie gathered his courage. After knocking twice and receiving no response, he pushed the door open. He found Golde, not in bed asleep, but standing before the window.

A pox on the wench. Why was she already dressed? He jerked his gaze from her back as she turned to face him.

Masking his irritation, he made his way to the bed with what he hoped was his usual blind deliberation. He felt his way around the mattress and sat on the edge of the bed, then pretended to reach for her.

"Mistress?" he queried softly when it became obvious he could not find her.

She did not respond for several moments, and he kept his gaze glued to the empty bed. 'Twas almost as if she were testing him.

"Here," she said at last, and he moved his gaze to fix on her.

His breath caught at her exhausted appearance. Dark half-moons hung beneath her eyes, lending an eerie luminance to their black and green colors. Like a flame that had burned itself out, leaving naught but glowing embers in its wake. The flesh beneath her cheeks looked hollow, while her colorless lips were drawn in a thin line.

He inclined his head, hoping that his face did not betray his shock at her appearance. "You are up so soon?"

She stared hard into his eyes, and he had trouble keeping his gaze blank.

"To what do I owe the pleasure of your company at such an early hour?" Her tone was cold enough to freeze fire.

"I've ordered a meal brought to us in hopes that we might talk," he offered meekly.

Her nostrils flared and she sneered. "We could easily have talked yesterday."

"Your forgiveness for my rude behavior. I had important—"

"Matters to attend," she interrupted. "Well, let us not waste your valuable time, sir. Of what do you wish to speak?"

Chagrined by his own words, which rang of overblown self-importance even to his ears, he tried a different tack. "You do not loo—er, you sound disgruntled this morn. Other than the honey mischief, did all go well in my absence?"

Now she glared at him. "Quite. You may have your chamber back. I shall return to Nicolette's room."

A knock sounded at the door. At his bidding, Roland and two serving boys entered carrying baskets, pitchers, and trays.

"Will you join me, or shall I eat alone?" he asked.

She inclined her head. "You are certain you have time?"

His patience began to erode. "Have I not said as much? Come and sit."

Stone-faced, she strode to the bed and sat stiffly on the side opposite him. Roland placed linen cloths on their laps and passed a water bowl, that they could clean their hands. Then the squire poured them each a cup of ale and placed the bread in front of Gavarnie.

"Shall I serve you, mi'lord?" he asked.

"Nay. Leave us."

He waited for Roland and the servants to clear the room, then reached for the bread. Its steaming, yeasty smell did nothing for his appetite, which had suddenly vanished. Careful to keep his eyes lowered, he broke a piece from the loaf and held it out.

"I find I have little desire for food," Golde said.

He allowed his gaze to travel to her face. "What must I do for you to accept my apology? Prostrate myself and kiss you toes? I did not mean to be abrupt yesterday, and I will admit that my excuse sounds full of bull's wind. Truth tell, I was overtired after the hard ride from the king's reception."

"Then why did you not wait until this morn to return, as you'd planned?"

He opened his mouth to speak, but she beat him to it. "Important matters to attend," she whined.

"Aye," he growled. "And I would not have to ride around in the dead of night were it not for the precautions I must take to ensure against another attack."

If she had been angry before, she fair seethed now. "You are a fool to take such risks. Think you any matters are more important than your life?"

"What would you suggest?" he returned hotly.

"Should I clothe myself in full armor day and night? Lock myself in my chambers? Mayhap I should surround myself at all times with a contingent of liegemen."

He crossed his arms over his chest. "'Twould be dimwitted, I suppose, to attempt to determine who is conspiring against me, that I might rid the earth of their wretched hides."

Abruptly her features crumpled and she turned away.

Christ's bones! She made him feel lower than a worm's belly. And he had done naught.

He took a deep breath, prepared to command her to wipe the broken look from her face, then clamped his teeth together. Witless get of an idiot. He was supposed to be blind. But God's blood, her actions were becoming more annoying by the moment.

Careful to speak evenly, he inquired, "What is this sudden concern for my welfare?"

She glanced around, and he froze at the naked despair mirrored in her eyes. He ordered his features to remain blank, to show no hint of shock, while his thoughts scrambled to make sense of her misery. She could not possibly summon such a bleak look on command. 'Twas as if death had claimed her closest kin.

Ignoring his question about her feelings for his welfare, she asked, "Did you not wish to speak with me?"

It sounded as if she were about to cry, so low and husky was her voice.

"'Tis not so important it cannot wait," he mumbled, unable to ask any questions that might further disturb her.

"Then, by your leave." She rose and headed for the door.

"A moment," he called, anxious for her to stay a

little longer. "Are you not interested in the events at Atherbrook?"

She did not break stride. "Perhaps some other time."

"You do not wish to hear how John, the Mad Breton, entertained us?"

She paused at the door and he hurried on, unaccountably desperate to cheer her. "It seems his wife had flown into a rage when he'd danced with a serving wench the night before. She'd thrown his clothing out the window of the second-floor hall and refused to fetch them for him the next day. You can imagine her embarrassment when he took his seat for dinner, wearing not a stitch, remarking on how drafty he found the king's castle."

She glanced over her shoulder and gave a smile, but 'twas so brittle he feared her lips might crack.

"Mistress, if you please," he persisted when she opened the door. "I can see—tell you are distraught by your tone. What is amiss?"

Though her back was to him, he saw her raise a hand and swipe at her face.

"Nothing." 'Twas almost a gasp.

"There is one matter of pressing importance."

Several moments passed before she slowly turned around and he saw resignation writ in her red-rimmed eyes. "Yes?" She made no move to come away from the door.

"I intended to ask ere now, but what with your injuries and all, it did not seem the best time."

Her eyes grew lifeless, as did her tone. "If 'tis pressing, then I am at your service."

Dread billowed in his gut and he took a deep breath. The time had come.

"Kindly recount for me, if you would, what my children told you concerning . . . their mother."

She blinked, then surprise flashed across her face. Apprehension followed in its wake. "You would not hurt them for telling tales out of turn?"

For a moment he stared at her. She must think him a monster to ask such. He fought the inexplicable pain her words wrought. Why should it matter what she thought? "I ask, that I may remedy the damage they have suffered."

GOLDE SWALLOWED HARD. She'd expected Gavarnie to hurl accusations at her, not ask after his children. She quickly relayed all she knew, anxious to be gone.

"As near as I can tell," she concluded, "Alory fears de Warrenne will spirit you away, and he will never see you again."

'Twas a dread of loss to which she could relate. Sperville would soon be seeing her to Atherbrook, and she would never see Gavarnie again.

"I have no doubt of your children's love for you," she couldn't help but add. "'Twill work in your favor when you speak with them."

There. She'd finished. She locked her trembling knees lest she collapse in a weeping heap. Though all she need do was turn and cross the threshold, she could not bring herself to leave. Gavarnie sat in brooding silence, still holding the piece of bread he'd torn from the loaf. Not once had he interrupted her with questions.

Why did he not defend himself? Tell her he'd not killed his wife? 'Twas what she longed to hear. Indeed, she prayed he would tell her it was all a mistake. A vast, ugly lie.

A muscle twitched in his jaw, an indication of his

anger. Doubtless, he was busy casting aspersions against himself with no consideration for the many hours he'd spent caring for his children. 'Twas far more than most lords of the realm. Still, he said naught, just sat there, his face growing more swarthy with each passing moment.

"Mi'lord?" she queried softly.

At last he balled the bread in his fist and flung it against the wall. He rose to stride toward her, black death in his eyes.

"I can scarce credit that my children would say all this to you, when they have said nothing to me, or anyone else."

Golde backed toward the corridor, feeling behind her for the door frame. Plague take her stupidity. She'd grown so accustomed to the charming Gavarnie, she'd forgotten his savage temper.

She spun and ran, scarce clearing three steps before he was upon her. Dragging her back inside the room, he pinned her against the wall beside one of the strange tapestries.

"'Twas you, and none other, who filled my children's heads with such vicious tales."

She started to struggle, to kick at his shins, then halted. 'Twas useless to pit her strength against his. 'Twould only fuel his fury.

She stared into his face. Darkened with heated blood, his jet eyes glowed like jewels in the midst of a fiery forge. Eyes that could see, but were blind to reason. Doubtless, he'd killed his wife while in just such a rage.

Drawing rein on the panic that threatened to overwhelm her, she forced an even tone. "Why would I tell your children such vicious tales?"

"Ha! You seek to poison my entire world with your scheming, deceitful tongue."

She already knew exactly what he thought of her. Had heard it from his own lips yesterday. His words should not have the same cruel power as they had then, but she felt anew as if her soul were being ripped from her chest.

Tears welled in her eyes, and she could not conceal the ragged disillusionment in her voice. "How think you I would gain such information?"

"You are most adept at gaining all you desire," he spat.

Her temper flared. 'Od rot the mean-hearted mucker. For once in her life, she'd placed another's needs before her own. And this was her payment? He spoke of her as if she were some baseborn slut.

Her hand shot up to grip his grizzled chin. "Unholy bastard. You rant and rave like a demented demon, then wonder why your children say nothing to you? You brag before an entire village how you murdered their mother, but the deed has filled you to bursting with poison. Every time you open your mouth, it spews forth. Why do you think you lost your sight?"

The enraged look on his face appeared to collapse in upon itself.

She dug her fingers in his hard jaw to be certain she held his attention. "You have had a fortnight and more to ask your children what they told me. Instead, you come to me for answers, then seek to place the blame for their worries everywhere but where it belongs. And that is with yourself."

His gaze solidified to frozen black emptiness. Dropping his hands, he stepped back.

"You are right, of course." His voice was flat and spent. "My thanks for bringing the truth to my attention.

Now, if you will, excuse me. I shall bathe, then set matters to rights with my children."

At his deadened response, concern absorbed her anger. Had she pushed him to the brink of madness?

"Mi'lord, I did not mean—"

"If you would locate Roland and send him to me, I would be grateful." He turned his back on her.

She pursed her lips. He'd directed his rage inward. Should she try to ease the self-loathing he obviously felt? She studied his rigid back.

Nay, she had brought his weaknesses to his attention. She turned and slipped from the room. He'd recognized the truth of her words, and someday he would truly be grateful.

Tears blinded her as she headed for the stairs. She'd lost him, irrevocably. Despite the fact he did not trust her, indeed, was convinced she was naught but a conniving slut, there had remained in her heart the small hope that she could convince him otherwise. 'Twould do her no good now.

Aye, he would appreciate her insight. But he would never be able to forgive her for it. He was far too proud.

She descended the steps, wiping her eyes. She must locate Sperville, that they could take immediate leave. The sooner she was gone from Skyenvic, the better she would feel.

TWENTY

GAVARNIE RESTED a booted heel on the lower slat of the pig pen. "Why did you say nothing until now?" he asked the swineherd.

"The witch-woman told me if I said aught, me seed would dry up and me shaft would wither 'til I had nothin' to piss with."

Nigel coughed, and Gavarnie hooked his thumbs in his sword belt while studying the ground. Humorous as Golde's threats were, he could find no pleasure in them. Not now.

Three days had passed since she'd disappeared, and never had he felt such misery. 'Twas worse than the first day of her absence, when he'd feared she'd gone to back to New Market.

He returned his attention to the swineherd. "She

gave you the coin to keep, regardless of the sow's condition?"

"Aye. But like I said, I can't be keepin' it. Not after what she done. Who would o' thought?"

The swineherd's gaze traveled to the sow where she lay on her side, suckling her litter. "A dozen and seven," he breathed reverently. "I'll wager there arn't another sow in the land wot's had so many."

Who would have thought, indeed. Gavarnie eyed the swineherd. For a peasant to surrender coin without being asked was a miracle unto itself.

"What is it you would have me do with this?" He gestured with the two silver pieces the man had pressed on him.

"Ye must give it back to the witch-woman, lest me good fortune turns bad. Would have done it meself, but she arn't been around."

"Why would she give it to you in the first place?" Nigel demanded impatiently.

Abruptly the swineherd's eyes shifted. "I—I—because I wouldn't let her in the pen to tend the pig."

The steward raised a brow. "What is this slop you attempt to feed us? The woman just happens to find the sow with a great splinter in her hind, then pays you to allow her to tend it? Come, my grimy friend. Let us have the truth."

Ronces' thin voice interrupted before the swineherd could reply. "'Twas no splinter. It was an arrow, shot from my bow."

Gavarnie spun to face his son where he stood flanked by Alory and Nicolette. The three regarded him with a mix of looks. Alory appeared fearful, though determined. Nicolette's small, square jaw jutted defiantly. Ronces' features displayed the resignation of a sick old man who knew he was about to die.

"You shot the pig?" Gavarnie asked.

"It was an accident," Alory offered.

Nicolette added, "We dared him to shoot the awwow, but not the pig."

Gavarnie scowled. "You are not allowed to use your bow unless . . ."

It struck him then. Golde had not forced the children to help her with the pig, as she'd claimed. 'Twas the other way around.

A sinking feeling pooled in his belly. "How did you convince Golde to aid you after pouring honey all over her?"

"We put dung in her boots, too," Alory said, lowering his head.

"Nicolette got her to help," Ronces intoned.

"She is a good witch, and she is gone 'cause of us." Misery claimed Nicolette's features.

Gavarnie felt his face flush, though whether it was from anger or chagrin, he wasn't certain. Without question, his children should be punished for their misdeeds. Yet he could scarce justify doing so. Their actions paled in comparison to his.

What a pompous thickwit he'd been. Accusing Golde of trickery with his children when she'd sought only to help.

"Is it true, Papa?" Alory pulled him from his thoughts.

Gavarnie sighed bitterly. "Is what true?"

"Can you see?"

Anger tore through Gavarnie, and he planted his fists on his hips. Despite his careful plans for keeping his sight secret, someone had informed his children.

Sperville, no doubt. Not only had the presumptuous chamberlain helped Golde reach Atherbrook, he'd told his children he could see. To think he'd only assigned the meddlesome dolt to cleaning the wardrobe these two days past. He should have made him muck the sheep pens.

"Where did you hear such?" he asked at last.

"'Tis being whispered all over the castle," Ronces answered. "Is it true? Can you see?"

Gavarnie gritted his teeth. "Aye."

"I tole you," Nicolette snapped. "The witch healed his sight."

Ronces eyed him with disbelief. "Why didn't you tell us? Do you not trust us?" He sounded betrayed.

"Of course I trust you. 'Tis just . . ."

His words trailed away as he realized the swineherd was listening. Whore's gleet. If the entire castle did not know of his sight already, they would now.

He turned to Nigel. "Fetch Sperville and meet me in my chambers."

He started forward to gather the children, but Alory scrambled from his reach.

"Is it also true what everyone says about Mamma? Did you kill her?"

Gavarnie halted in his tracks. Words deserted him. He could do naught but watch as a terrible battle between hope and loathing played across Alory's chubby features. *Tell me, Papa. Tell me you did not do it.* His youngest son's upturned face implored him.

Nigel moved quickly to capture the boy. "All of you, come with me," the steward ordered.

Nicolette held her ground. "Is it twue that you awe not my fathew? Is that why you killed Mamma?"

"Come on, Nicolette." Ronces grabbed her arm and dragged her backward.

"The night you tole us what the witch said," Nicolette taunted, "when I was sitting on your lap. I was the one who lied. Ever'thing the witch tole you was twue."

With that, she turned and followed Nigel toward the great hall, casting accusing looks over her shoulder.

And still, Gavarnie could not move. He'd known for some time that Golde had spoken the truth, and 'twas not that which mattered to him now. Nay. 'Twas the fact that Nicolette was deliberately trying to hurt him that clawed at his soul.

To what purpose did he live? Isabelle dead by his hand. His children's thinking torn and bloodied as surely as if he'd taken a blade to their heads.

And Golde. Only three days gone, yet it seemed an eternity.

He'd not yet had a chance to speak with the children about Isabelle. He'd spent the first day of Golde's disappearance searching for her, fearing that if she'd gone to New Market, the villagers would kill her. Indeed, when he'd been unable to locate her, he'd grown frantic.

'Twas then that Sperville had confessed his misdeeds. "She was in the wardrobe during our conversation. She was determined to leave, and I thought it best to see her to Atherbrook, where she would be safe."

Gavarnie kicked a clod of dirt and attempted to recreate the rage he'd experienced at the chamberlain's admission. Anything to save himself from thinking. But all he could recall were Sperville's other words.

She is in love with you. Imagine how she felt upon hearing your talk of her. 'A conniving slut. An agent of the king.'

The chamberlain had then gone on to tell him everything he knew of Golde. *She is Celt, not Saxon, and the last in a long line of great mystics. Rather than develop her real abilities, Golde practices all manner of deception, which dis-*

*turbs her great-grandmother to no end. While money was her
reason for coming here, 'twas not any coin she would receive
from William. Rather, her intent was to trick you into paying
her.*

Before Gavarnie could demand why the chamberlain
would bring such a woman into Skyenvic, Sperville had
continued. *The old woman wished to teach Golde a lesson
and promised to heal your sight, provided I brought Golde
here. It seemed a good bargain.*

Aye, Gavarnie mused, stubbing his boot toe in the
dirt. He should be angry. Angry enough to kill the chamberlain. Not only did Golde know his thoughts concerning her and the king, she was also aware of his idea to
align himself with the Danes.

Yet she'd apparently told no one. Had she done so, he
would currently be standing before the king's execu-
tioner.

Instead of rage, a forlorn and desolate loneliness
clutched at his heart. He stilled, and gazed out over the
bailey.

Would life be worth living if he were to discover
beyond doubt that the king was against him? 'Twas scarce
worth living at present, and would be less so in the future
without Golde.

He scowled. Worst of all, he supposed he would now
have to admit he'd been wrong and apologize to Spindleshanks.

TWENTY-ONE

❦❦❦

THE CLANGOR of a hundred royal guests and
their servants reverberated with ferocity from the interior
of Atherbrook's gray stone walls. And the lords and ladies
camped at Skyenvic had yet to arrive. Positioned between
Sir Varin and his giant underlord, Arnulf, Golde stared at
the oysters piled high on her trencher.

She could not have refused Varin's offer to dine with
him and Arnulf, especially when he'd gone to the trouble
of making arrangements for her seating. But her stomach
roiled at the thought of food. Instead, she sipped upon
the king's fine wine, her second full goblet.

Four days had passed since the clever Spindleshanks
had spirited her away from Skyenvic, right beneath
Gavarnie's nose. Dressed like a man, she'd walked
through the gates in the direction of New Market. Meanwhile, the chamberlain had saddled a mount and followed

her on the pretext of fetching more salt from the village. They'd met on the road, where they'd changed direction and headed for Atherbrook.

"The oysters are not to your liking?" Sir Varin's deep voice pulled her from her thoughts.

She gave him her attention, affecting a bright smile. "My stomach has been a bit unsettled of late, but this wine is proving quite the tonic."

The concern in Varin's blue eyes melted, and a wicked grin lit his tanned countenance. "Mayhap your time at Skyenvic was spent in quarters too close to Sir Gavarnie."

He winked over her head at Arnulf, his rough tone loud enough to split the wooden beams overhead. "Those blind bastards must e're grope about for purchase. 'Twould not surprise me in the least to hear you are expecting—"

Varin gasped when she drove her elbow in his ribs. "'Twould seem to me," she summoned a haughty tone, "that were a tournament held for groping, you would be the winner, mi'lord lecher. Five babes in seven years, is it not? Poor Roscelyn must run screaming at your very approach."

Arnulf's laughter trilled beside her, unbelievably high and sweet for a man so large. The sound was grating with the intensity of its good cheer.

Varin snorted. "'Tis I who suffer Roscelyn's groping. She cannot keep her hands from me."

Inexplicably, his good-natured banter left Golde feeling weepy. Clinging to her teasing mien, she rolled her eyes. "I was present during each of your children's births, save this last. As I recall, Roscelyn requested a blade with each delivery that she could slit you throat to groin."

Arnulf fair strangled on his merriment.

Varin scowled at the redhaired giant. "I wonder if you recall what yon ox's wife said at the birth of his son?"

A squire refilled her goblet and Golde drained it, hoping to ease the sudden constriction in her throat. "I believe she requested a potion from Mimskin that would induce violent cramping, that Arnulf might experience the thrill of childbirth."

Golde's spirits sank at the loud guffaws that erupted from Varin.

Why could Gavarnie not love her the way Varin and Arnulf loved their wives?

Because you are fearsome to look upon.

Even as she thought it, she studied Arnulf's mirth-filled face. Never had God created an uglier man. His red hair sprouted in every direction, his nose had suffered numerous clubbings, and his forehead was furrowed with scars. Yet his wife, Dunne, worshipped him, regardless of her spiteful words during childbirth.

Golde returned her gaze to the oysters before her. Who would not love the overgrown Arnulf? He was as gentle as he was fierce. He loved children, even those who were not his. He was courageous and honorable, and possessed the patience of a saint.

All virtues, none to which she could lay claim, she thought morosely. 'Twas not her looks that frightened Gavarnie, as if aught could scare the miserable cur.

Nay. Rather, he found her lacking in all things decent.

Abruptly she rose from the table. "If you will excuse me, sirs." She struggled for levity. "Our immediate vicinity suddenly seems to reek of bull's wind. If I do not take some fresh air, I will surely be overcome."

Varin's brows swooped down. "You are truly ill," he accused, his gaze worrying over her features. "You grow more wan with each passing day. Let us all retire, that you may rest."

He half rose from the bench before she placed a restraining hand on his shoulder. "Take your ease, mi'lord." It required every bit of will to plaster a smile on her lips. "'Tis but my way of saying I must visit the latrine."

"Why did you not say so?" he boomed, relaxing.

She heaved an exasperated sigh. "I'd hoped to be discreet."

"Oh." Varin looked chagrined, while Arnulf clutched his belly and tittered.

Simpletons, she thought, turning her back and heading toward the open entrance to the hall. *Let us all retire, that you may rest.* The last thing she needed was to sit in Varin's tent and listen to him and Arnulf sing their wives' praises. 'Twould do naught but remind her of her own shortcomings.

Her steps slowed as harried servants rushed around her to attend their lords' shouted demands.

If she could not abide hearing such avowals of devotion from Varin and Arnulf now, how would she manage once she was home? Surrounded by families, seeing Roscelyn and her new babe, watching Arnulf and the village children. All would be reminders of what she could not have, would never have.

Her shoulders slumped and she bowed her head. Gladly would she give her life to hear Gavarnie say he loved her. And though she would deny it to her dying breath, 'twould be immensely pleasurable to hear Ronces claim affection for her. Not that he ever would. Nor would Nicolette, the little curmudgeon. But Alory. There was a kindred soul. She could see it in his dreamy features.

However would Gavarnie manage the three little imps with no woman about to help?

As she neared the hall's entrance, a high-pitched squeal disrupted her thoughts. A greasy-haired woman tumbled from a bench directly into her path. Golde swerved to avoid the wench, a baud from the looks of her.

Without warning, she collided with a servant bearing a tray. Down she went, sprawling over the baud. The tray of oysters landed on her head.

Laughter rang about her as she scrambled to her feet. Swiping slimy lumps from her hair, she glared at the woman.

The wench's painted mouth rounded and she scooted backward, much like a crab. Clambering to her feet, she crossed herself and fled.

Only one man continued to laugh, and Golde stabbed him with her best demon-eyed look. "'Twould serve you well to cease your cackling, lest you find yourself keeping company with the devil."

Two other whores sat with the man, one upon his lap. Both took a sudden interest in the table before them, avoiding her gaze.

Not so the man. He tilted his head back and cast her a bleary grin. "'Tis hell-bound I am, pretty hag. If you can expedite matters, I shall put in a good word to Satan on your behalf."

'Twas clear from the man's seating nearest the doors that he held little favor with the king. His ginger-colored hair was unkempt and frosted with gray, while his freckled countenance was florid.

But 'twas not that which held Golde spellbound.

Nay. It was his eyes. Rimmed by red, but gray all the same.

She studied him. He was much changed, thinned by

worthlessness, worn with debauchery. But she knew him as well as she knew the sun would rise, or that the stars had once shone upon two lovers on a dark, secret moor.

Abruptly she sneered. "Poor, unfortunate wretch. 'Tis a pity how you are forced to gorge yourself on fine drink and food. How miserable to abide in royal accommodations with three women to appease your desires."

Unaccountably, tears stung her eyes. But they did naught to stop her tirade. On the contrary, they lent it impetus.

"Mayhap you would prefer a drafty hovel and cold floor to sleep upon. Mayhap 'twould be your pleasure to work at mean tasks the entire day long while suffering all manner of cruel invective. Mayhap you would enjoy going to your rest hungry and alone."

In the silence that suddenly descended over the immediate surroundings, she hissed, "Mayhap you should visit your *son*. His name is Lull. He lives in New Market and knows all about hell."

Her vision had grown so blurred with tears, she could scarce make out the selfish lord's features. Blinking, she turned and hurried toward the open doors. She did not reach the threshold before a hand clamped over her shoulder and spun her about.

Shoving her backward against the wall, the lord flourished his carving blade in her face. "Think you to frighten me, witch? I have wrestled with demons far more powerful than you."

He leaned in close and pressed the knife to her throat. "Mayhap it is time I dispatched one of your unholy kind to your infernal maker."

She winced, not at the threat, but at the sight of Varin and Arnulf bearing down on the bellicose lord. Heedless of the blade's sharp edge, she bobbed her head and swiped at her eyes. 'Twould be the final humiliation for her two friends to discover she cried.

The lord misinterpreted her actions. "Ho, not so free with your hell-borne tongue when your life is at stake."

"Do you seek to have me killed, Hugh?" Varin thundered merrily, clasping the lord's arm and forcing it down.

"What?" The lord swiveled his head about and looked up, for Varin topped his height by half a head.

"De Brionne!" He grinned happily. "And Arnulf. I shall attend you shortly, once I have killed this brazen devil's spawn."

Golde smothered a sniffle and concentrated on preventing new tears from seeping into her eyes.

"I cannot allow it, Hugh." Varin waved a hand. "Mean-tempered as she is, she is my wife's dearest friend. Roscelyn would have my head if aught befell her."

"She is with you?"

Varin nodded.

"But she has insulted me to my very toenails!"

"I doubt it not. Her tongue is more venomous than an adder's. Come. Let us sit and talk. It has been long since I last laid eyes on you."

"But—"

Varin wrapped an arm about the man's shoulder. "Faith, Hugh. If 'tis your wish to kill the wench come morn, then I shall see what can be done to accommodate you. For now, let us share some wine, that I can learn what has befallen your miserable hide. You look mangy as any cur."

Shaking his head, the lord grinned. "How could I refuse such a sweet offer?"

With that, Varin led him back to the table, and Arnulf took Golde's arm.

"You are all right?" the giant asked as he escorted her from the hall.

She nodded and managed several paces beyond the open doors before the torrent burst. Tears rushed from her eyes and sobs gushed from her chest.

"What is it?" Arnulf's voice rose to greater than normal heights. He clutched her waist and halted. "Are you hurt? Should I call for the king's physicians?"

She shook her head doggedly. "Mean-tempered. Venomous as an adder." Choking, she staggered forward, drawing Arnulf with her.

"Varin was but jesting," he soothed in the echoing darkness. "Why . . . he loves you like a sister."

"Nay," she gulped. "No one loves *meeee*." The last word sailed upward in a gusty wail.

Arnulf shrilled to be heard. "Of what do you speak? Cyning has not been the same since you left. Roscelyn bemoans your absence hourly. Your father wears a perpetual frown. Your great-grandmother is more sour than ever, and wanders about the day long, heaping curses on everyone's head. Even the shrew, Dorswyth, sings your praises. She has found a husband and claims 'twas all your doing."

"Oh, Arnulf, you are so *kiiind*."

Even as she blubbered, she told herself sternly that she must cease. What must Arnulf be thinking? If anyone behaved thus while in her company, she would spit in their eye and tell them to shut their whining mouths.

She took several deep breaths and managed in a trembling voice, "I can find my way to the tent. Go back to the hall and enjoy yourself."

"What, and miss my rest? It takes no little amount of sleep to maintain such beauty as mine. I would look my best for the tourney next week."

Sobs tore from her anew.

"What have I said now?" Arnulf again raised his voice to be heard.

"Would that I were as handsome as *youuu*!"

"Please, Golde. You have said naught that makes sense to my slow reasoning. Mayhap if you explain—"

"Can you not see how ugly I am?" She bawled like an ungainly cow. "I hate children. I feed on people's frailties. I'm a deceitful thimblerigger and—and—" She sniffled loudly. "And I smell worse than dead *fiish*!"

Arnulf loosened his grip about her waist and patted her back. "There, there. You are . . . overwrought. Aye," he said, as if convincing himself. "Overwrought. A good night's sleep will set matters to right."

A good night's sleep! She near strangled on the emptiness that billowed in her chest. She hadn't slept in a week. Gavarnie did not love her. Could not abide her. Heavenly hosts could herald her innocence, and still he would not trust her.

Pools of yellow light flooded the area around the castle gates, and she did her best to stifle her lamentations. She did not wish to embarrass Arnulf before the guards who stood attendance. But once they were through the gates, she again dissolved in a weeping fit.

By the time they reached the tent, her body felt spent and pithless. Arnulf waited outside while she lit a lamp and stripped off her damp, fishy clothing. Cold water from a bucket provided some relief for her hot, swollen eyes, but a bath would have to wait 'til morn. Falling on a pallet that Varin's squire had donated for her use, she pulled a cover over herself.

"I am finished," she called to Arnulf.

Though the tent was quite large, it was not near big enough to accommodate the giant's height, and he had to stoop when he entered. "Do you need aught?"

"Nay." She stared at the yellow-brown oilskin of the tent overhead.

"If all is well, then, I shall take the lamp and await Varin outside."

Doubtless, he was anxious to avoid her company. Tears again welled in her eyes, and she wondered sourly if they might spring eternal.

"Arnulf?" She stopped him before he got through the tent flap.

"Aye?"

"My thanks. You have been a good friend this night."

He did not turn around. "You have e're been a good friend to me."

The moment the flap closed behind him, the tears slipped down her temples. She did not deserve Arnulf's considerate regard. The stinking bastard. If he would cease being so nice, mayhap she could stop crying. Her nose was so clogged it felt as if an anvil were buried inside her head.

She rolled on her side and closed her burning eyes. Before God, she would not shed another tear. She would not think of . . .

Gavarnie's dark visage loomed behind her lids. His black eyes beheld her with loathing.

More tears.

'Twas bad enough that he did not trust her. Worse that he believed her a conniving slut. But neither could compare to the crushing void she felt at the thought of life without Gavarnie.

She covered her face to muffle her ragged cries. Would that she could hate him. Would that she could despise him. Would that she could cease thinking of him.

Abruptly her breath caught on a sniffle.

". . . do something," Arnulf whispered urgently from outside the tent.

"You exaggerate," Varin's low voice responded. "She is made of iron. I cannot imagine her crying thus."

"I tell you, she is completely undone."

"Did she say what troubled her?"

Wiping her eyes, Golde sat up, wrapping the covers about herself.

"She took exception to your calling her mean-tempered, and comparing her to a venomous snake."

"I have called her worse," Varin defended himself, "and she did naught but laugh. Indeed—"

Arnulf interrupted. "Then she went on to say how she was deceitful and hated children. She was most upset by how handsome I am—"

"Handsome!" Varin's voice rose. "You?"

"Shh. She is finally quiet. Do not get her started again."

"Handsome?" Varin hissed.

"It makes no sense to me, either. And the thing that distressed her most was that she smelled like dead fish."

"Fish?"

"From the oysters that were spilled on her. I did my best to soothe her, but my words only made her weep more."

For a moment all grew silent, and Golde held her breath. Arnulf must think her daft. She had not realized how moonstruck she'd sounded.

"Mayhap she drank too much wine," Varin offered.

Arnulf snorted. "Come. She has kept apace with us on more than one occasion."

More silence. Golde rubbed at her eyes and nose. Plague take Gavarnie Delamaure, Baron of Skyenvic.

How could one man cause such great misery in so short a time?

Varin spoke at last. "The only other explanation I can think of is . . ."

"Is what?" Arnulf urged.

"Nay. It could not be."

"What?"

"Think on it, my dullwitted friend. Have you ever seen your wife act thus?"

"Nay, praise the saints."

"Well I have seen Roscelyn behave in just such a manner, more than once. Five times to be exact."

Golde covered her mouth and her eyes rounded. Did Varin dare to imply—

"You are making no more sense than Golde," Arnulf groused.

"Each time Roscelyn conceived, she did naught but cry, for no reason a'tall."

Arnulf's tone conveyed no little hint of horror. "You mean Golde is—"

TWENTY-TWO

I AB NOD WID CHILD, dungheads." Though Golde strove for a haughty tone, her plugged nose ruined it.

Abruptly the tent flap parted and Varin entered, carrying the lamp. He, too, was unable to stand upright, though he did not have to slouch as much as Arnulf. "You are awake?"

"Who could sleep wid two bulls bellowink at the door? Do nod give me thad concerned look. I can cry wheneber it suits me."

"Of course you can. 'Tis just uncommon—I mean . . . For you, it is uncommon. I—" Suddenly his features grew harsh. "What has the Baron of Skyenvic done to you?"

Golde shook her head, afraid to speak lest she break down again.

"Do not deny it. He has committed some grave offense. I can see it in your eyes."

Her bottom lip quivered and she bowed her head.

"The worthless get of a snake. His blindness has stolen his wits. To think I agreed with your great-grandmother and sent you to the bastard."

"Neider you or Bimbskin could have known . . ."

Her words trailed off at the sheepish look that overcame Varin's countenance. "Whad have you and Bimbskin been about?" she demanded suspiciously.

"Nothing terrible." Varin held up his hands as if to show he had nothing to hide. "I'd heard of Gavarnie's troubles and asked your great-grandmother if she could help. When she said Gavarnie was the answer to her prayers, I contacted Sperville."

Rage near strangled Golde. She'd been duped, and by her own Mimskin. Just wait until she returned—

She narrowed her eyes and sniffed, her nose clearing a little. "Did Mimskin say whether or not Gavarnie had regained his sight?"

Varin nodded. "Aye. Said that not only could he see, his life was completely changed by your presence."

So, Golde thought. 'Twas Mimskin who'd cured Gavarnie's sight the night of the attack. She'd likely had to use her Mad Rye spell to heal Gavarnie from such a distance.

She glared at Varin. "Gavarnie was right. You indeed risk losing your wits each time you empty your bowels."

Varin blinked, then his nostrils flared and his features hardened. "He said that, after all I have done on his behalf?"

"He also believes you sent me to kill him."

"Wha—"

"The king has decided to rid himself of Gavarnie.

You are the king's agent in the affair, and by your order, I was sent to accomplish the deed."

Once she began, she could not stop. She told Varin everything that had occurred during her stay at Sky-envic—with the exception of her wanton behavior and Gavarnie's ridiculous notions concerning the Danes.

"So I am returned to you by Sperville's good hand," she finished.

Varin, his legs cramping, had long since taken a seat on the ground.

"Delamaure should be hung, the lowly coward. You say he admitted to killing his wife?"

"Admit it he may, but he did not do it."

She frowned the moment the words left her mouth. She'd felt his innocence in her bones that night when they'd been attacked. Yet she'd allowed self-doubt rule her intuition.

"Who—" Varin began.

Golde breathed deeply, then exhaled. "I do not know who murdered his wife. I only know it was not Gavarnie."

Varin gave her a look of strained patience. "Your forgiveness, but I fail to see your logic. Murderer or no, the man arouses public sentiment against you until you are nearly killed in an alehouse. I would not wish to be the bearer of that news to your great-grandmother. He abuses your good nature and treats you with naught but contempt. Yet you would defend him?"

She raised a brow. "You know better than any that there is little good in my nature. Gavarnie would have to be blind, deaf, and dull of wit not to notice such. Though he may have drawn the wrong conclusion concerning the king, 'twas not because of faulty reasoning. Someone murdered his wife, and is now trying to kill him."

"Well, it is not the king," Varin snapped. "Nor is it

you or me." He rose to stomp his feet, ducking when his head hit the tent top. "With the morn's first light, you and I shall proceed to Skyenvic and inform the dunderwit of his errors."

"There is not enough gold in all the world to make me return to that wretched place," she huffed. "Let us send the information by messenger and be done."

"Messenger!" Varin gave her a disbelieving look. "I will have the satisfaction of confronting the ill-mannered lout with his stupidity."

An image of Gavarnie and Varin locked in mortal combat struck Golde. "Nay!"

Realizing she'd shrieked, she immediately forced a more moderate tone. "If aught befell you, I would never forgive myself."

Varin gaped. "Think you the bumptious clod could take me?" Again his head hit the tent and he ducked. "Why, I would have him beaten before he could draw his blade!"

"Please! Gavarnie is the victim in all this, not you or me. 'Twas the murder of his wife that begat this entire sordid mess, and he has suffered the torments of hell."

"But he did not murder his wife?"

It was so clear, no amount of self-doubt could sway her belief. "You forget, I have developed the true gift of sight. And verily am I right in this."

Varin stared at her a long moment. Then a sly look slid over his features. "You love him."

Golde gasped. "I most certainly do not!"

A grin charged across his face. "So that is what all this moaning is about. You are in love. I never thought to see the day *you* would be humbled by such foolish sentiment."

Sitting up straighter, she drew the covers about her

shoulders as if she were donning royal robes. "I tell you, I have no feelings for the oaf, other than pity."

Varin chortled gleefully as if she hadn't said a word. "Poor Gavarnie. I'll wager he hasn't a clue. To think I was prepared to leap to your defense. 'Tis Gavarnie who needs aid, more than he can guess."

Golde's lip curled and she narrowed an eye. "You are worse than a cackling old hen. I do not love the man, and if you are not careful, I will see to it that Roscelyn has a blade to hand at the birth of your next child."

Her threats did naught but make the imbecile laugh harder. At last she threw herself back upon the pallet and rolled to her side, giving the merry fool her back. Faith, all men were dungheads.

Abruptly Varin's laughter ceased, and she heard the flap ruffle as he exited the tent. "Come, Arnulf. Let us return to the hall."

"But—"

"Golde needs some time alone for now."

Time alone? 'Twas the last thing she needed. Yet she could not bring herself to ask Varin and Arnulf to remain. Both men doubtless looked forward to escaping her miserable company.

Did Gavarnie feel the same? Was he glad that she'd taken leave of Skyenvic?

Her breath caught. Would he attend the tourney at Atherbrook, now that he could see? Might she have an opportunity to speak with him?

Why, oh why, had she allowed self-doubt to ruin her belief in Gavarnie's innocence? Had she trusted her feelings, her swevyn, she would have been more understanding and patient, more kind and gentle with Gavarnie. Then mayhap he would have grown to like her, if only a little.

But nay, she'd given her waspish tongue and sour disposition full rein. And she would suffer for it the remainder of her life.

Mimskin had indeed taught her a lesson, more than she could ever know.

❧❦☙

IT SEEMED HALF THE NIGHT would pass before Arnulf and Varin returned to settle themselves. And though Golde had not thought it possible, sleep she did; so heavily, that she did not realize what was happening until it was too late.

One moment she was dreaming. *Ye are a fool for leaving when ye could have him*, Mimskin was saying. *He loves ye.*

Before she could sigh wistfully, something was strapped over her mouth. By the time she managed to gather her slumber-dulled wits, she was already bound and gagged.

TWENTY-THREE

GAVARNIE SAT MOTIONLESS in the dragon-carved chair. After a sumptuous breakfast, most of the lords and ladies had hurried to their tents to prepare for the great exodus to Atherbrook.

He, too, should be preparing to leave for the king's castle. Though William did not expect him to participate in tomorrow's tourney, Gavarnie would be expected to attend the huge feast that would be held this eve.

But he could not seem to stir himself just yet. He stared at the distant oak doors, open to air the hall. No sunlight shone on the bailey beyond, for the day had dawned overcast and chill.

What would King William think if the guardian of the Solent did not appear? Would he notice? Or would he be too busy entertaining his newly favored barons?

Mayhap, at Golde's behest, Sir Varin de Brionne would be whispering in William's ear the reason for his absence.

No sooner was the thought complete than he blinked and sat up straighter in his chair. By the rood, but it appeared de Brionne was coming in through the doors— followed by his giant underlord, Arnulf. The few servants that remained in the hall froze midtask to ogle the ugly giant.

What in the name of all that was holy? The two were shouldering a huge rolled tapestry. Gavarnie rose, clutching the hilt of his sword.

"I will not have it," de Brionne announced as they drew to a halt at the foot of the dais. "I send you a gift and you dare to return it." He and Arnulf deposited their burden on the dais.

Gavarnie squinted at the frayed roll of faded yellow-gray material, uncaring whether or not the pair knew he could see. Faith, it stank worse than dead fish. "What trickery is this? I have never laid eyes on that flea-infested pile of offal."

De Brionne drew himself up as if he'd been slapped. "I will admit, 'tis a bit rough around the edges, but 'twas given with the best of intentions. A steady hand and thorough cleaning will do much to bring forth its worth."

Was the man serious? Gavarnie snorted. "The thing could be hung on a line and beat for a week, and it would yet be a useless heap of filth."

Gavarnie's gaze shifted as the chamberlain came through the screens passage. "Sperville. Come and confirm for his daftness here that we never received this *gift*. And if we had, we would never have returned it. We would have used it to keep the crows from our fields."

The chamberlain hurried forward, gaping. "Sir Varin! And Sir Arnulf. Come and take your ease." He gestured, indicating that the two should seat themselves upon the dais. "Wine," he commanded the nearest servant.

De Brionne shook his head and huffed, "We will not linger where we are not wanted. Faith, Arnulf. One would think we were lepers."

If Sir Varin had planned to empty the hall, he could have picked no better way to go about it. At his mention of the flesh-wasting disease, the servants quickly found tasks that would carry them from the room.

As if he hadn't noticed the peasants' departure, de Brionne continued to address the chamberlain. "First, the king seats us as far from himself as possible while entertaining the likes of de Warrenne. Then we are insulted by his rudeship here. Come, Arnulf. We will take ourselves off."

The two turned to leave, and Sperville shot Gavarnie a harried look that begged him to call them back. Gavarnie scowled. Judging from Sperville's behavior, one would think the two were royalty. Still, his curiosity was piqued.

"De Brionne," he snapped. "Come and have some wine."

Varin halted, then turned to face him. "We would not wish to impose ourselves on your hospitality." The satisfied note in his voice indicated the opposite sentiment. "But if you insist."

It seemed the man fair skipped up the dais steps, dragging Arnulf behind him. Doubtless, some heinous scheme accounted for the lowly cur's good cheer. Plopping on the bench beside Gavarnie's chair, Varin inclined his head. "Are you going to stand there looking sour, or will you join us?"

Gavarnie curled his lip and seated himself with great

deliberation. "What is your purpose in coming here? And do not pretend 'twas to deliver that sorry rag."

De Brionne affected a coy look worthy of the cheapest baud. "We have come to gossip."

Gavarnie hid his interest behind a smirk. "Gossip?"

Sperville hustled up the steps to deliver their wine, then positioned himself at Gavarnie's elbow. Varin took a hearty gulp and smacked his lips. "'Tis quite good, Arnulf. Do you not agree?"

The giant's cheeks bulged as he made a show of swishing the wine in his mouth. "Aye. It rivals the king's. Mayhap our host could send—"

"Get on with it, de Brionne," Gavarnie interrupted.

Abruptly Varin's teasing mien vanished and his features grew harsh, along with his tone. "Were I you, baron, I would endeavor to remain civil. 'Twould be much easier to kill you than try to convince that thick head of yours what is right."

Gavarnie slammed his fist on the table and rose. "Then let us have done. 'Twas your plan all along."

"Mi'lord!" Sperville pleaded, reaching out. "At least listen."

Gavarnie shook the chamberlain's hand from his shoulder. "Admit it, de Brionne. 'Twas you who perpetrated the ambush on me."

A muscle twitched in Varin's stubbled jaw. "You are an even greater idiot than Golde has relayed."

"So," he sneered, "the magpie has chattered."

"And more is the good fortune to you. Hear me out—then if 'tis yet your wish to draw swords, I will be most content to oblige your dullwittedness."

Abruptly Arnulf jabbed an elbow in Varin's ribs, and a look of . . .

Gavarnie narrowed his eyes. Was it apprehension

that crossed de Brionne's features? Aye. He looked like a small boy about to receive punishment for some mischief he'd caused.

The man cleared his throat. "There are greater schemes afoot than even your twisted thinking can invent." His voice was low and hurried. "I have it on good authority that there are those who would see themselves as rulers in William's stead, which is why the king entertains the whoresons. Better to keep the vipers before him than be bitten from behind."

Gavarnie frowned. Had not de Warrenne and Gundrada shared William's table at the king's reception? Was it possible the two were . . .

He had no time to finish the thought, for Varin was blathering on. "You risk much to hold de Warrenne in such contempt. He is no simpleton, and what he cannot think of, Gundrada will."

Arnulf began to fidget, and de Brionne drained his wine. The two rose hastily as a loud thump distracted Gavarnie. He glanced at Sperville to see if the chamberlain had bumped the table.

"Oh, I near forgot," de Brionne called.

Gavarnie looked back, astonished to see that Varin and Arnulf had already reached the dais steps and were rapidly descending.

Varin spoke over his shoulder as he and the giant hurried toward the doors. "If you persist with your absurd imaginings concerning my supposed plan to kill you, William says he will be happy to rid you of the dust that has collected between your ears. He wishes you to know that 'twas not he who sent the messages warning of betrayal. And he sends his congratulations on the return of your sight."

White-hot rage flashed through Gavarnie, and he shot to his feet. "You went to the king!"

"'Twas necessary. I would never have returned such a lovely gift without first consulting the king. And I have it from William's mouth that if he truly believed you guilty of Isabelle's murder, he would never have pardoned you. He suggests you concentrate your efforts on recalling the events of that eve, rather than wasting your time on plots that do not exist."

Gavarnie gripped the hilt of his sword, prepared to give chase, when Sperville grabbed his arm.

"Leave go!" Gavarnie snarled. "De Brionne has breathed his last."

"Shh!" the chamberlain hissed. Clutching Gavarnie's arm more tightly, he inclined his head at the tapestry, his eyes round with apprehension.

The lump of material jumped, and Gavarnie took an involuntary backward step.

"Unholy son of a goat!" he roared at de Brionne. "What demons have you brought into my house?"

The man turned, but he did not slow his retreat. Instead, the bastard scurried backward, waving and grinning. "No need to the thank me. Your face says all. 'Til next we—"

His words were cut off as Arnulf jerked him through the doors.

"Stop them," Gavarnie ordered the chamberlain.

Sperville started forward, then halted as the tapestry wiggled.

Whore's gleet, Gavarnie swore. Had de Brionne wrapped some huge serpent within the folds of material? He waited until it stilled, then sidled toward it. Drawing his blade, he took a deep breath, prepared to stab the thing.

Nay! a voice screeched.

Gavarnie froze. The same voice from the alehouse, the same voice from the lane during the attack.

He spun about, his sword raised. "Who is speaking?" he demanded, surveying the area.

Sperville's Adam's apple bobbed. "You are hearing voices?"

"Did you not?"

The chamberlain's face paled as he shook his head.

Gavarnie clamped his teeth together against a shiver. 'Od rot. He was not mad. Someone had screamed at him. And though it was much higher in pitch, it *was* the same voice he'd heard when . . .

The shiver finally rushed up his back to claim his body.

On both occasions when he'd heard the voice, Golde had been endangered. Indeed, the second occasion had heralded the return of his sight.

He narrowed his eyes in thought. What had Sperville said about Golde's great-grandmother? That she had promised to heal his blindness? Was it possible that—

He blinked and jerked his gaze back to the tapestry.

Nay. 'Twas absurd to imagine that some old crone had cured him from afar. 'Twas even more fantastic that she would be aware of events she was not present to witness.

Still, he could not bring himself to stab the tapestry. Instead, he raised his foot, then shoved the thing with all his might. It flew off the dais, landing with a thud on the rush-strewn floor. To his horror, the coarse material began to flop about and unravel.

He should have killed it before kicking it from the dais. He braced his legs and raised his blade, ready to leap on the thing once it was free.

With a writhing flourish, the creature at last burst forth.

Gavarnie clamped his teeth together lest his jaw fall from his face to the floor. Joy consumed him, so fierce it near buckled his knees.

"Mistress," Sperville whispered.

Just as quickly, fear coursed through Gavarnie's blood. He could have killed Golde! Shuddering, he staunched the unbearable flow of his thoughts.

At the very least, de Brionne should be whipped for trussing Golde thus. Faith, she was dressed in naught but her undergarments. He jumped from the dais and hurried to her aid as she thrashed about in an attempt to sit. Though her chest heaved and she grunted mightily, the ropes that bound her from head to toe precluded the possibility.

Upon spying him, she stilled.

"Here. Let me loose this gag."

He grimaced at her soiled state. Her hair was matted and greasy beneath the knot of the gag, her white chainse stained with grayish blotches, and her . . .

Legs. Long and sleek, they were bared to mid thigh where the chainse had rucked up. He recalled the soft, lush feel of them, underlaid with corded strength, to be sure. Had he not felt the pleasure of their power when lust held the wench in its grip?

He eyed her bottom. His *coillons* tightened as he remembered the smooth round flesh there, the way she'd strained for his touch.

The flatness of her belly, the perfect curve of her breasts, the demanding thrust of her hard nipples.

"Toad-eating dunghead," she spat the moment he removed the gag. "If you stare a little harder at my person, mayhap the ropes that bind me will burn away."

Gavarnie drew back. Had he heard a'right? Did the wench dare to curse him, even as he helped her?

He glanced at the gag in his hand. Swiftly he replaced the wad of material over her mouth and tied it behind her head.

Her smell wafted upward and he wrinkled his nose. "You reek worse than a buzzard's dinner."

A strangled noise issued from her, and it took no little effort to hide his satisfaction. "I see de Brionne had the good sense to secure your flapping mouth."

The color drained from her face to collect in her eyes. The green one glittered and shot poison at him; the black turned hard as jet and swore vengeance upon him.

Indeed, at the moment, she appeared most capable of destroying anyone and everything that crossed her path. No wonder Sir Varin and Arnulf had beat such a hasty retreat.

He shook himself. De Brionne and his giant underlord were cowardly simpletons. No woman was going to unsettle him thus. Ignoring the hair that bristled at his nape, he bent and scooped up Golde.

"Sperville," he called as he headed for the screens passage, "have bathwater sent up. And do not bother heating it. Methinks the lady needs cooling."

By the time he reached the stairs, she was struggling. The feel of her warm, squirming body melted his fear. "Have a care, mistress. You are hardly a tiny burden and I would not wish to drop you on your she-goat head."

More strangled sounds from behind the gag, though she calmed. In the semidarkness of the stairwell, he smiled. Despite her soiled state, she was the most desirable female he'd e're laid hands on. Her bare legs felt whisper-soft. The manner in which her hands were tied arched her back so her breasts rubbed against his chest.

Feline. An intense ache spread through his groin until he feared he might split his braies.

He caught himself as he reached his chambers. What was he thinking? The wench likely hated him.

He halted before the tub and all but threw her in. Ignoring her grunt, he turned his back on her thrashing form. Most wenches would be grateful that a lord of the realm displayed such interest in their persons.

Not Golde.

He stomped to the drawing point and hauled on the rope.

Nay. Not only did she disdain him, she had had the gall to lecture him on his lack of self-restraint, as if his temper were responsible for all the ills that had befallen him.

He snatched at the bucket of water to release it from its hook.

What did she know of being blind? Of being incapacitated and unable to control her own destiny . . .

A slow grin spread over his lips as the bucket came loose. Ha! Was she not incapacitated at present? Had she any control over what befell her? 'Twas time and past the little wasp took a sting from her own tail.

Wiping the smile from his face, he turned and strolled to the tub. He clenched his jaws to keep from chortling at the vicious look she gave him.

Then he stilled. She'd managed to work herself to a half-sit, using the side of the tub for purchase. And what a chore it must have been. She'd near unclothed herself in the process.

Against his will, his gaze traveled to her legs. She was bent at the knees where she'd pushed herself up, and her movements had caused the chainse to bunch about her hips. Her underdrawers, too, had ridden upward, baring her thighs. He eyed the juncture where they met.

She straightened her legs and wiggled about, trying to scrape the material downward.

He arched a brow and gave her shoulder a pointed look. Turning her head, her gaze followed his and her eyes widened. Where she'd levered herself against the side of the bath, the chainse had slipped halfway to her elbow. The delicate line of her collarbone was exposed, as was the upper swell of one breast.

Her enraged snarl distracted him and he blinked innocently. "You must learn to control that foul temper, mistress. All this writhing about makes you appear most unwholesome."

Her nostrils flared and he took the opportunity to dump the water over her head. Her body went stiff as ebony hair cascaded over her face, covering her eyes and shoulders. A terrible noise, something between a bleating goat and a bull in rut, erupted from behind the gag. Without another glance, he strode back to the drawing point, clamping his teeth together at the guffaw that threatened to choke him.

Latching the pail on the rope, he spoke over his shoulder lest the sight of her destroy his composure. "I had nothing to do with your current predicament, just as you had nothing to do with my blindness."

He lowered the bucket. "Indeed, my only wish is to give you aid, much as you wished to restore my sight when you first arrived here. But I now understand the difficulty of dealing with one whose rage precludes all reason. I confess, you have inspired no little fear in me."

He retrieved the pail and returned to the tub. Bending, he pulled dripping strands of hair aside to peer at her face, then clucked his tongue. "There, you see? You have turned a most unbecoming shade of red. And the way your eyes are rolling in your head makes me think some demon inhabits your person."

Releasing the curtain of thick hair, he poured the full pail over her head and sauntered back to the drawing point. "I could scarce be persuaded to release you under such circumstances. There is no telling what injury you might do yourself, not to mention my person."

The bucket full, he again moved to the tub. "You shall remain bound until you exhibit some modicum of control. Only then will I loose you."

He drenched her a third time, noting the gooseflesh that had risen on her legs. His fist clenched around the bucket's handle as she shuddered.

Nay. He would feel no sympathy.

Marching to the drawing point, he refilled the pail. She deserved much more than this small amount of discomfort, which was naught in comparison to the misery she'd wrought upon him.

Approaching the bath, his steps slowed. The rhythm of Golde's breathing rapidly increased until great strangled gasps filled his ears.

He hurried forward. The black hair that draped over her face jerked eerily each time she sucked air. Her legs were tinted purple. In contrast to her upper body, they appeared immovable. Hard and lifeless as marble.

The pail thumped to the floor as he dropped to his knees. Dear God! Had he drowned her?

He flung the hair back from her face. Glazed and unblinking, her eyes stared past him with all the disinterest of the dead.

Like Isabelle's eyes.

"Prithee, Golde," he whispered frantically, "do not do this to me."

He snatched at the knot that held the gag. "'Twas but a jest. I meant no harm."

If she heard him, she gave no indication.

He yanked the wad of material from her mouth. "By all that is holy, Golde, you are more dear to me than life."

She did not speak, but only continued with the hoarse choking sounds.

Nay! he wanted to scream. What had he done?

TWENTY-FOUR

GOLDE FLINCHED. The cursed light was growing ferocious. She narrowed her gaze at the shadowed shape that wavered in the midst of the glare. Shades of purple, near black at the heart of the figure, faded to pastel hues at its extremities.

'Twas the person who'd murdered Gavarnie's wife.

Blue-white shafts of brilliance pierced Golde's eyes like red-hot needles. Still, she did not look away. If she could capture some small detail, something that would give her a clue to the figure's identity.

A whiff of . . . was it lavender?

Nay, 'twas blood. Sickly sweet.

She shuddered as all was obliterated by the searing flash. 'Twas as if a hell-borne gale blew through her soul. Her eyelids squeezed shut, despite her command for them to remain open. Hissing her frustration, she gulped air. She'd been so close.

Then blessed darkness settled about her, dragging at her limbs. As her breathing eased, so did the ache that throbbed behind her eyes.

Abruptly she realized someone was patting her cheek. And with more force than necessary.

"Mule-headed hag," Gavarnie ground. "If you dare to die, I will follow your demon hide to hell and hound you for eternity."

She cracked an eye to see him leaning over her, his swarthy features grim. Could the simpleton not see she was exhausted? She opened her other eye to discover she lay in his bed. How had she come to be here?

For a moment the answer glimmered before her. But she was too tired to pursue it. Besides, the only thing that mattered was Gavarnie's irritating treatment of her.

Summoning her strength, she grumbled, "Strike me again and there will not be enough left of you to reach hell."

Before she could roll to her side and get comfortable, Gavarnie had yanked her to a sitting position and crushed her to his chest. Her eyes felt as if they might pop from her head, so tight was his hold.

Just as quickly, he pushed her away to arms' length. Gripping her shoulders, his black eyes studied her face. "You are well?"

She tried to shake off his grasp, but what little energy she possessed was quickly spent. "I would be fine if you would cease battering me and allow me to rest."

He inclined his head and gave her a steady look. "Know you who I am?"

She scowled. Whatever ailed the imbecile, that he would ask such? "Of course I . . ."

Her words trailed away as she recalled the vision. Doubtless, it was the reason for his peculiar behavior. She must have appeared mad.

Her mouth suddenly felt dry. She must tell him—

Her thoughts continued to tumble backward before she could speak. Did memory serve correct? Had she been bound and delivered to Skyenvic with less dignity than an old cow about to be butchered?

Oh, but Sir Varin and Arnulf would pay for their scurrilous abuse, the lackwits. As would Gavarnie. That he had dared to leave her trussed like a hare on a spit. Then near drowned her. And all the while, he'd babbled on, comparing her shackled state to his blindness, as if one had aught to do with the other.

She affected a confused look. "You wish to know who you are?"

He raised a brow and nodded.

She gave him a dazzling smile. "You are the Pope."

His brows swooped down and he cast her a penetrating look. "Where are we?"

"We are in Rome."

Dread and pity warred for dominance of his features. Pursing his lips, he leaned forward until his face was no more than a hand's span from hers. His eyes burned with intensity. "How did you come to be in Rome?"

She could stand no more of his patronizing tone. Her nostrils flared and her smile soured. "I was transported by two spineless worms, who shall soon rue the day they were born. As will you, mi'lord dunghead, if you do not release me at once."

She near laughed at his stunned expression. His features clouded, and it appeared thunder would roll any moment. Then his mouth abruptly crooked in a half smile. "Clever wench. You e're amaze me with your cunning."

She eyed him warily. Why was he being so even-tempered?

"Never have I met a female with such an aversion to bathing. Is there aught you will not do to avoid soap and water? You had me scared half unto death with that pretentious fit."

Her mouth dropped open. "Bumptious lover of sheep. 'Twas no pretense. And do not attempt to disguise your lecherous intent with insults."

She scrambled from the bed, pausing long enough to sneer at him. "Think you I did not see the gleam in your eye at my defenseless state? All that blather about wishing to help me, and how I must learn to control my temper."

She spun and tromped toward the door, gesturing at the ceiling. "Drool fair spilled from your mouth at the thought of having me at your mercy."

"Mistress," he called, the edges of his voice curled with amusement.

The odious buzzard. She did not look back. "Save your breath, mi'lord knave. All the wealth of England could not convince me to suffer your company another moment. Nor will you ever know what I have seen."

"Golde," he called again.

"Do not hope to play on my sympathies with that sweet tone," she huffed, nearing the door. "Though it might have wings and a gilded snout, a pig is yet a pig, and easily identifiable."

"I could not agree more," he purred as she reached for the door latch. "Despite the odor you emit, one could never mistake you for a fish. Particularly when your charms are so clearly displayed."

At his cheerful tone, she jerked her head around. Following his gaze, she peered over her shoulder and down. Her eyes rounded. The bastard! All the while he'd been ogling her rear, which, indeed, the clinging wet chainse did naught to conceal.

"Both halves of your bottom are easily identifiable," he commented smugly, "as is the line that separates—"

"Out," she snapped before he could finish.

"Come, mistress." He sounded like a cat who just happened to be in the vicinity of the dovecote. "You cannot order me about in my own chambers."

Turning sideways, she pointed at the door. "Out!"

He shrugged and sighed heavily. "Very well."

Rising from the bed, he shuffled toward the door, his shoulders hunched. Faith, he looked exactly like Ronces, the spoiled brat.

Except there was nothing boyish about him.

She retreated toward the wall, her gaze slipping from his face to his broad chest, to his narrow hips and long legs. Though less than a week had passed since she'd last seen him, he appeared to have developed a great deal more brawn.

A tingling sensation pooled in her groin, stealing the warmth from the rest of her body. She shivered.

"You are certain you do not need my assistance?" He paused before the door.

She jerked her gaze to his face and nodded her head emphatically. "Ab—abso—" She cleared her throat. "Absolutely."

He raised a brow. "Well, if you change your thinking, do not hesitate to call."

With a most reluctant glance, he fair drooped across the threshold, the latch clicking as he closed the door behind him.

She released her pent breath. Getting rid of him had been easier than she'd expected, though why she should feel so deflated, she knew not. Shivering again, she turned toward the bath. Some hot water and fresh clothing . . .

Her bare feet halted. Of all the despicable—

There would be no hot water. And what clean clothing she possessed lay in her chest, which, last she'd seen, was in Nicolette's chamber.

She spun about and did her best to pull the door from its hinges. "Lowly son of a serpent," she shrieked into the corridor. "Hie yourself back here."

As if he'd been awaiting her summons, Gavarnie's head appeared at the top of the stairs. "Is there something you require?"

"Do not give me that innocent look. You know very well that I require hot water and clothes."

His steps purposely laggard, he came up the stairs, then sauntered along the corridor. Drawing to a halt, he crossed his arms over his chest and leaned against the door frame. "I shall be most happy to accommodate your wishes, provided I am well paid." He held out his palm.

She slapped it. "Fool. You are mistaken if you think I will not fetch my own clothes for fear of being seen by some lowly liegeman."

He stared pointedly at her breasts.

She glanced down to see her nipples poking against her wet chainse. Again, warmth spread through her groin and she fought to keep from wincing. Gathering the soaked material in her frozen fingers, she held it away from her body and made to sweep past him.

He grasped her upper arm and gave her an over-affected leer. "'Twould be most remiss of me to ignore your icy discomfort."

"I am not cold."

"Then can I presume your nipples have hardened in response to my touch?" He pulled her close and wrapped his arms about her. "Come, my redolent blossom. Let us get you cleaned up."

He lifted her off her feet and hauled her back inside the bedchamber, kicking the door closed behind him.

Despite his buffoonery, warm wisps of unwelcome desire curled through her body. Squirming for release did naught but increase the horrid yearning. Commanding her body to stillness, she strove for an imperious tone. "Leave go, lout."

"In a moment, fragrant flower." He grunted and staggered, as if he were performing some great feat of strength in carrying her weight.

Her eyes widened when she realized he was headed toward the tub. "If you dare return me to that icy—"

The backs of her knees hit the padded rim of the bath. Before she could blink, he'd tilted her backward until she was forced to bend her legs. Then over the side she went. She gasped as she landed with a great plop in ankle-deep water that felt colder now than it had before.

"You were saying?" He straightened, making a show of rubbing his back as if she'd broken it.

"Misbegotten son of a cur."

He smiled benevolently. "No need to express your appreciation. Let me help you remove that filthy garment."

She crossed her arms over her chest and scooted as far from him as the opposite side of the tub would allow. "Touch me, and before God, I will break every bone in your hand."

"Here, here," he chided. Leaning over, he grabbed her chainse at the waist.

He jerked it up with such force, she toppled forward as the material was snatched from beneath her. The moment she moved her arms to catch herself, he clutched the neckline and hauled it over her head.

"There. Mayhap now you can be properly cleansed."

"Son of Belial," she hissed, again crossing her arms over her chest. "You will pay with your life for the indignities you have perpetrated."

He clucked his tongue and shook his head, eyeing her underdrawers. "Those will have to come off as well." He dropped her chainse on the floor and made a grab for the undergarment.

"Nay!" she screeched, swatting at his hands.

"Do not be difficult, mistress," he admonished, ignoring her flying fingers to pull on the drawstring. "I seek naught but that which is best for you."

His knuckles brushed her belly, sending jagged bolts of lust straight to her woman's core. She redoubled her efforts to forestall him, to no avail. Thrash and slap as she might, it seemed he possessed ten hands.

"Have done!" she cried at last. "I am most capable of bathing myself."

He raised his head to stare at her, his black eyes full of deviltry. "Did I not know better, I would think you were averse to my touch."

"You have the right of that, mi'lord toady-fingers. I would sooner bathe with eels than suffer your slimy ministrations."

At last, she congratulated herself. Judging from the swift glint that sparked in his eyes, she'd succeeded in pricking his temper. Mayhap now he would leave her in peace.

He sneered. "If you detest me so, why does your gaze e're linger on my person?"

Heat crawled up her face. The bastard. Aye, she'd looked, more times than she could count. Not that she would admit such. She cloaked her embarrassment with an indignant reply. "Your pardon for my looking upon you. I did not know 'twas forbidden."

She scooted around, pointedly giving him her back. "I suppose 'twould better suit your pompous sensibilities were I to prostrate myself at your feet when speaking to you."

"Now, there is a thought, though you would doubtless take the opportunity to tie my boot buckles together."

"And well do you deserve such. Always skulking about, accusing innocent folk of the foulest deeds."

"What was I to believe? Under my roof less than three days, and you throw yourself upon me with ravenous abandon. Mayhap you could explain why a virgin would behave thus. To my thinking, such sacrifice can be based on naught but deceit."

"So now you would discuss deceit?" she hissed. "What of the fortnight you spent trying to burrow your way into my heart? Who insisted on carrying me from tub to bed, and bed to tub, that no man would see my bare body?"

She snorted. "Blind, my ear. All the while, you filled your eyes to brimming."

"Your pardon, Mistress Celt Soothsayer, but 'twas you who arrived upon my doorstep intent on parting me from my coin."

She gasped and glowered over her shoulder at him.

"Do not deny it. Sperville has told me much about your person."

"And well you Normans deserve to be parted from

your coin, the bulk of which you have stolen from English peasants."

"Hmph. So much for your second sight. My ancestry lies with the Moors, not the Normans, a fact you would know if you truly possessed any gift for prophecy."

She heard the water swish behind her, then Gavarnie ran a lump of soap over her head and began scrubbing her hair. "I can scarce credit what I am about to offer," he grumbled, "but since 'tis obviously money you covet above all else, then name your price for your maidenhead."

"Mon—name—price!"

"Do not pretend outrage," he snapped, pushing on her head when she would have risen. "You have beaten me. Faith, I can think of little else. Give me your demands and let us have done."

His fingers stilled on her scalp when she made no reply. "Well," he prodded.

Her voice trembled with rage. "I am not in the habit of speaking to dead men. And rest assured, though you may yet draw breath, you are as good as buried."

"Pff." He yanked her backward and scooped water over her head, splashing soap in her eyes and mouth. "I would offer you marriage, but you would doubtless mock me for it."

She came up spitting and swiping at her eyes. The idiot! Was he proposing?

"Which is as well," he continued, with no consideration for her stinging eyes or the foul taste in her mouth, "for though I was able to last many years with my first wife before killing her, God knows I would likely murder you within a fortnight."

She fought the compassion that swelled in her chest. How was it the man could pull her heartstrings so?

Because, she answered herself, he feared she would not have him. He felt himself unworthy of her. The oaf. 'Twas no wonder she loved him.

She scowled. "You did not murder your wife, and I will not tell you so again."

He shifted her hair over her shoulders and ran the soap over her back. "From whence comes this conviction of my innocence, wench? And do not say you have seen it in some magical vision."

"Ha. Who was complaining most recently about hearing voices? I distinctly heard you comment on it to Spindleshanks, despite my incapacitated state. And how do you think you recovered your sight?"

"Mayhap 'twas my fear for your life that restored my sight."

"'Twas fear for my life all right. My great-grandmother's fear. She planned to teach me a lesson, and your blindness was not about to hinder her. Had I been killed during the ambush, I would have learned nothing. Thus, she decided to heal your eyes, that you could save me."

"Your pardon if I have a hard time grasping all this. Even you will admit, it sounds fanciful."

She blew an exasperated sigh. "Very well, then. If you yet believe you murdered your wife, look at the people about you. Never have I met a person who so frequently deserves gutting as does Spindleshanks. Yet you have not killed him. And what of your children. At the very least they should be flogged daily, but you have never lifted a finger against them. Indeed, though 'twas certainly within your rights, you could not rid yourself of Nicolette."

His hands slowed to trail over her shoulders, warm and slow. Gooseflesh sprang up in their soapy wake, though she felt less cold by the moment.

"Must you e're be contrary?" he murmured. "One would think you are most eager to wed a murderer."

His hands slipped along her ribs and it seemed she could feel his gaze scorching her back. She shifted uncomfortably at the heaviness that settled between her legs. "You are not—"

"Hush," he whispered, his breath near enough to stir the fine hair at her nape. Then his lips nibbled her neck. "Save yourself. Tell me to go."

She near wept with frustration. Why did he leave the decision to her? As if she could deny him aught with her tongue firmly plastered to her teeth to prevent herself from begging him to stay.

His hands swept around to her breasts, gently kneading. "Have you any idea what torment you have caused me?" His voice was a low tomcat growl.

She placed her hands atop his and felt her own hard nipples as he rolled them between his fingers. The soap made everything slippery and so very achy. Her breathing quickened and she leaned her head back against his shoulder. Never had she witnessed such a delicious sight as his hands on her.

"The many hours I have spent imagining this," he breathed in her ear.

He tugged gently on her hand, drawing it down over her belly, then lower. Blood, hot and pulsing, filled her woman's flesh. He slid his fingers over her collop and she pressed her hand hard atop his. 'Twas unbearably alluring to watch him stroke her, and know that he, too, was watching.

She groaned and spread her legs, anxious for him to feed the raging hunger that slavered for his touch. His finger dipped inside her and she heard his breath catch.

Abruptly he hauled her from the tub and cradled her

in his arms. Exhibiting none of his previous difficulty with her weight, he fair sailed to the bed.

He landed on the mattress, dragging her atop him. Pulling her face to his, he ran his tongue over her lips, as if he would drink her. His hands moved to cup her bottom and he pressed her against his groin.

Blazing tendrils of fire licked at her core. "Please," she panted into his mouth. "I can stand little more."

"Then mayhap you should remove my clothing."

She moaned and straddled his lap so he could sit. Grasping his tunic, she fair tore it over his head. But before she could get his undertunic, he bent his head to suck her nipples.

Quivering, she pushed his head away and yanked the undertunic off.

He grabbed her hands and pressed them to her breasts, then watched as she stroked herself. 'Twas heaven and hell to see the scorching look that darkened his features. She arched her back, begging him silently to suck her nipples again. It took little urging, and when he grazed his teeth across them, she shuddered.

Instantly his hands were on her bottom, kneading and separating the flesh so she was further exposed to his rigid shaft where it filled his braies.

She could wait no longer. Shoving at his shoulders, she forced him down, then snatched on the drawstring at his waist. She slid backward on his thighs and did no more than pull the material below his groin. For a moment, she eyed his engorged state. Then she moved back up and rubbed herself against him.

Faith, his shaft felt like an exotic silk from a faraway land. Sleek and slippery, and hard as an iron post. She raked herself over it, trembling with each stroke.

"Have a care," he cautioned, his tone raw. "You are yet a maid."

He attempted to grab her writhing hips. "You are like to feel—"

She gasped. Too late. She had impaled herself. "Ohhh."

She curled her fingers into the hair on his chest, grimacing. "Ohhh."

"Easy, sweeting." He covered her hands and squeezed them. "'Twill pass. Be still."

"Ohhh." She closed her eyes, certain she would never recover from the pain. Even if she did, the crutch of her thighs had surely been split to her waist, which would make walking impossible.

The thought made her open her eyes and look down. Her face must have reflected her horror, for Gavarnie was instantly soothing her.

"'Tis naught but a little blood, Golde."

"A little—I am bleeding to death."

"Hush, witchwife. You know more about the nature of women than most. Virgins bleed. You will live to enjoy fulfillment."

"Nay." She shook her head. "You are bigger than any man I have e're seen. I'd wager there are few bulls that compare." Her voice shook. "If I die, promise you will not spread the manner of my demise."

She looked up, begging with her eyes, then frowned. Was that a smile that flitted across the oaf's lips? She snatched her hands from beneath his. "Pig! You find some amusement here?"

Before she could raise herself from him, he clutched her waist and pulled her chest down against his.

"A bull," he chuckled. "Have a care with whom you

share such information, else I will have women coming from far and wide to sample my charms."

"Worm-eating mucker. Let me up."

"Umm," he purred. "'Tis most appealing when you wiggle about thus. I believe the worst of your discomfort is past."

It was, but she would never admit it. Instead, she opened her mouth to berate him. But before she could issue a word, his lips clamped over hers.

By all that was holy, she would not succumb.

But, oh, how sweetly he kissed. And how gentle his touch. Within moments, his mouth had drained her of anger. And the void it left behind was quickly filled with aching desire. Try though she might, she could not keep still.

His tongue stroked the inside of her mouth, hot and hungry. With great deliberation, he began to move, the length of him riding hard and slow against her collop. With each thrust, her woman's flesh coiled tighter. She rubbed her breasts over the coarse hair on his chest, moaning her need at the intense friction.

His pace increased slowly and the coiling sensation between her legs grew tighter. She ran her hands over his shoulders and down his arms, marveling at the strength in his taut muscles. For a moment he reached to entwine his fingers with hers, then his hands slid beyond her reach as he clutched her bottom.

He pressed her hips down as he thrust upward, his breath blowing hard against her lips. She tried to follow his withdrawal, but he would not let her. Holding her hips, he raised her from him until only the tip of his arousal remained inside her.

She whimpered and nipped his lips, making her disappointment clear. His arms shook, and he thrust again, pushing her hard against him, only to withdraw.

Groaning, she bore down on his next plunge. The coiled sensation grew acute and she writhed on his hardness. If he dared withdraw again—

Abruptly the coil snapped, and she was flooded with pleasure so pure, her body quaked.

At her cry, his muscles went rigid. His chest rumbled, the sound vibrating through her as if she were a bowstring from which an arrow had just been released.

For long moments afterward, he did not move, and she was content to lie where she was, sprawled atop him. Indeed, she would have passed the night in the same position had a knock not sounded at the door.

"Mi'lord," Sperville called.

"Take yourself off, man," Gavarnie ordered. "I am not here."

"Yes, your grace. But there is a lord, a Sir Hugh, who demands an audience with mistress."

TWENTY-FIVE

GOLDE CLAMBERED for cover, accidentally jamming her knee in Gavarnie's groin. His legs snapped together, and she winced at his gasp.

"A little caution would not be remiss, wench," he grumbled as she rolled onto her back beside him. "Who is this Sir Hugh?"

She rucked the sheets to her chin. "A lord of the moors."

He rose on his elbow, glaring suspiciously. "How is it you know him?"

"I met him yestereve at Atherbrook."

"What is it he wants of you?"

Golde pursed her lips. What indeed? Was the lord yet determined to visit vengeance upon her?

Nay, she reassured herself. Sir Varin must have told

him where to find her. He would not have done so if the man were a danger.

"Well," Gavarnie prodded. "Is he another of your culls?"

She shot him a withering look. "If you would fetch me some clothing, I will go and see what he wants."

Abruptly Gavarnie became a churning fit of motion. Kicking at the covers, he flung them heavenward. "Whore's gleet." He thrashed and scooted toward the edge of the mattress, yanking up his braies. "Not bedded but moments, and already men seek you out."

Heat swept Golde's face, though it had little to do with his words. At the moment, her embarrassment far outweighed her anger at his remark. She could scarce credit her wanton behavior.

She eyed his leathery back, the lighter flesh of his buttocks. Bad enough that she'd been unable to deny him. Worse that she'd sat astride him like some domineering she-goat. But worst of all, she'd not even allowed him to remove his braies and boots before she'd taken . . .

She looked away as his feet hit the floor. Aye, she'd taken him, not the other way 'round, as was natural. There wasn't a hole on earth deep enough for her to crawl in.

He paused at the door. "You will stay where you are, witch. I will determine whether or not this lord has need of your presence."

Her lips parted at his peremptory tone. Had she heard a'right? "Your pardon?"

He exited the room without a backward glance, banging the door behind him.

She blinked, then narrowed her eyes and gritted her

teeth. The gall! Did he think 'twas his right to take charge of her affairs just because she'd lain with him?

Throwing the covers aside, she leapt from the bed to grab her chainse where it lay in a wet heap beside the tub. She would fetch her clothes from Nicolette's chamber and be downstairs before he could break wind.

The overbearing thickwit. She sucked in her breath as she jerked the cold material over her head. He was not swift enough to race with snails.

She stomped to the door and threw it open. A pox on any who crossed her path. She slammed down the corridor, making no attempt at silence. Let Gavarnie hear. By the rood, let him come rebuke her for not staying put as he'd commanded. She would give him an earful.

She halted abruptly upon crossing the threshold of Nicolette's room. Sitting upon the bed, cradling a doll, the girl looked up at her.

Golde forced a tight smile. "Your pardon, mistress. I have come to see if—ah, yes, there is my chest." She kicked the door closed and swept forward.

"Why awe you all wet?" Nicolette asked.

Golde snatched fresh clothes from the trunk and draped them over the lid. "I took a bath."

"In youw undewcloves?"

"'Twas the best way I could think to wash this filthy chainse," she responded evenly.

"Why did you not take dwy cloves to youw bath?"

"I forgot." She clenched her teeth against the cold and stripped the chainse over her head.

Nicolette gasped. "You awe huwt!"

Golde looked to see the girl cover her mouth, then followed the child's gaze. Blessed Mother of God, she'd forgotten the blood that stained her thighs. A rush of heat ravaged her face. Dragging a hand through her hair, she stifled the urge to pull it out by the roots. What was she to say?

Your dear father just tumbled me?

She raised a brow as an idea struck her. "'Tis my monthly course."

Nicolette eyed her as if she knew better.

"All women have them," she snapped defensively, then caught herself. The child could not possibly know. She moderated her tone. "Well, most women have them, except for the very young and very old."

Nicolette appeared as if she'd just discovered a worm in an apple after taking several bites. "Does it huwt?"

Golde paused as her inwit pricked her. Doubtless, the only knowledge the child would ever receive would come from lewd remarks made by serving maids.

She chose her words carefully. "I would not say it hurts. 'Tis more like a dull ache that passes quickly. If it bothers you, there are tonics to help ease the discomfort."

She returned to her chest and rummaged about, withdrawing a rag. "And you wear a bit of cloth, like this, to keep from soiling your garments."

Nicolette wrinkled her nose. "Ugh. I do not think I wool have these couwse things."

Golde struggled to keep a grin from her lips. "You will have no choice in the matter. 'Tis what makes you a woman." Then the devil caught her tongue. "Otherwise, you would be an arrogant, toad-eating man."

The child gave her an assessing look. "Has Papa—I mean Schiew—been mean to you again?"

Why was the child calling Gavarnie "sir"? Golde padded the inside of her underdrawers with the rag and pulled them on. "Your Papa is meaner than an old goat."

"He is not my Papa."

Golde pulled the chainse over head. "Did he say he was not your father?"

"Nay. But everyone knows." Nicolette gave her a sullen look.

Golde opened her mouth to deny the statement, but changed her thinking. Nicolette was not stupid, and she deserved the truth. Though how best to tell it?

"Silly girl." Golde drew her tunic over her head, pretending anger. "The man calls you daughter, does he not? If everyone knows that such is not the case, does he not risk appearing foolish? Yet he does not seem to care what others think. Indeed, he must love you beyond measure to claim you as his own."

Nicolette pursed her lips. "Do you weally think he loves me?"

"Of course he loves you."

"As much as Alowy and Wonces?"

"Every bit."

Abruptly Nicolette changed the subject. "Awe you leaving?"

Golde blinked. Though surely she was mistaken, the little girl appeared sad. "Not right away, but soon."

The child suddenly became inordinately interested in the doll, plucking at the threadbare material that covered it. "Schiew—Papa—wool turn souw again, just like when you left before."

Eyeing the girl, Golde secured her girdle about her hips. "When I left before?"

Nicolette nodded. "That one time, when you huwt your wibs. Then last week. Evwyone says Papa is smit with you. He is suwly when you awe gone."

Golde snorted. "Your Papa is always surly."

Misery claimed the child's features. "Awe you afwaid Papa wool kill you, too? Is that why you awe leaving?"

Golde stilled, her gaze roaming over matted, honey-colored hair. The dirt-smudged chubby cheeks, the square little chin that trembled.

She quickly sat and wrapped an arm about the child's shoulders. "Your father did *not* kill your mother."

Nicolette's eyes rounded. "Weally? Who—"

"I do not know who did it, only that it was *not* your Papa."

Nicolette's glowing countenance suddenly reminded her of Lull, whose father was sitting with Gavarnie in the great hall even as she spoke. Rising, she inclined her head. "Listen to your heart, Nicolette. Do you truly believe your Papa could have done such a thing?"

She strode to the door, realizing belatedly that she had no shoes. Plague take Sir Varin and Arnulf. At the very least, they could have tucked her boots in the filthy tapestry.

Just wait until she told Roscelyn of Varin's underhanded treatment. He would never hear the end of it. Nor would that dolt, Arnulf. With luck, his wife Dunne would take a kitchen mallet to his thick skull.

Opening the door, she hurried into the corridor, anxious to retain some measure of irritation for Gavarnie. Mayhap she had been hasty in judging his actions, but by the rood, he'd not hesitated to pass judgment on her. *Not bedded but moments and already men seek you out.* His reasoning was suspicious as ever.

Her steps slowed as she descended the stairs. *How could he help but be suspicious?* her inwit inquired.

Blind, believing himself a murderer. What coincidence that she should have arrived on his doorstep? A witchwife, not a nursemaid.

Then she'd flung his children's words in his face, and

when he'd not believed her, what had she done to convince him? Discussed the matter in a reasonable manner?

Nay. She'd done her best to seduce him, at least to his way of thinking. Meanwhile, he'd received missives warning of betrayal, had been attacked returning from New Market.

Her thoughts tumbled forward to his recent treatment of her in the tub. *My only wish is to give you aid, much as you wished to restore my sight.*

She winced. How smug she must have sounded those first few days at Skyenvic. How trite her advice to a man struggling to conquer his affliction. Had she not learned firsthand how it felt to be at another's mercy? Indeed, she'd grown so enraged at her incapacitated state, she'd brought a vision upon herself.

Coming through the screens passage, she paused. Where was he? With the exception of a few servants, the great hall was empty.

She picked her way to the entrance, cursing the prickly, dry rushes that stabbed the soles of her feet. Upon reaching the doors' threshold, she gazed out over the bailey. The day was overcast, and though servants scurried over the yard and men-at-arms manned the wallwalk, she saw no sign of Gavarnie.

Strange. She had grown accustomed to the many guests billeted at Skyenvic, but now the place fair seemed deserted. She strode forward. Halfway across the bailey, she stopped a youthful liegeman.

"Have you seen Sir Gavarnie?"

He nodded and pointed at the gates to the keep. "Left just moments ago with another lord."

Golde bobbed her head and continued on. Reaching the open gates, she scanned the expanse of ground that rolled away from the castle. Only a few tents remained, straggling relics among the beaten earth where so many had camped. Her gaze followed the road that led to New Market. There, in the distance, she spied two riders heading in the direction of the village.

Which was well and good. She needed some time to herself, away from the castle and the gossiping castlefolk. She strode down the path, welcoming the heavy sea air. *Not bedded but moments . . .*

She concentrated on her ire. If the cur thought he would return to find her lying in his bed, he'd best think again. How dare he gorge himself on her charms, then desert her? Did the arrogant bastard think himself so great a lover that she would remain enchanted to her dying breath?

Her steps slowed as she watched two gulls glide overhead, underbellies white against the gray sky. Ah, but he was more than she'd ever dreamed. She shivered at the memory of his touch. His eyes filled with black heat. The way he'd driven himself into her.

Not that she would ever comment on it to him. She rolled her eyes. And she certainly would never, ever, fill his ears with the sounds of aching pleasure he'd wrought in her. 'Twould be like congratulating the fox for raiding the henhouse.

Her pace increased. She should have named a price for her maidenhead. Should have made it exorbitant. She glared at the tree line ahead of her, gray-green before the brackish sky.

But nay. Carried away by the dream that the simpleton might care for her, she'd given him her most precious possession.

She grimaced. Truth tell, her virginity was her second-most precious possession. When had Gavarnie acquired the first, her very soul?

She hugged herself while she walked. He'd spoken no words of love, only lust. And he'd led her on with his mention of marriage. Playing on her secret hopes.

Her lip curled. 'Twas naught but a game to him. Now that he'd had her, he would cast her aside.

She reached the edge of the forest, grateful for the shelter it provided, for she suddenly felt frozen. And empty. She moved off the road, deeper into the protection of the trees, where no one could see her. Where no one could witness her anguish. She felt certain that even in death, her soul would hunger for Gavarnie.

He is smit with you. She recalled Nicolette's words. If only such were true. She slumped down against a tree, too drained to go farther. Closing her eyes, she envisioned Gavarnie's face, his lips. Hot and demanding. His swarthy flesh, hard and unyielding. The slow, hammerlike thud of his heart, solid and sure. There were no truces, only complete, delicious surrender. . . .

❧❦❧

GOLDE MUST HAVE DOZED, for next she knew, the quiet hiss of voices disturbed her. Opening her eyes, she judged it to be midafternoon, though 'twas difficult to tell by the overcast sky. A whiff of lavender, sickly sweet, wafted through the trees.

She bolted to sit. Where had she smelled it before?

The fine hair at her nape rose. 'Twas the odor in her vision. Instantly she rose on her haunches and eased forward, that she could better hear.

". . . are a fool." Sir Nigel's voice carried low and angry. "If your husband discovers us together—"

"He so chafed to reach Atherbrook," came a dulcet, feminine response, "that I sent him ahead while I saw to our belongings. None will know we have met. And after what you told me of Gavarnie's plans to join with the Danes, this cannot wait."

Golde clutched the front of her tunic, concentrating on slowing her racing heart. The voice. The lavender. 'Twas Lady de Warrenne!

"And what of your liegemen?" the steward demanded. "Surely your husband did not leave you unattended."

"A half-dozen servants to pack, and two men-at-arms whom I made certain are sotted. Take your ease, Nigel. You begin to sound more womanish than I."

"Womanish? You?" Sir Nigel snorted. "Come, mi'lady. There is nothing feminine in your nature. I saw how you butchered Lady Isabelle. Few men possess the stomach for such."

Golde covered her mouth. *Lady de Warrenne!* She felt as if a bare-fanged snake were coiled at her feet, ready to strike. An urge to run seized her. But she dare not. She must remain and learn all she could.

"Have a care with your tongue, steward." The timbre of Gundrada's voice cooled with disdain. "You shall rule Skyenvic only by my will. Indeed, 'tis only my sweet pleas that have prevented Walther's killing you."

The slap of a hand against flesh cracked the air, and Golde started.

"To whom do you think you speak?" Nigel demanded. "I am no serving boy to be ordered about. You shall rule Skyenvic only through me. And be forewarned. There are sealed documents, along with a goodly benefaction, in a remote church in Normandy. They shall be read upon my death. Can you guess what they say?"

Golde imagined the fiery imprint of Nigel's palm on the woman's cold, white cheek. 'Twas a moment before

Gundrada managed in a quiet, shaken tone, "Whatever possessed you to do such a thing?"

Though the steward doubtless thought the woman's voice trembled with fear, Golde recognized the rage it held. Sir Nigel had just made a bitter enemy.

Nigel's tone dripped caustically. "Those mysterious warnings to Gavarnie. Mayhap 'twas you who sent them. 'Twould be the perfect device for ridding yourself of me without giving yourself away. Meanwhile, you could cozen another to do your bidding—one more easily beguiled with your charms than I."

Branches creaked and leaves rustled in the short silence that followed. An odor rose from the forest floor, decayed as rotting flesh. Golde squeezed her eyes shut.

Gavarnie had not killed his wife. She clung to the thought. She must tell him, tell his children, tell anyone who would listen. Not only did she have proof of his innocence, she knew who'd actually murdered his wife.

Gundrada spoke at last, venting a small portion of her anger. "'Twas that imbecile, Walther, who sent the messages. I cannot make him see that in ruining you, he ruins himself." She paused, then her tone grew sly. "But his grand schemes have provided me with the means to make Skyenvic ours. Look."

Sir Nigel laughed bitterly. "What are these? More warnings to Gavarnie of impending danger?"

"Read them. They are writings of treason explaining how William can be overthrown."

Another pause followed, and Golde massaged her thighs. Her muscles burned with tension and her bare toes felt frozen. She tilted her head back to ease the ache in her shoulders. Patches of leaden sky showed through the canopy overhead. 'Twould rain ere long.

She lowered her head. 'Twas easy now to understand

her strange feelings toward Gundrada. And Nigel. His actions made chilling sense. His smirk when Gavarnie had appeared in ill-matched rags after dressing himself for the first time, how the steward had conveniently left Gavarnie during the attack on the road to raise the hue and cry, his agreement with Gavarnie in the bedchamber that she was the king's agent.

Nigel chortled, recapturing her attention. "Your audacity knows no bounds. The king will not be fooled by forgeries."

"Rest assured," Gundrada intoned, "they are genuine and easily proven such. When combined with your testimony of Gavarnie's thoughts on the Danes . . ."

Nigel's voice grew hushed, avid with interest. "Where did you come by these?"

"They were written to Walther, who is fool enough to believe the king can be beaten. All you need do is place them in Gavarnie's chambers where they can be found by William's agents."

Golde narrowed her eyes. The cunning bitch. 'Twas the perfect plan.

Abruptly suspicion laced Nigel's tone. "Why do you not use them against your husband, if, as you claim, you despise him? He is a greater threat at present, and we would be well rid of him."

"Are you so afraid, that you would throw away all we have worked for? Think! We need Walther to claim Skyenvic. The king will not give my hand and Adurford unto you if my husband is convicted of conspiracy. I will become royal chattel. Adurford will go to some favored baron. You will never rule Skyenvic."

Her tone grew placating. "Patience, Nigel. All is within our grasp."

"Words I have heard before," the steward returned

flatly. "First Isabelle's death, then the attack on the road from New Market. Your schemes fail with such regularity that I begin to wonder if you are not cursed. Meanwhile, Gavarnie regains his sight, making it more difficult to manipulate him."

Gundrada sniffed. "Gavarnie's sight will do him no good when the king receives all of this evidence. If 'tis your wish to withdraw, say it. I cannot do this without you."

Golde clamped her teeth together. The impulse to race to the castle was raw. Cease, she commanded her twitching muscles. She could take no chance on being discovered. Gavarnie would know soon enough.

"And if I agree?" Nigel queried.

"Gavarnie will be hung, along with the other conspirators. Walther will appear the cleverest and most loyal of men for reporting the matter, and the king will reward him with Skyenvic."

Gundrada sighed gustily. "Then poor Walther will suffer a terrible wasting sickness. Once I am in control of his affairs, I will appoint you to guard Skyenvic on my behalf—with the king's permission, of course. When Walther dies, 'twill only be natural that you and I marry."

In the quiet that followed, the muffled sound of crunching underbrush could be heard. Golde cocked her head, then tensed.

"Shh," Gundrada hissed in the same instant.

'Twas difficult to determine exactly from whence the noise issued, but Golde thought it to come from behind her. And it was fast drawing nearer. Gundrada's men-at-arms?

What was she to do? The sound was coming straight at her. *Please, God.* She rose to her feet. *Do not let me be discovered.* If only she knew which way to run.

Abruptly two cur hounds burst from around a tree. Their noses were to the ground and their tails wagged fiercely—until one of them looked up. Startled, it jumped backward a pace, drawing its companion's attention. Both dogs stilled.

Golde pressed a finger to her lips in a silent gesture for quiet. In that moment, it seemed the entire forest held its breath.

Then both hounds set to baying.

TWENTY-SIX

FOR A MOMENT Golde froze, unable to believe her misfortune. Then she glanced about. There stood Sir Nigel and Lady Gundrada, no more than a quarter furlong distant. Their faces, too, reflected disbelief.

Abruptly Gundrada screeched. "After her, fool!"

Golde spun and ran. Lifting her skirts over her knees, she sprinted over fallen logs and dodged tree trunks. Her heart rode in her throat, near strangling her. She must not be caught. 'Twould mean the end for her, and Gavarnie.

She zagged left, then forward, then left again. If she set an intricate pattern, it would be more difficult for Nigel and Gundrada to follow.

She glanced frantically over her shoulder. Though no one was in sight, she felt little comfort. She was making enough noise to raise the dead.

Gasping for air, she concentrated more on stealth and less on speed. What had become of the wretched hounds? Plague take their flea-ridden hides. Could Sir Nigel use them to track her?

The thought again set fire to her heels and she crashed ahead, uncaring of the noise she made. She chanced another glance over her shoulder, and had barely looked forward again when, suddenly, white-fanged pain bit into her head. It was accompanied by a deafening thump.

She staggered backward, grasping her forehead. Who had struck her? She widened her eyes as her vision blurred. Was it Gundrada or Nigel? She could see little, only hazy grays, browns, and greens.

"A curse on you, and your seed," she rasped as her legs buckled 'neath an onslaught of dizziness.

She swayed on her knees, waiting for the blow that would claim her life. Strangely, she felt naught but roiling anger. "You shall never enjoy your tenure at Skyenvic. I will haunt you to your dying breath."

Panting, she did her best to remain upright, but within moments even that grew impossible. Her lungs felt seared and blackness encroached upon her vision. Collapsing on her belly, she pressed her cheek into the damp, decayed leaves that layered the forest floor.

She had failed. Gavarnie would die.

Nicolette's face swam before her, little doe's eyes filled with inconsolable loss. Then Alory, his sweet features blighted by grief. Finally Ronces, fearful and accusatory. He would embrace his father's death as if he were to blame, as if there were something he could have done.

Never once had she told them how wonderful they were, she thought groggily. What strength they possessed. Gavarnie was so very fortunate to have such children.

How could she have thought to leave them?

Nay. She was confused. 'Twas they who wanted her gone. *Dragon-hag . . . Grendelskin . . . I would offer marriage, but you would doubtless mock me for it.*

Wild images stole through her thoughts.

She and Gavarnie at the altar. The priest raised his cowl to reveal a goat's head. She should have told Gavarnie of her wicked nature. He could not know she was the devil's spawn.

But she wasn't in church after all. Instead, she was in Mimskin's cottage, though it more resembled a cavernous tomb. Gundrada was roasting a pig on a spit. Only, the pig turned out to be Nigel, or was it Lord de Warrenne . . .

Then there was noise. Great tearing sheets of sound. Wetness splattered her face and she cracked her eyes open. What—

She forced herself to sit, blinking. Rain. So heavy it crashed against the forest canopy until she thought the reverberations might split her head in two.

Nigel and Gundrada! Her eyes widened. Where were they?

She scrambled to rise, grimacing at the pain that shot through her feet. A blessed numbness carried throughout the rest of her body. She squinted at her surroundings. The forest had grown darker, but not so dim that she couldn't see a fallen tree directly in front of her. The huge trunk angled upward to rest upon the branches of another tree.

Witless get of an idiot! No one had hit her. She'd run full speed into the dead wood and knocked herself senseless.

Her relief was short-lived, though. Was it dusk, or were the clouds so thick that they concealed the day? How much time had passed? For all she knew, Gavarnie could be dead by now.

A feeling of dread billowed in her chest, snatching the air from her lungs. Not only had she obviously lost her pursuers, she'd lost herself. However would she find her way back to the road?

Cease! She clutched her head. Standing about sniveling like a babe would do no good. So long as she lived, Gavarnie had a chance. Whatever it took, she would find her way to Skyenvic. She had the sight. And by all that was holy, she would make it serve her needs.

❧❧❧

THE RAIN HAD SLACKED to a slow drizzle as Gavarnie stood beside the bed in his chamber. No lamps were lit and as twilight descended, the room darkened. 'Twas what he awaited. The cover of night.

Behind him, Roland climbed atop a stool and tied Gavarnie's hair back with a leather strip. He would not so much as chance a stray wisp obscuring his vision.

Sperville paced the floor before him, shaking his head. "You cannot go," he repeated for the hundredth time. "'Tis naught but a trap."

Weary and sick to his soul, Gavarnie demanded, "What would you have me do? Await the return of my sons' body parts?"

"Send someone else," the chamberlain pleaded. "Once we discover where Gundrada and Nigel hold the boys, then we can plan."

Gavarnie eyed Spindleshanks. The rush of rage at the missive he'd received a short while past had dwindled. Now only fear, raw and frostbitten, remained.

Your witch-woman has told you all by now. Nigel and I will send our demands for the return of your sons once we reach France. Bide quietly until then, or your children will be returned to you in pieces.

It was signed "Gundrada."

Gavarnie scowled. Where was Golde? What did Gundrada mean when she said his witch-woman had told him all?

Sperville pulled him from his grim musings. "At least wear your armor."

"And alert all to my presence?" Gavarnie shook his head. "The sound of ringing mail is more than I will risk. If I stand any chance, 'tis to arrive by stealth."

Roland eased off the stool and Gavarnie nodded at the youth in the dim light. "Go and feed yourself, then rest. I will have need of you later."

Roland bowed and quickly took himself off, closing the door behind him.

"Let me accompany you," Sperville persisted.

Gavarnie crossed his arms and shook his head. "I would that you remain. There is much that will need your attention if I do not return."

Sperville grimaced, his teeth gray in the failing light. "Do not speak thus, lest you curse yourself."

"I am already cursed." Gavarnie strode to the narrow window beside the bed and surveyed the lowering sky.

Was Golde's absence a result of her revulsion for him? Had she again flown to Atherbrook? He could not blame her. Yet he could not believe Golde would leave if she had information concerning his children.

Unless her hatred of him was so great that . . .

He rubbed at his neck. Would that he could take back his offer to pay for her maidenhead. Would that he had not forced himself upon her. But she would never consider marriage to him. Taking her had been the only way he could think to bind her to him.

He stared at the murky twilight. *Prithee, God—and any other Being that might watch over Golde—let her be safe.*

He should not have left with Sir Hugh. Everything—Ronces and Alory, Golde—had happened in his absence. But he had not been able to resist proving Sir Hugh wrong. At Golde's instigation, the man had become determined to travel to New Market to find his son.

He searched the glomung sky. Truth tell, he'd insisted on accompanying Sir Hugh to the village to discredit Golde, to prove to Sir Hugh that she'd lied, to throw her false abilities in her face. Then she would feel . . .

He stiffened. Feel what? Dependent upon him?

He clenched his jaw, disgusted with himself. Aye. If he proved her a fake, ruined her reputation as a seeress on the mainland, she would be unable to fend for herself. She would need a man. Him.

And it had all been for naught. Were Sir Hugh younger, he and the village boy could pass for twins.

How had Golde known? Had the boy's mother been one of her culls? Or did Golde truly possess the gift of sight?

Have done, he commanded his thoughts. He must prepare himself for the task at hand. 'Twas well and good that the evening was overcast. 'Twould be dark sooner. He had no intention of sitting idle while his children were whisked off to France.

Suddenly the door crashed inward. Gavarnie spun, clutching the hilt of his sword, his body vibrating. There stood Henri, flanked by Bogo and Lund. And sweet Mother of God, they had Golde.

"Mi'lord," Henri's voice quavered, "you must listen to mistress."

Gavarnie's brows drew together. Golde's forehead appeared bruised before the flickering rushlight Henri held. He strode forward, his lips thinning. Was that a puddle of water at her bare feet?

Faith, she was soaked! And filthy, as if someone had dragged her through mud. Then it came to him. His liegemen must have beaten her.

"Lowly worms," he growled. "You will pay for your abuse."

He jerked his blade from its sheath. They would lose their feet first, then their—

Golde held up a hand. "Cease." Her voice sounded thick and hoarse. "Your men have done naught to me."

He reached out and jerked her against his chest. Mean-tempered, sour-tongued little she-goat. He held her tight. Even if it meant chaining her arms and legs and locking her in his chamber, he would never let her go again. She would learn to love him or he would thrash her senseless.

"If you would leave go," she grumbled against his chest, "there is much I need say to you."

He glanced up to see the trio of liegemen watching him. Faith, one would think they'd never seen a man hold a woman. He cleared his throat. "That will be all."

The men bowed and backed out of the room, closing the door behind them.

Blackness engulfed the chamber at their departure. "We waste valuable time." Golde attempted to pull from his grasp.

Refusing to release her, he called to the chamberlain. "Sperville, a light."

Flint was struck and a candle flared. He realized Golde was shaking. Not trembling, but fair convulsing. He held her away and brushed tendrils of wet hair from her face. Her flesh was clammy and she smelled of rain. "Sperville, a blanket, and fire some coals."

Golde brushed his hand from her face. Her gaze darted over his features, anxious. "Henri told me of Alory and Ronces' disappearance. I fear I am to blame."

Gavarnie clutched her shoulders, studying her eyes. Now that he'd placed his faith in her, she would admit that she'd deceived him?

"What are you saying?" he whispered, scarce able to draw breath.

He would not believe it. Could not. He loved her.

TWENTY-SEVEN

GOLDE ROLLED UP a sleeve while hurrying from the wardrobe where she'd helped herself to one of Gavarnie's black tunics. "Sperville, we must be quick."

The chamberlain gave her a patient look. "You will abide here, mistress, just as his lordship has commanded."

Golde headed toward the door, rolling the other sleeve. "Shoes, Sperville. I need shoes."

"I cannot allow you to leave." The chamberlain stepped in front of her, arms crossed over his chest.

Golde spun about and raced back for the wardrobe. "My girdle. I'll not be tripping over this hem all night."

She snatched her corded belt from the pile of rain-soaked clothing and began tying it about her hips. Faith, but Gavarnie's tunic swallowed her, and she was no small girl. She sailed from the wardrobe and again headed for the door.

Sperville grabbed her arm. "Have your ears failed? I tell you—"

"Your wits have flown if you think I'll lounge about while Gavarnie and his sons are butchered."

Spindleshanks winced and his grip tightened. "I cannot let you go. Sir Gavarnie would have my head if aught befell you."

Golde leveled a deadly stare at him. "Release me, or you will not live long enough for Gavarnie to kill you."

The chamberlain shook his head. "Be reasonable. You cannot wield a blade. You cannot fight. You would be naught but an added burden for Gavarnie to worry over."

Golde raised her free hand and pretended to scratch the back of her head with irritation. Men could be so foolish, she thought, grasping the hilt of a small dagger she'd hidden in her bound hair. In one swift move, she pulled the blade free and pressed it to the chamberlain's throat. "I have not all night. Die now, or live to deal with your lord's idle threats later."

Spindleshanks couldn't cease blinking. "What . . . Where? How did you . . ."

"Leave go or I will slit you ear to ear."

Sperville recovered quickly and his eyes narrowed. "Very well. I will release you on one condition."

"You are in no position to—"

"I will accompany you."

Relief flooded Golde. What would she have done had the chamberlain refused to let her go? She could never have killed him. She lowered the blade and nodded. "As you will. But I yet need shoes."

❦❧

GAVARNIE'S HEART WARRED with his belly for possession of his chest. It had taken an hour to reach on foot what would have been a quarter-hour ride on horseback. But there was no help for it. Mounted, he would present an easy target. As it was, he hugged the lane's edge, prepared to dive for the forest's cover should he be detected.

Considering all that Golde had overheard, 'twas possible Gundrada's missive had been straightforward. That she wanted no more than to ensure his silence until she and Nigel were safely away.

Still, he could not shake the feeling that he was walking into a trap. Like as not, Gundrada was counting on him to come for his sons. Then, once he presented himself, she would kill him.

He crept forward around a tree trunk, feeling for brush and skirting it. Would that he had wings. His head could do naught but create vivid images of Ronces and Alory in the throes of death.

He grimaced. It did no good to think of such.

He paused to listen. The rain had stopped, leaving a cool mist in its wake. The whir of crickets and croaking frogs were the only stirrings.

He continued on. His head yet spun with the knowledge that he'd not killed Isabelle. What if he'd never discovered the truth? And who would have believed that de Warrenne would warn him of danger? Yet that was what the Baron of Adurford had done, if what Golde had overheard were true.

Golde. 'Twas only by the grace of God that she had been witness to Nigel and Gundrada's meeting. And God had delivered her safely unto him. Was it too much to ask that Ronces and Alory be returned unharmed?

He halted and cocked his head. It sounded like . . .

Voices. Gooseflesh rippled over his body. Whispery snatches of conversation from the road. They wove about his ears like spider's webs. His muscles tensed and he crouched lower. What were they say—

"Must you walk on my heels?" Golde hissed.

"'Twas not done a'purpose," Sperville snapped in return.

Gavarnie rose, scowling. Of all the dimwitted . . .

Even as his jaw opened to chastise the simpletons, a man ordered, "Hold, baron."

Gavarnie froze. The voice was nowhere near him. Rather, it came from the same vicinity as Golde and Sperville.

"Take his sword, Rolf," the man commanded with ill-concealed contempt. "Lady Gundrada will be most pleased."

"Wha—wha—" the chamberlain spluttered.

"Mi'lord." Golde's tone was underscored with double meaning. "Do not protest. Give them your blade."

Gavarnie narrowed his eyes. He had been right. 'Twas a trap. Clearly, the assailants thought Sperville was he. And Golde was doing her best to confirm the mistake, the little fool. 'Twould cost Sperville his life.

"This way, baron," the man ordered. "One false move and we'll gut you where you stand."

"Do as they say, your lordship," Golde begged.

"Shut your mouth, wench, or lose your tongue."

Gavarnie slid his sword from its sheath. There were only two men. 'Twould not be difficult to slip up behind them and slit their throats. Yet . . .

He eased forward, following the slogging sound of footsteps in the muddy lane. The men were taking Golde and Sperville to Gundrada. Ultimately they would lead him to his children.

It was easy to track the foursome. Keeping to the tree line, Gavarnie prowled along behind them. If ever his blindness could have been considered a blessing, 'twas now. His balance was as secure as if 'twere full daylight. Though no one spoke a word, he could distinguish the men's heavier breathing from Golde's, could smell the acrid odor of sweat from the men-at-arms. And all the while, he used his sword to avoid ruts, his steps sure and silent.

After some bit of time, one of the liegemen let loose a warbling whistle. Obviously a signal, though even a deaf man wouldn't be fooled into believing it was a bird. The group continued more slowly now, the whistling more frequent, until at last there came a muffled response.

"Maegus," a liegeman grumbled. "Give us a light, fool."

"A moment, sir."

At the sound of flint being struck, Gavarnie leapt forward. By the time the tinder caught, one liegeman had been dispatched. The second could only blink once at the light before Gavarnie's blade found his throat.

Sperville had the wherewithal to clamp a hand over the lamp-bearer's mouth—a lowly servant judging from his coarse, hole-filled tunic.

Gavarnie placed a finger to his lips, signaling for silence. Then he shook a fist at Sperville and scowled at Golde. She took a deep breath, her eyes filled with . . . if not adoration, then certainly gratitude, and tearful at that.

He couldn't resist. Pulling her against him, he pressed a hard kiss on her mouth. Her nose wrinkled when he set her away, and his gaze followed hers.

Faith, he was covered with gore from the dead liegemen. That he had not noticed it, or its odor, was grimly exhilarating. He had not been reminded of Isabelle. Had not been rendered witless with guilt, or immobilized by fear.

He raised his gaze to Golde, unable to keep a savage grin at bay. Or mayhap 'twas a sneer, a contemptuous farewell to the horror that had bound him for so long. It mattered not. He was whole again.

Golde laid a hand on his chest and leaned forward to whisper in his ear. "Take your ease, mi'lord. Ronces and Alory are safe."

Relief near buckled his knees. "They are returned to Skyenvic?"

Golde placed a finger to his lips. "Lower your voice. They are not at Skyenvic."

"Then where—"

"Trust me. They are well and unharmed. But I know not for how long."

He studied her eyes. Even the black one appeared most sincere. 'Twas difficult to doubt her. Yet before he could comfort himself with solid reassurance, she forestalled any further questions by covering his mouth with her fingers. Her eyes shifted in the lamp-bearer's direction, a silent reminder.

Jerking his head at the servant, he gestured with his sword for the peasant to lead on. Sperville retrieved his blade and stood at the ready.

By the Blessed Virgin, his sons would be rescued. Then those responsible for their abduction would die.

❧❧❧

NEVER HAD GOLDE felt such discomfort in the wood. This night she felt suffocated by the gnarled trees, clammy from the cool mist. Like she'd been buried.

She stared at Gavarnie's broad shoulders as she and Sperville walked behind him along a narrow footpath. The servant who led them had not uttered a sound, was doubtless incapable of speech. And she could not blame him.

Gavarnie appeared ferocious. Indeed, the unholy, slavering look of triumph that had claimed his features moments ago had frightened even her. 'Twould not surprise her in the least were he to raise his face to the heavens and howl.

She longed to reach out and touch his back, to temper the wild bloodlust that fair pulsed about him. But she dared not. To tame the beast would weaken him. Instead, she cast sidelong glances at Sperville, who seemed unaware of her existence.

God's will be done, she thought, recalling the vivid images that had assailed her when she and Sperville had left the castle.

Ronces and Alory. A campfire illuminated their frightened little faces. Gundrada paced before them. She was going to kill Gavarnie.

Though Golde could not see Nigel in her vision, she'd felt his presence. Confident and secure, he was busy planning his rule at Skyenvic, which would never happen. Gundrada would kill him, too. Golde had felt it as surely as if Gundrada's thoughts were her own.

She'd drawn Sperville to a halt outside the castle gates. In the dark, she'd concentrated until she'd felt herself drawn squarely to Alory's mind, could feel the boy's fear and confusion.

Gundrada was going to kill him. Kill his father. Hopeless. He was so small. Lady de Warrenne was so big. And Sir Nigel had always been so kind. Like an uncle. Why was Papa's steward being so mean?

Twist your wrists, Golde had commanded. *The ropes that bind you will fall away, fall away.*

She'd repeated it over and again until it felt as if her head would split. And all the while, she'd felt Gundrada pacing, a spider with an appetite.

Then it had happened. Alory's thumb was free; next, his forefinger.

Patience, she had counseled. *Loose your brother. Keep your hands hidden.*

And they had!

Her inner eye had settled on a fallen branch behind the boys. *Pick it up, Alory*, she had urged. *That's it. When Gundrada next passes before you, hit her!*

Run! Run!

Golde blinked, her thoughts returning to the present, and focused her gaze on Sperville's back. The chamberlain walked ahead of her now, the footpath too narrow to accommodate more than single file.

What had distracted her? Was it voices she heard?

Aye. Faint at first, they grew in volume with each step she took. And as they grew, so did Gavarnie's pace quicken.

Abruptly he shoved the servant aside and lunged forward. The peasant scuttled back in the direction of the road, the light from his lamp quickly swallowed in gloom.

She hesitated a moment to watch the man flee, but Sperville was hard on Gavarnie's heels. By the time Golde rushed to catch them, both men had reached the middle of a clearing where a small fire burned.

Two young serving maids shrieked, and the man-servants who'd sat huddled beside them half rose. "Sit!" Sperville commanded in a surprisingly hard-edged tone.

Golde halted and searched the shadows beyond the

fire. There. Gavarnie had pinned Gundrada to a tree, his blade pressed to her throat.

"Where are they?" he snarled.

Gundrada spat in his face, then sneered, "You are too late. Your demon children are halfway to France."

Golde quickly scanned the clearing again. Ronces and Alory were nowhere in sight. Nor was Sir Nigel to be seen. A pithless feeling clutched her stomach. Without question, the boys had escaped. But had the steward recaptured them?

"You lie!" Gavarnie roared, an animal sound filled with unspeakable pain. "You have killed them!"

Grabbing the neckline of Gundrada's tunic, he spun her about and flung her toward the fire. Horror-stricken, Golde watched as the woman stumbled and fell. Would Gavarnie kill her?

"They are bound for France," Gundrada whined, raising her arm as Gavarnie advanced on her. "I swear it!"

"Liar!" Gavarnie bellowed. "You would be with them."

"I—I—"

"Cursed whore. You will speak the truth or I will cleave you in two."

The servants scooted backward en masse, looking like a flock of sheep bound for the banquet table. Gavarnie moved to tower over Gundrada, his twisted, swarthy complexion burnished orange before the fire. Blood yet smeared his blade from the liegemen.

And Golde knew at once that he would not harm Gundrada.

Nay. He needed a worthy opponent to spend his rage upon, not some puling woman.

"They escaped!" Gundrada screeched at last.

"Escaped?" Gavarnie thundered, raising his blade. "You have spoken your last."

"'Tis true!" Gundrada jerked her skirts up to reveal her shins. "Look what the little bastards have done to me."

Golde squinted to see a thick purple welt on each of her legs.

"What have they done, wife?" came a coarse demand from behind Golde.

Even as she swiveled about, Golde knew 'twas Lord de Warrenne. And he had Ronces and Alory. They were restrained by grim looking men-at-arms, as was Sir Nigel.

"Walther!" Gundrada cried.

Golde glanced back to see the woman grow still as Gavarnie placed the sword tip beneath her chin, forcing her head back.

"Have a care, husband," she croaked. "He can see."

Golde's flesh crawled as de Warrenne strode past her into the clearing, a great, ponderous bear walking on its hind legs. His liegemen hung back at the edge of the clearing, eight in all. Her spirits sank. Gavarnie and Sperville could not possibly hope to win against so many.

Reflexively she checked the dagger in her hair. Could she reach de Warrenne and sink the blade in his back before one of his minions captured her? Or should she aim for the men-at-arms who held Ronces and Alory?

Before she could decide, Gavarnie threatened, "Release my sons or your sweet wife will die before your eyes."

De Warrenne halted, his back to Golde. "Sweet wife," he growled. "Women are poison, one and all."

He turned and signaled for Nigel to be brought to him. It required two men to perform the task, for the steward put up a valiant struggle. His grunts and frantic cries rent the forest night like obscenities.

Realizing de Warrenne's intent, Golde sidled to her right, blocking Ronces and Alory's line of vision. The boys should not witness such brutality.

Without batting an eye, de Warrenne drew his blade and split the steward's head in two. Sperville made no move to stop Gundrada's servants as they scrambled from the clearing.

Golde shifted her gaze to Gavarnie. His nostrils were flared, his black eyes pitiless at the steward's demise. He yet held his sword to Gundrada's throat.

"What think you of your lover now, sweet wife?" de Warrenne demanded.

"'Tis not what you think," Gundrada rasped, her eyes round with pleading. "He was useful—"

"Shut your flapping mouth," de Warrenne spat. Turning, he inclined his head at the men-at-arms who held Ronces and Alory.

A low, threatening rumble crawled from Gavarnie's mouth, and Golde snatched the dagger from her hair.

"Release them," de Warrenne ordered.

Golde blinked, then stared at the Baron of Adurford. Had he said—

"Papa!" Alory cried, racing for Gavarnie. Ronces was fast behind him.

Sperville dropped his sword and grabbed both boys before they could get past him.

"Leave go!" Ronces shrieked, even as the chamberlain began pulling them toward one side of the clearing—away from de Warrenne and his liegemen.

Golde moved quickly to help, for the children struggled hard to free themselves. Gripping each boy by one shoulder, she leaned close enough to hiss in their faces,

"Distract your father now, and he could lose his life. Instead of squirming about, think how you can help should he need you."

"Nay!" Gundrada shrilled.

Golde straightened to see that Gavarnie had removed his blade from the woman's throat. And now she rose like an angry squall.

"Fool," she snapped, stomping toward her husband. "Know you the effort I have put forth—"

De Warrenne clubbed her before she could finish, a blow so stiff she staggered. "Await me at the roadside," he commanded his men.

"Mi'lord," a liegeman queried, "are you certain?"

"Leave us!" the baron roared.

Within moments silence had settled over the clearing, eerie and strained. Then de Warrenne turned his attention on Gavarnie. "Fate has e're smiled on you, Delamaure. Take your children and begone."

Sperville was already ushering the boys away. Golde noted their retreat from the corner of her vision, but kept her gaze trained on Gavarnie. Bewilderment struggled with distrust to claim his harsh features. His blade hung in his hand, a weapon with no direction.

"I beg you, husband," Gundrada pressed, though she kept her distance from de Warrenne. "Do not let them go. You could yet have the king's favor, and Skyenvic."

"Mi'lord!" Golde inclined her head at Gavarnie, urging him with her eyes to come away. Something terrible was about to happen. She could feel it. Death. Its rancid smell engulfed the clearing. And it had naught to do with Sir Nigel's corpse.

Suddenly de Warrenne lunged forward. 'Twas amazing the speed with which the big man clutched his wife's throat. He used but one hand, the other yet holding his sword. Gundrada clawed at his great wrist and her lips moved fervently, but only choking sounds issued forth.

"De Warrenne!" Gavarnie's tone was appalled.

"Mi'lord," Golde called again, shivering. "Let us be-gone."

Gavarnie shook his head at her, the fool. What was he about? He was free to go, yet he would remain?

"Walther," Gavarnie said in a most reasonable tone. "You do not want to do this."

If de Warrenne heard, he gave no indication. Gundrada's strangled gasps were growing more feeble.

"Listen to me, man," Gavarnie persisted. "She is not worth the suffering you will visit upon yourself."

Golde stared at him, unable to believe her ears. Was de Warrenne not his sworn enemy? Had not the evil baron and Gundrada near destroyed Gavarnie? Yet he felt compelled to save them from tragedy?

Gundrada's legs gave way and her eyes were begin-ning to bulge. De Warrenne's wrist and forearm were bleeding where she'd gouged him with her nails.

"I tell you, Walther, you do yourself a grave injustice. The memory of this will haunt you unto death." Gavarnie edged close enough to lay a hand on de War-renne's arm.

"Gavarnie!" Golde cried. If the witless imbecile got himself killed, she would never forgive him. Still, she could not bring herself to physically interfere. In her heart, she knew Gavarnie had the right of the matter.

"Send her away," Gavarnie coaxed. "You need never lay eyes on her again."

Abruptly a sob tore from de Warrenne. He threw Gundrada from him, then took several reeling steps. Wip-ing his mouth with the back of his hand, he circled his wife where she lay unconscious.

Golde started forward to see to the woman, but one look from de Warrenne's glittering, close-set eyes stalled her. He yet had a steady grip on his blade.

"Convents are e're in need of patronage," Gavarnie said in an emotionless tone.

At last de Warrenne halted. "I am not without honor," he spat.

Gavarnie held up a hand. "No one has said—"

"Think you I know not how it feels to have a son held hostage?"

Golde frowned. What was the man talking about?

Gavarnie's visage grew cool. Apparently, he understood. "Do not think I will say I am in your debt for releasing my sons."

De Warrenne snorted. "Do not hope I will say I am in your debt because my wife yet lives."

"Do not believe," Gavarnie shot back, "that I will not bring charges against you on the morrow for the murder of my wife."

De Warrenne's chest expanded. "You will not."

Unable to hold her tongue a moment longer, Golde blurted, "Then I shall."

Both men looked at her as if they'd just realized she were there. De Warrenne scowled and turned away as if he would ignore her. Then, just as quickly, his gaze swung back to regard her.

Refusing to give in to the impulse to cringe, Golde crossed her arms over her chest and presented what she hoped was a fearless mien.

"Your witch-woman," de Warrenne remarked sourly, returning his attention to Gavarnie. "She has done much for you, has she not?"

He paused to study Gavarnie's stony features. "What if she roused you in the dead of night, her clothes soaked with blood? Then she rants wildly how she has just murdered another man's wife. What would you do?"

"Golde would not—"

"Think you I ever dreamed that Gundrada was capable of such?"

"Do not attempt to excuse your actions," Gavarnie sneered.

At his contemptuous tone, the Baron of Adurford stiffened. Golde winced and gazed heavenward. Did Gavarnie yet spoil for a fight with the man?

"You are a simpleton." Spit flew from de Warrenne's mouth. "My precious honor once cost me a son. Forgive me if I am not as swift of wit as you. I could scarce think when Gundrada presented me with Isabelle's murder. I only sought to protect her."

Gavarnie's eyes narrowed. "You expect me to believe your woebegotten tales?"

There must be some purpose to Gavarnie's cruelty, Golde decided. Poor de Warrenne was baring his soul.

"I tell you," de Warrenne spoke through clenched teeth, "Gundrada spread her legs for your steward to gain his aid. 'Twas Nigel who poisoned your drink the night Isabelle died so your sleep would be deep. He let Gundrada in through the pantry. Once she had murdered Isabelle, they managed to drag you to your chamber—"

"Where they left me," Gavarnie interrupted. "And all, I suppose, without your knowledge." His tone dripped sarcasm.

De Warrenne inclined his head. "Believe what you will. I never intended for matters to get so far beyond my control."

"Charging me with murder—was that beyond your control?"

De Warrenne took a deep breath, and Golde saw sullen resignation writ on his swollen features. "The king had assigned me a task. There are benefits to being perceived as greedy and slow of wit. Such a man would never be suspected of being William's agent by those plotting against the king."

De Warrenne eyed Gundrada's prone form, and his shoulders slumped. "I'd been ordered to bind myself to Roger de Breteuil. To gain information on the insurrection he and his brother-in-law, de Guader, are planning. I could hardly be involved in scandal. 'Twas an important matter. It is still an important matter. You might wish to consider such before carrying this tale to the king."

At last Gavarnie appeared stunned. Praise the Goddess Danu. Mayhap now, Golde thought, he would realize the Baron of Adurford was not as stupid as he appeared.

"I would not have allowed you to be convicted of Isabelle's murder," de Warrenne grumbled. "I did my best to appease your anger by offering to foster one of your sons. When I learned that Gundrada and your steward were scheming yet again, I warned you. I had no clue the two would take your children hostage."

A muscle twitched in Gavarnie's jaw. Fearing he might continue to prick de Warrenne's temper, Golde spoke up. "I overheard them plotting in the wood this afternoon. They saw me and must have panicked, knowing I would tell Gavarnie."

Ignoring her, Gavarnie demanded, "What of the treasonous documents Nigel was to have planted in my chambers? According to your wife, they were missives written by you to de Breteuil."

"And so they are—written at the king's behest. Think you I would be fool enough to tell Gundrada the true nature of my business after all she has done?"

Gundrada groaned and coughed.

Gavarnie did not soften one whit. "Mayhap you should kill her after all, if what you claim is true."

"Nay. You are right. She is not worth the misery."

Gavarnie strode to clutch Golde's arm, and herded her to the footpath. "I have located the missives," he said to de Warrenne. "Rest assured, they will be delivered to the king. If you have lied—"

"One more word," de Warrenne's tone grew menacing, "and one of us will die here and now. Do as you will."

TWENTY-EIGHT

❧❧❧

GOLDE FELT SUFFOCATED and wanted no more than to rest her weary bones. It seemed days had passed since she'd last slept. Ducking her head, she backed from the tangle of castlefolk that surrounded Gavarnie and the children in the great hall. Doubtless, she would be returned home on the morrow.

"I know'd it all along," she heard a kitchen maid remark. "His lordship arn't the kind o' man wot would kill his wife."

"Oh go on," another woman huffed. "'Twas me wot said he didn't do it."

Golde rolled her eyes. One would think Gavarnie was the only person who did not know he was innocent.

"De Warrenne should pay for his crimes," a liegeman cried out.

Shouts of agreement rose to the rafters, and Golde

headed for the screens passage. Now, she supposed, plans would be laid for the Baron of Adurford's demise. Not that the man did not deserve it. But faith, 'twould be less difficult to hate de Warrenne had Gavarnie not been so cruel.

She paused, realizing her feet were carrying her to Gavarnie's chamber. What was she thinking? She could not sleep there.

Mayhap Nicolette's room.

Aye. The girl's chamber would be quiet. Nicolette was happily ensconced in Gavarnie's embrace amidst the gaggle of castlefolk. She was halfway to the child's room when a hush fell over the hall below.

"There will be no retaliation against the Baron of Adurford." Gavarnie's voice rang hard and uncompromising. "He had naught to do with his wife's schemes."

Golde's steps slowed. After his mean treatment of de Warrenne, she'd wondered if Gavarnie intended to ruin the man.

"'Twas Sir Nigel who would see himself as lord of Skyenvic," Gavarnie continued, "and he is dead."

At his words, a collective gasp wafted over the hall.

"It was de Warrenne who ensured Ronces and Alory's safe return."

Golde's shoulders slumped and she dragged her feet along the corridor. 'Twould have been easier to return home if Gavarnie had left her with some disgust for his person. But nay. The great lout had to be noble and extend his protection to the Baron of Adurford, instead of decrying the man.

By the time she reached Nicolette's room, Golde's eyes were watering. She pitched herself on the little bed and curled into a ball.

'Od rot Gavarnie. He was to blame for these incessant weeping fits. *I would ask you to marry me, but you would doubtless decline.* Her eyelids drooped.

"Hmph." Let him ask. She would accept his proposal with such speed, 'twould make his head spin.

She sighed. Would that it were so. But now that he knew he'd not murdered his wife, now that his sight had been restored, his confidence had returned. He no longer needed her. . . .

She could not have slept more than a few moments when she felt arms sliding beneath her shoulders and knees. Cracking one eye, she found Gavarnie bending over her.

Joy leapt about in her heart and head. Had he come for her?

Just as swiftly, doubt replaced her ebullience. "What are you about?" she grumbled.

He lifted her in his arms. "You cannot sleep here, mistress. Your great weight will break Nicolette's bed."

She blinked, then glared and shoved against his chest. "Put me down, thickwit."

"Nay, 'tis in my bed that you belong." He had the audacity to grin.

Acute disappointment near strangled her. "You want naught but another sample of my charms."

"Kindly cease thrashing about. It only arouses me and we have more important—"

"Matters to attend," she spat. "Say it and I will knock your teeth from your head."

"Nay. 'Tis family matters to which we must attend."

Family matters? Did he think she would allow him to get her with child without marrying her? She stilled, and eyed him as he carried her across the threshold into his bedchamber. He deposited her on her feet beside the bed.

Golde glanced about. Ronces, Alory, and Nicolette

sat sullenly upon the beautiful red coverlet. Hesper and Roland stood nearby.

"Now," Gavarnie addressed the children. "You will do as mistress instructs, or she is like to place a spell on you that will raise great, green warts on your faces."

"But Papa," Alory whined. "'Tis not fair."

Ronces elbowed him in the ribs. "You sound like a baby."

"Do not."

"You awe both bwats," Nicolette accused.

"I'll leave you to it, mistress." Gavarnie bowed to her, then headed for the door.

"Leave me to what?" she demanded of his back.

"They need baths," he called over his shoulder.

"'Tis not my place to see to such. They are your children."

"You will soon be their mother, so you had best accustom yourself to the chore."

The imbecile fair sprinted from the room before Golde could say aught. Of all the gall. Did he think she would marry him just because he said so?

And he'd left her with the dirty work.

"Roland," she snapped. "See to the tub."

"'Tis already filled, mi'lady."

A tingling sensation swept over Golde. *Mi'lady*. It sounded so . . . wonderful. Not that she would never admit it.

"I am not bathing with her," Ronces groused.

Golde affected a horrified tone. "I should hope not. You are far too old for such."

Ronces' small chest appeared to swell.

"Me, too," Alory declared.

Golde pursed her lips and regarded the boy. "What think you, Ronces?"

The older boy heaved a sigh. "I suppose he can bathe with me."

"A moment," Golde commanded.

Both boys halted where they'd slid off the bed.

"Ladies first."

"Yea. Ladies fiwst." Nicolette tilted her head back and stuck her tongue out.

Golde rolled her eyes.

Mi'lady. Lady Golde. Baroness of Skyenvic. Her lip curled. Washer of Soiled Children would be a more apt title.

Still, by the time Gavarnie returned, her spirits were revoltingly bubbly. After inspecting faces, necks, and ears, he kissed the children and bade everyone a good night.

Once alone with Gavarnie, Golde crossed her arms over her chest. "I believe there is one important family matter you've neglected, mi'lord."

"Indeed?" His black eyes twinkled and he sauntered toward her.

Golde held up a hand. "Was there something you'd intended to ask of me?"

"Aye. Could I have my tunic back?" He reached out to pull at her girdle.

"Dolt." She swatted his hand. "That is not what I meant."

He gave her an innocent look, but continued to work at the belt. "Ah, yes. Did the children behave?"

The girdle fell to the floor and Golde gave him a sour look. "If I am to be a mother, I will have to be married."

"Oh, that." He pulled her into his arms. "The deed but awaits the blessing of a priest."

"What if I do not wish to marry you?"

His lips found her neck and she shivered at his gentle

kiss. "It matters not what you wish in this instance," he whispered in her ear.

Golde closed her eyes and wrapped her arms about his waist. "You are an arrogant brute." Her breathing quickened as his hands caressed her back.

"Yea. I can see you are greatly distressed."

She drew back and searched his face. "Make no mistake, mi'lord. Your cruelty toward de Warrenne, when the man sought only to explain himself—"

"Willful wench," he grumbled, though he yet clasped her back. "You must e're spoil the moment with your flapping mouth. I see you will require much kissing during the years ahead."

"I have not agreed to any future between us," she declared.

"Very well. If your reservations are a result of my actions toward the Baron of Adurford, then you may rest easy. I but wished to leave the man with his dignity. He would have interpreted any sympathy on my part as pity."

Golde scowled. "Sympathy! 'Twill be years before he recovers from your mean treatment."

"Exactly. Meanwhile, he owes me naught for my shrewd observations. A trick I learned from a clever witch."

Golde raised a brow. "I am clever, am I not?"

"Pff. I speak of your great-grandmother, who was clever enough to send you here. Though I wish she would cease jabbering at me. 'Tis unsettling to hear a voice when no one is about."

Abruptly Golde's mood soured. She didn't doubt that Mimskin spoke to Gavarnie. Nor should she be surprised. Was there anything her great-grandmother did not interfere with? "What does Mimskin say to you?"

"She says you should return my tunic. It is far too large and does little to flatter your shape."

"Liar," she snapped.

Gavarnie heaved a great sigh. "Your great-grandmother speaks to me only when you are in danger."

Golde pursed her lips to keep from smiling. While it was comforting to know that Mimskin would e'er watch over her, 'twas most satisfying to think that Gavarnie would now have to share the burden of Mimskin's needling.

"If you would," Gavarnie redirected her thoughts, "kindly return my tunic."

She hedged. "You will have to wait. I have nothing else to wear."

He grinned, a cat eyeing a fresh fish. "You need wear nothing." He began rucking the material up.

"I have not yet said I will marry you."

"You will."

"Why is that?"

"Because I love you."

"Should I not love you as well?"

His hands halted their busywork with the tunic. "How could you not? I am handsomely pockmarked, I am willing to curl my hair if that is your wish. And I am very good at satisfying your desire."

"'Tis no wonder your tunic is so large. It has to fit over your swollen head."

"Hear, hear, mistress. You love me well, and you may as well admit it."

His hands again tugged the tunic upward.

"Very well," she admitted. "I love you. But do you not think we should await our nuptials before we—"

"Faith!" He gaped. "Is this some new fashion? Where are your underdrawers?"

"They were soaked. 'Twas the only pair I had."

"Well . . ." His hand roamed over her bare bottom. "I suppose 'tis not so bad. Indeed, I can see where it might prove just the thing."

She forced a stern tone against the heat that stole through her body. "Does your sense of propriety always vacillate thus?"

"Nay." He rubbed himself against her front, watching her eyes. "Only when I am presented with difficult females."

"I am difficult?" Doubtless, he could see her desire quicken. She fought the urge to plaster herself to him. "Already you are trying to bed me, and you have yet to propose."

A spark of challenge lit his eyes. "Take off my tunic, and I will ask for your hand."

Good lack, she would show some restraint, she vowed. "Ask first. Then I will think on your tunic."

Her breath caught as he ground his leather-clad hips against her. "Think you to best me at the game of seduction?"

"We shall see." She grasped his hips and held him tight.

"Since you are a novice," his words sounded labored, "I will tell you the most important rule."

"What?" Golde breathed hard, staunching the urge to tear the tunic over her head.

"Never oppose your opponent."

About the Author

A native Floridian, Sandra Lee received a B.A. in elementary education, and promptly moved into the field of freelance writing without ever teaching a day of school. It has been Ms. Lee's experience that a twisted sense of humor goes a long way toward straightening out the dangerous curves on the highway of life, especially where romance and children are concerned. When she's not writing, Ms. Lee's time is spent with her husband and two daughters, none of whom appreciate her pointless lectures. Ms. Lee is also ruled by two dogs and three cats, none of which obey her commands.

Don't miss these novels by
Kay Hooper

~~~~~~

AFTER CAROLINE ___57184-2 $5.99/$7.99 Can.

"Kay Hooper...knows how to serve up a latter-day gothic that
will hold readers in its brooding grip." —*Publishers Weekly*

AMANDA ___56823-X $5.99/$7.99

"Provides all the requisite thrills, chills,
and hot-blooded romance." —*Kirkus Reviews*

THE WIZARD OF SEATTLE ___28999-3 $5.50/$6.50

"The always outstanding...multi-talented Kay Hooper
again demonstrates her incredible gift for telling unique
and imaginative stories." —*Romantic Times*

FINDING LAURA ___57185-0 $5.99/$7.99

"Kay Hooper is a multitalented author whose stories always
pack a tremendous punch." —Iris Johansen

And now available in hardcover:
HAUNTING RACHEL ___09950-7 $22.95/$29.95

- -

Ask for these books at your local bookstore or use this page to order.

Please send me the books I have checked above. I am enclosing $_____ (add $2.50 to
cover postage and handling). Send check or money order, no cash or C.O.D.'s, please.

Name _____

Address _____

City/State/Zip _____

Send order to: Bantam Books, Dept. FN 8, 2451 S. Wolf Rd., Des Plaines, IL 60018.
Allow four to six weeks for delivery.

Prices and availability subject to change without notice.   FN 8 11/98